TOUR OF DUTY

TOUR OF DUTY

KENNEDY SHAW

URBAN BOOKS

www.urbanbooks.net

URBAN SOUL is published by

Urban Books
10 Brennan Place
Deer Park, NY 11729

ISBN-13: 978-1-59983-103-9
ISBN-10: 1-59983-103-1

First Printing: December 2009
10 9 8 7 6 5 4 3 2 1

Printed in the United States of America

TOUR OF DUTY

Prologue

Senator Seth McCaffrey sat in his appointed seat in the Joint Chiefs of Staff meeting. The defense committee was questioning his suggestion about the drug for soldiers listed in the recently approved military defense bill. He had a good plan two years ago when the plan was originated, albeit there was a snag or two in it, but in the end it was for America.

"Mac, have you lost your mind? This drug hasn't been approved by the military. You can't start administering it to soldiers without telling them."

Seth looked at Howard Burns. *Coward.* "Look, Howard, it can work and it will work. All you have to do is okay the testing. You don't have to tell anyone that it's going on. That's my department. You just keep the president out of our business."

Howard turned his cold eyes on Seth. "You can't kill innocent soldiers," he hissed. "I'm not going to be a party to this. The serum has serious side effects."

"It has probable side effects," Seth corrected. "That's

why we need to test it. Send a regiment to the war zone, and if someone gets sick, kill 'em."

"What?"

"Look, it's real simple," Seth whispered. "Pick a unit. Send them to Iraq for a year. We can monitor them, and no one will be the wiser. If any of the men exhibit any symptoms, they'll have a tragic accident. Spoils of war. You know the routine."

"What about your end? What about your mistress? She knows your whole plan. You got sloppy, leaving top secret documents at her place, and now we're all paying for that. What are you going to do about her?"

"Kill her."

"Another tragic accident?"

"Of course," Seth said confidently. "But this time I'm going to be the one pulling the trigger. It's going to be my pleasure to end that reporter's life."

Chapter 1

Six months later, somewhere on the East Coast

"Carter, will you just shut up and listen?" Mikerra Stone bellowed into her prepaid cell phone.

"Okay. I'm listening," he said finally. "What's going on with you? You're totally off the grid. I've been trying to get in contact with you for over a week. I heard about your gig at the magazine. I'm sorry."

"Getting fired is the least of my worries now. I'm in trouble and I need your help. Can you help me or not?"

"If you lose some of that attitude in your voice, I'll do anything you ask. Where are you?"

Mikerra tried her best not to lose it on the phone in the parking lot of a gas station, who knows where. She had no idea where she was or how she got there. "I don't know." She wiped nonexistent tears from her face. "Seth is trying to kill me."

Carter sighed. "I told you to break it off with him years ago. Not only is he married, but he's married to one of the richest women in the nation. He can't afford to divorce her."

"Carter, I didn't call for a lecture. I called for help.

Are you with me or not?" Mikerra knew the consequences of dating a married white senator from Massachusetts, but now wasn't the time to dwell on that monumental mistake.

"I told you about that attitude, Mikerra. Look around you. Tell me what you see."

She glanced around the desolate area. It was dark on the two-lane highway. The only light illuminating the road came from the full moon and the lights of the motel across the street. "I see the lights of a motel called the Bainesberry Inn. It looks like a rattrap."

"Right now that's going to be your best friend. More than likely they're not going to ask for a credit card. I think I know where you are. How did you get to Maryland?"

"I don't know," she admitted.

"I see where you are."

"How can you track me if I'm using a prepaid cell?" Could Seth track her as easily?

"I have my ways. You're still using a tower to use the cell, so yes, I can find you. The average man isn't as smart as me," he said. "I'm about four hours away. I need for you to follow my directions, and don't ask questions, okay?"

Like she had an option. "Okay."

"Good. You have cash?"

"Yes."

"Check in to the motel under the name Mikerra Stone and sit tight. I'll call back in one hour. Don't answer your phone unless it's my cell. Got it? I'll be there as quick as I can." He ended the call.

Mikerra looked at the small phone and pondered how her life had spiraled out of control.

* * *

"Okay, start from the beginning." Carter sat on the bed, facing Mikerra. "Why is Seth after you this time? I know in the past when you tried to end it, he threatened you. So what's got you running?"

"My car," she whispered.

"Your Benz?"

"Yeah. I decided to sell it, since Seth bought it for me, anyway. I wanted to get rid of everything he'd ever bought me. So I sold the car to this guy."

"So?"

"Three days ago this guy's mother called me, asking about the title."

Carter looked at her with intense brown eyes. "Mikerra, I'm an attorney. This sounds perfectly normal."

"She explained to me that two days before, her son was killed in an explosion in the car that he bought from me. The police told her the bomb was professional level. That's when I went into hiding. My gut feeling tells me Seth was behind this, or someone acting on his behalf."

"That's some strong accusation, Mikerra. Why would he care if you sold the car? It was in your name." Carter opened his laptop and turned it on.

"I know what I'm talking about, Carter. He knows I know about the military defense bill that was just passed. Project Perfect One-ninety-two."

"The bill to increase military enrollment?"

"On the surface, but a less obvious part of the bill is the part about research and development. No one reads the last page of a three-hundred-page document. There's one clause about research, but it's not good research."

Carter's fingers flew across the silver keys on his laptop. "If it's in the bill, it's public knowledge."

"But that's not the right bill. Seth slipped in duplicate

pages, taking out the part about the real research. And I'm the only one who knows. I have a copy of the original document."

"Damn."

"Tell me about it," Mikerra said. "Since that call, I've been afraid to go back to my condo."

"What about your work?"

"Who do you think got me fired?" She stood and started to pace the room. "Seth made a call, and the next week I was unemployed. And to make this even sicker, I was in the room when Seth called my boss and threatened him with a scandal if he didn't fire me. They gave me a nice severance package, but my name is mud in New York."

"Your name is mud in the tristate area. I mean, Karen Mills's name is mud." He turned the laptop screen so she could look at her own picture. "You have a BOLO on your head."

"Why is there a 'be on the lookout' on me?"

Carter turned the laptop back in his direction. "Says in connection with a suspected terrorist."

Mikerra sat on the bed. She was not going to let this man take her down like this. As if she didn't matter. If it took her dying breath, Senator Seth McCaffrey was going to pay for what he was doing to her and the men and women of the United States military.

Her only saving grace was Carter. "Okay, what's my next move?"

He glanced at her over his laptop. "All roads point to home. I think this is a perfect time for Karen Mills to disappear and Mikerra Stone to reemerge."

"Carter, all my possessions are at my condo. What am I supposed to do? Nothing has Mikerra Stone on it. What am I supposed to do for credit?"

He smiled. A plan was already forming in that devious mind of his. No wonder he was senior counsel in the Justice Department. "You let me take care of that. You just take the most scenic route to your home-town. Give me two weeks, and I'll wipe Karen Mills to-tally off the grid. Now, aren't you glad you listened to me when I said Mikerra sounded too country?"

"Yes, and I still hate you for that. But at least now I have something to fall back on. Seth never knew my legal name."

"Well, that's a point in our favor. I'll plant as many roadblocks as I can, but he'll eventually find you. Even I'm not that good. Maybe by then we'll have come up with a plan to get rid of Seth for once and for all."

Okay, so she had a little cushion. She wished she knew how long she had before Seth tracked her down. "What about my money?"

"I'll take care of it. Trust me," Carter said. "I hide people all the time."

Three months later, Wright City, Texas

Safe.

Mikerra Stone finally felt safe.

Safe was definitely good for the former journalist, who had reached the tender age of thirty-nine. The last few months of her life had been one wild ride, ending with a two-week journey across the United States. Carter had been a godsend. He'd managed to sell her condo and moved her money without leaving much of a paper trail. Talk about miracles. She owed her life to Carter.

Her front door opened, and her brother walked

in her newly purchased house like he owned the joint. "Hey, sis."

"Hey, yourself," Mikerra shot back. "You're late."

"So? I'm here. What's the problem?"

This was her baby brother. Quentin Stone made no apologies for being late. He simply flashed that million-watt smile, and all was forgotten. She decided against chastising him about not being on time. It wouldn't do any good, anyway. "Forget it. Let's go to the furniture store." She grabbed her purse and headed for the door.

Quinn, as Quentin was called, stared at her. "I know I haven't said this since you moved back to Wright City, but it's so good to have you back home."

"It's good to be back." And it was true. The familiar knot in her stomach had begun to loosen. "I never thought I would come back here to live. I guess it was meant to be."

"Did I miss a conversation?" Drake Harrington shoveled the eggs onto his plate, adding bacon and toast to the ensemble.

His mother sat down opposite him, placing a few more strips of bacon on his plate. "No, I've just decided to do something special for your father since he's going to be retiring in a few months. So I've decided to get him that chair he's been eyeing at the furniture store."

He devoured his breakfast. This was his price to pay for three home-cooked meals every day for the last few weeks. "Look, Mom, I don't mind taking you. I just would have liked a heads-up."

"Don't you use that military lingo on me, Drake Alexander Harrington. This is a heads-up, as you call it. I think it would be nice for you to help pick out this gift for your father."

Drake met his mother's gaze. "Mom, you know you don't have to cook like this for me every day."

Shirley Harrington smiled at her son. "I promised myself that when you came home from that place, I would show you how much I love you. I still don't know why you picked the most dangerous occupation in the army. You just had to go jump out of planes, didn't you? Why couldn't you just be a paper pusher like your father?"

Drake didn't want to get into a debate about being an airborne ranger. He loved his job. It gave him a rush. Or at least it used to. "I'm thinking about retiring next year, when my hitch is up."

Shirley gasped. "Baby, really?"

"Yeah, I can retire. My twenty years was up last year. Who knows? Maybe I'll decide to settle down." Drake knew that was highly unlikely. The last thing he was looking for was a woman.

"That would be nice," Shirley said. "But won't that mean you'll have to go back to Iraq before they'll let you out?"

"You know, with the military, anything is possible."

"Well, I know I've been preaching these last few years about you getting out. But if that's the case, I'd rather you stay in until this excuse of a war is over."

He knew how hard it was for his mother to admit that. But he also knew the army was what he needed right now in his life. He patted his mother's hand. "Don't worry, Mom."

"I'll always worry. I'm your mother. It's what I do."

An hour later Drake accompanied his mother to Wright City Furniture Store in downtown Wright City.

Shirley led her son to the leather section of the store. She stopped in front of an oversize red leather chair.

It would look great in his father's office, he thought. "Mom, are you sure about this? This chair is over two grand."

His mother caressed the chair. "What's your point?" She looked at him. "Are you trying to tell me the man that gave you life isn't worth two grand?"

He knew she was teasing. Or at least he hoped she was. "No, Mom. I've just never seen you spend that kind of cash without consulting Dad first. He's going to blow a gasket."

"Not unless you tell him."

"How are you going to explain this to him?"

"I don't have to explain anything to anyone. Besides, I have my own money."

Drake raised his hands in surrender. "Okay, Mom. I think it's a cool chair."

Shirley smiled at him. "Much better." She signaled for the salesman. "Why don't you look around and see if you find something else for your father?"

Drake glanced around the large showroom. "I'll do a walkabout while you wrap things up."

His mother waved him away as she headed over to meet the aging salesman.

Drake slowly ambled his way across the showroom floor to look for a present for his father. He stopped cold halfway to the recliner section of the store. The woman lying on the plaid couch, with her eyes closed, captivated him. The rapid beat of his heart told him it was her. He'd been dreaming about her for only the last two years.

He quietly stepped over to where she was lying to get a positive ID. Even if he hadn't recognized her from high school, his heart would have told him he was correct. It was her. "Surely you're not Mikerra 'I've got bigger fish to fry than you' Stone?"

He smiled as her eyes sprang open and she jumped off the couch, dropping her leather purse in the process. It was her. She had filled out in all the right places. She was as tall and regal as ever, but now she had a healthy look to her. She wasn't skinny by any means, and he liked that. She was what people would describe as thick, with curves galore. Just the way she should be.

She was dressed in blue jean shorts and a snug-fitting white blouse that hinted at her full cleavage. Her smooth brown legs seemed to go on forever.

"I'm sorry. Do I know you?" She stared at him blankly.

Oh, that hurt. She didn't remember him. He sure remembered her. "Yeah, I guess you wouldn't remember me." He extended his hand to her. "I'm Drake Harrington. I was your first."

Mikerra fought to find her voice. He was the last person she'd thought she'd see. True, he was her first, and she'd thought of him often over the years. Drake Harrington was standing directly in front of her. All six feet three inches of him. His rich chocolate skin seemed to intensify with each second the silence stretched between them. He was dressed in shorts and a T-shirt that hugged those bulging biceps and that wall of a chest too well. What was he doing in town?

"Drake, it's been a while." Was that the best she could do? After all, she made her living with words, or at least she had until six months ago. A simple explanation should have been a snap.

He crossed his large arms across the big, broad expanse of a chest and smiled down at her. He was enjoying this. "I'd think a prizewinning journalist could do a lot better than that."

Mikerra hated being on the receiving end of his sarcasm, but after all, she probably deserved that and a whole lot more. "True. Last I heard, you were jumping out of planes."

"Still am. I just got back from Iraq. I'm home on leave for another week."

Mikerra took a deep breath. The situation was going from bad to worse. They were in the same place at the same time. What were the odds? "Why don't we just start over?"

"Over from what? From the last time you told me that you didn't have time for someone entering the military or from when you broke my heart?"

Chapter 2

Mikerra stared at Drake, incredulous. "Can you please get over yourself? We were eighteen at the time. I told you I was going to college, and I did. Just like you were going into the military. We both made a choice. You could have come after me if I was that important to you."

"How do you know I didn't?"

"Did you?"

"Well, no."

She reached for her purse, which had fallen to the floor. A few of the contents were scattered about. She quickly grabbed her cell phone, lipstick, and hairbrush. She straightened and faced her opponent. "Look, Drake, I have some shopping to do. It's nice to see you, but I have some furniture to buy."

He stood rooted to the spot, breathing hard, like he was seconds from blowing his stack. "I'm not moving, woman."

"Well, fine. Stay there. I have a house to furnish. I can come back and look at couches later."

"Why are you buying furniture, anyway?"

Mikerra had figured everyone in town knew the

answer to that. "I just bought the Henshaw place. I moved back home a few months ago."

He rubbed his forehead in confusion. "Why? I thought you were doing so well at the magazine. Last I heard you were the senior editor and reporter."

"I was. I just wanted a change," she lied.

"Sounds like a load of bull to me," he said. "You're a big-time city girl now. Why would you want to come live in Hicksville?" He eyed her skeptically, as if he already knew her secret. "Somebody after you?"

His question was too close for comfort. "No," she said quietly. "My parents do live here, Drake. Quinn moved back a year ago."

Drake nodded. "Yeah, Mom told me that."

"Well, it's been great talking with you." *Not.* "But I do have to finish shopping."

A slow, easy smile crossed Drake's handsome, chiseled face. "Why don't I join you? Mom is still shopping, so I got time."

Why was he doing this to her? Was this his version of revenge? "You don't have to. I'm sure you have better things to do."

"Yes, I do. But at present, none of them would be as delightful as hearing what you've been up to since you trampled my heart like it was a spider under your foot."

Mikerra shook her head. She wasn't going to get out of this fool's reach until she told him what she figured he wanted to hear. She might as well get it over with now. "I can sum it up for you right now," she said. "I graduated with a bachelor's degree in journalism. Got a master's in creative writing and political science from Syracuse. Then I interned at *New York* magazine for two years. After that they hired me. I was on the political and the society beat. The last five years I was in the editorial department and did a lot of reporting."

She left out the horrible events of the last few years. "Never married. Have a dog. His name is Terror."

Drake laughed. "You're kidding, right?"

"No, I'm not. His name fits him. He is a terror, but in a good way. He's a Yorkshire terrier."

Drake shook his head. "No, I mean you didn't mention getting the Hannah Prize. That's a big deal, and you don't even mention it."

"Because I got that for my coverage of September eleventh, and I didn't do anything. I just got some quotes from people whose lives were shattered by some horrific events."

He looked as if he understood. "I hear you. I wasn't in the country when that happened, but I wished I had been. I would have been right there, doing whatever I could to help out."

She knew there must have been a compliment in there somewhere. But she didn't want to talk about the series of articles she had written on the devastation on 9/11. "Well, I really must get back to shopping. Quinn is helping me shop."

He nodded. This time he moved out of her way and let her pass.

Mikerra thought she was home free until she heard him say, "If Quinn needs help, tell him I'm happy to lend a hand. I'll be over as soon as I take Mom home."

"Did I hear someone mention my name?" Quinn walked up to his sister just as he spotted Drake. "Hey, man. You're going to help me with all this stuff. She's bought like two truckloads of stuff. The delivery truck is already full, and we'll probably have to make two trips back here as it is."

Mikerra shook her head. Leave it to her brother to make a horrible situation worse. "Quinn, I'm sure

Drake has something better to do than help us move furniture. I wouldn't want to occupy all his free time."

"Oh, I don't have anything else going on. I'll be glad to help," said Drake.

Quinn slapped his hands together in celebration. "Hey, this will be fun. Mikerra is an awesome cook. She's volunteered to cook one of her gourmet meals for me, since I'm helping her. You don't mind one more, right, sis?"

What was she supposed to say? No? "I don't mind."

Drake smiled in satisfaction as Mikerra agreed to fix both him and Quinn a gourmet meal for moving her furniture. It felt almost as good as jumping out of a plane. He even felt a little light-headed at the victory.

But Mikerra was trying to back out gracefully. "Don't feel that you have to, Drake. Quinn has an annoying habit of backing people into a corner by not giving them a chance to refuse."

Her reluctance was starting to eat at Drake. Why didn't she want to talk to him? It wasn't as though they were complete strangers. They had a history. "And I told you, I want to catch up with what's going on in your life."

She nodded. "Of course."

Drake glanced around the showroom, looking for his mother. She was walking toward them, with a smile on her face. It could only mean she had got the chair for a steal. "I'll just take Mom home, and I'll come help you guys."

His mother joined the trio. "Hello. Aren't you Carolina Stone's daughter?"

Mikerra nodded, hoping this didn't turn into a

journey down her family tree. Luckily, Drake's mother spared her.

"You and Drake were inseparable your senior year of high school," said Shirley. "I was proud to hear of your accomplishments over the years. I told Drake he should have gone after you when he finally got out of college, but he was stubborn, just like his daddy."

"You graduated from college? I thought you went into the army." Mikerra's voice was filled with awe, which infuriated Drake.

"Yes, I went to college on the military's dime. I have a master's degree in information technology," said Drake.

Mikerra nodded.

Quinn cleared his throat. "Well, I don't have a master's. I barely got my bachelor's, but I think I still have enough brains to know when I'm the odd man out."

Mikerra tore her gaze from Drake and laughed. "I guess you're right," she told Drake. "Maybe we do have a lot to catch up on."

Drake decided it was time for a little button pushing. She used to hate that, he remembered. "Oh, I get it. Since I went to college, now it's okay for me to move furniture with your brother?"

Mikerra gasped. "Don't you dare talk to me like I'm some kind of gold digger or something! First, you're all up in my face about something that happened so long ago that I can barely remember it. Now you're calling me names."

Drake stepped toward Mikerra, ready to read her the riot act and a whole lot more, but both Quinn and Shirley stepped between them. Quinn stood in front of his sister, and Drake was looking down at his mother.

"Hey now, Mikerra. Chill. You know how it is. Well,

maybe you don't," said Quinn. "Anyway, you guys need to sort all this out, but not in a public place. Wright City is too small for you guys to start a fight here and not expect Mom and Dad to hear about it. And you know how they hate drama. After we finish moving your stuff, I suggest you and Drake talk about your situation."

Mikerra nodded.

Drake did the same, struggling to keep a smile from forming on his face. Not only was she going to cook for him later, but he was going to have her alone later tonight. "Okay, Quinn."

Shirley motioned for her son to follow her. "It was nice seeing you, Mikerra. When you and my son get through fighting, you have to get me up to speed on what you've been doing."

"Yes, Mrs. Harrington," called Mikerra as she and Quinn headed to another section of the store.

His mother looked at him with that "I raised you better" look. "Now, my mule-headed son, could you please tell me why you deliberately picked a fight with that woman?"

He wished he had an answer for his mother. "I don't know. Well, actually, I do know. I offered to help her brother move her furniture, and she was all like no thank you. But the minute you said I had a college degree, her tune changed. How dare she think I was less?"

His mother continued walking to the rear of the store, with Drake on her heels. "Oh, don't get your boxers in a knot. That woman is just like every other independent woman. She's looking out for her interests. A woman wants to know a man has plans and aspirations, especially an accomplished woman like that. She has no idea what you've been up to for the last twenty or so years, but she is supposed to welcome you with open arms."

"No, but she just assumed I was less, because she thought I didn't have a college degree."

"She was only going on the way you presented yourself. You were acting like some brute. I would have done the same. That woman has been through enough without you and your macho act."

"I guess you told me." Drake rubbed his head. Yeah, his mom was tearing him a new one, because he deserved it. He had been a jerk. His little verbal skirmish had cost him another headache. "You got anything for a headache?"

"Another headache? I think you need to go to the doctor. I know your body is adjusting from being in Iraq for eighteen months, but you've had a lot of headaches in the last three weeks."

He knew his mother was right, and this headache was worse than the others. But not even the sharp pain pounding in his head would keep him from having a gourmet meal with Mikerra Stone.

Four hours later Drake was beginning to rethink the whole dinner plan. He'd naturally assumed Mikerra had bought a few pieces of furniture, but she'd practically bought out the entire store. The delivery truck, Quinn's truck, and Drake's father's truck were all loaded to the hilt. And the delivery truck had to return for a second load.

Mikerra politely directed the deliverymen to place the couch in a corner of the room. Initially Drake had thought it was not going to work, but it did. The plaid couch made the large room seem cozy.

Quinn sighed when he saw the second load arrive. "Who's installing the plasma TV?"

Mikerra laughed, directing upstairs to the two deliverymen carrying her very heavy bed frame. "First door on the right," she told them. To Quinn, she said, "Daddy. You suck with tools."

"Do not," Quinn shot back. "You suck with directions. Are those wonderful men going to put your bed together?"

"Yes," Mikerra said. "Dinner will be ready in about an hour." She walked into the kitchen.

Quinn plopped down in the love seat as soon as his sister was out of sight. "I don't know about you, Drake, but I'm beat."

"Yeah, this has been a real workout for me, too." Drake sat in an oversize recliner. "I think this is the most I've done since I've been home." He felt the pounding in his head increase, and the room began to whirl and slip in and out of focus. He closed his eyes against the motion. "I guess I was more tired than I thought," he groaned, opening his eyes and feeling twice as bad.

"I'll go see if Mikerra has anything cold to drink," Quinn announced as he rose from his seat.

Drake nodded and closed his eyes. Maybe if he took a quick nap, the little black dots would stop dancing in front of his eyes.

Mikerra watched her brother rush into the kitchen, instantly alerting her reporter's senses. Quinn generally ambled. He never rushed anywhere. "What's wrong?"

Quinn opened her refrigerator and took out two bottles of imported water. "Drake looks overheated. Maybe it was that last load of furniture. You know, you didn't have to buy all the furniture at once."

Mikerra didn't like the sound of that. She followed her brother into the living room and found Drake sprawled out on his back on the floor. "Oh, my gosh." She raced to her former high school sweetheart.

Quinn said more, but Mikerra ignored him, focusing on Drake, who was out cold. Quinn looked over her shoulder. "He was in the recliner when I left. He must have passed out. He didn't look too good. And he was slurring his words. You know, like he was drunk."

She kneeled beside Drake and patted Drake's face to wake him. Nothing. She took one of the bottles of water from her brother. After she opened it, she poured the water on Drake's face, hoping to revive him.

"Hey," Drake sputtered, rolling his head from side to side. "What gives?"

"You were out cold." Mikerra tried to help the large man stand up, but it was useless. He was too much man for her. Quinn had to help him to the couch.

"I'm fine," Drake growled. "Just a little hot, that's all."

Mikerra didn't believe him for a second. But being around pigheaded men all her life, she knew it was a losing battle. "Okay, Drake. You're right. You're probably just hot. Why don't you lie down until dinner is ready?"

Drake shook his head. "I'm fine."

Mikerra rose. "I know. It's a man thing. I'll wake you when dinner's ready." She went back to the kitchen.

She was taking out the fixings for shrimp scampi when Drake stormed into the kitchen, looking like hell's fury.

"Look, Mikerra, I don't need you all up in my business. I can take care of my own damn headaches without you playing nurse. I've been handling them just fine for the last three weeks."

"You've been having headaches for three weeks,

and you hadn't seen a doctor? Drake, it could be a warning sign for something serious. You should go to a doctor."

"I'm a grown man, and I can handle my own business," he grumbled.

She didn't want to fight with him. She wanted to find out why he was having so many headaches. So she tried another tactic. "I'm sorry if I offended you, Drake. Do you still want dinner?"

"No, I think I'd better go before you try to dump me again." He strode out of the kitchen without another word.

She leaned against the counter and let out a sigh. Some days it didn't pay to be concerned about a man.

Chapter 3

After Drake left in a huff, Mikerra decided to forgo cooking and surf the Internet. Something about Drake's headache had nudged a memory she was trying to forget.

She opened her laptop and clicked on the file labeled "Terror," so named for her dog. The file opened and there it was. Project Perfect 192, a military project so secret, it had cost her her job, her relationship with a married man, and quite possibly her life.

Information on PP 192, as it was more commonly known to the Joint Chiefs of Staff and the members of the defense committee, had been unknowingly leaked to her by her former lover. Once Senator Seth McCaffrey realized she knew about PP 192, she became expendable, and that was when she knew her life in New York was over.

She searched the Internet for information and found little. She was hoping for more leaks, but there was nothing. It was as if the project didn't exist, which meant only one thing to a journalist; namely, it had existed.

Given their severity, Drake's headaches seemed

more like very intense migraines than anything else. She looked up migraine symptoms and decided that that wasn't what he was experiencing. But she'd witnessed only one isolated incident. Not even the most experienced physician would diagnose something this serious after only one episode.

She would have to see how and when the headaches occurred. Drake's headache could have been triggered by the Texas heat, the physical exertion of carrying heavy furniture, or the fact that they'd been quarreling earlier in the furniture store. It was the first time they had laid eyes on each other in over twenty years.

All those factors could have brought on a headache for even the average person.

She reached for her cordless phone and dialed a familiar D.C. number.

"Hey, Sloan. It's Mikerra."

"Girl, you know my mama already called me and told you and Drake were arguing in the furniture store earlier today," Sloan Duncan said. "I can't believe it. Mom says it's all over town. I still can't believe that you actually moved back."

She couldn't either. But something had pulled her back to Wright City, and she was going to find out what it was. She could have moved anywhere to hide from Seth, but all signs had pointed home. "Yeah, thanks to Carter, it was pretty painless, until I ran into Drake. Can you believe he's still whining about our senior year?"

"What can I say? You broke my man's heart. He might not tell you that, but you did."

Mikerra laughed. "Oh yes, he did. In the furniture store. The big, bad army ranger told me just that today. You'd think a career soldier would have more pride. He jumps out of planes, for Pete's sake! And he's still whining about me breaking up with him on graduation night."

Sloan gasped between bouts of laughter. "Stop, girl. You know you guys got some unfinished business, and until you settle it, it's always going to be like World War III with the two of you whenever you get together."

She knew that. Knew from the moment their eyes met. But was that what had pulled her home? "I know, Sloan, but that's not why I called."

"What's up?"

"Remember last year about PP One-ninety-two?"

Sloan's voice was suddenly serious. "Yeah. And?"

"What were the requirements?"

"Oh, you mean what's what?"

Mikerra reached for a pen. "Yeah. Who got chosen?"

"I'm not saying that such a program exists, but if it does, it would have to be for the best of the best," Sloan answered in his official role of junior administrative assistant to the Joint Chiefs of Staff.

"I think Drake may be a part of it. How can I know for sure?"

Sloan paused, probably weighing his options.

"He's been home about two or three weeks," Mikerra went on quickly when Sloan remained silent too long. He was definitely hiding something. "He's been having some kind of headache every day since he returned from Iraq."

"How do you know all this? Does this mean you guys are reconciling already?"

Mikerra grunted. "No, you didn't. Quinn backed me into a corner, and I was going to cook dinner for them for moving my furniture, but Drake passed out from that drug that is the focus of PP One-ninety-two."

"Passed out?"

"Yeah, I remember that the Project Perfect drug

has some kind of crazy side effect that can lead to a brain tumor."

"I really can't talk about this now. I'll get back to you." Sloan ended the call.

Mikerra's heartbeat accelerated as she pushed the end button on her phone. She hoped with all her might she was dead wrong, or Drake would be dead in a matter of months.

The next morning, after an hour of letting Cora Barnes, the owner of the Wright City Florist, suggest a floral arrangement, Drake was on his way to Mikerra's with a large bouquet of bluebonnets, the state flower; sunflowers; and daisies.

He parked in front of her house and took a deep breath. *Damn.* His headache was getting worse. He opened the glove compartment and found a travel pack of aspirin. He tossed an aspirin in his mouth and swallowed without the benefit of water. A little trick he'd learned in the desert.

He reached for the flowers and angled them around the steering wheel of the truck. As he walked up to her front door, he realized he probably should have called and asked if she had plans for the day. That would have been the mature adult thing to do. *Too late now,* he thought as he rang the doorbell.

She answered the door, dressed in shorts and an oversize New York Mets T-shirt. Her glossy black hair was pulled back in a ponytail, and he heard Etta James belting out "At Last" in the background. Drake realized he must have caught her in the middle of a cleaning fury.

She looked him up and down. And down and up. Apparently, she approved of his casual outfit of a

T-shirt and shorts. "Drake, what are you doing here? How's the headache?"

"Long gone," he lied. He pushed the vase of flowers toward her. "These are for you. It's a combo offer. Part apology, part thanks for yesterday."

She motioned him inside the house. "Well, you don't have anything to apologize for. But thank you just the same. I love flowers. I was thinking of planting a rose garden in the front yard." She closed the door. "Have a seat on the couch, and I'll be right back." She headed for what he figured was the kitchen.

Drake took a deep breath and took a seat. He willed the headache away and waited patiently for her to return.

She returned with a glass of water for him.

"I didn't ask for this," Drake said. He was defensive and didn't know why.

Mikerra nodded. "It's pretty hot outside, and you look like you could use a little refreshment." She handed him the glass.

Okay, maybe she was right about the heat. He just didn't know if he was feeling the heat outside or the heat within his own body. How could this woman have that kind of effect on his body even though they hadn't seen each other in over twenty years?

"What are you doing today?" She sat beside him on the couch.

"Not much," Drake said, trying to sound casual. "I thought we could have lunch or something. You know, a clean slate kind of thing. Maybe get to know each other as adults, versus horny teenagers." And just maybe he could repay her for breaking his heart all those years ago.

Mikerra smiled at him. "Lunch sounds nice. I am in the middle of cleaning and can always use a deterrent."

Drake knew something was definitely wrong. Had it not been just twenty-four hours prior that they'd argued like old lovers? Now she was being nice to him. He knew not to look good luck in the mouth. "All right. How about lunch at Jay's?"

Mikerra nodded and rose. "Like we have a choice?" Jay's was the only diner in town. It also had the best home cooking in town. "Can you give me about thirty minutes to get ready?"

Drake knew he should offer to leave while she changed, but that would give her the advantage. If she wanted him out of her house, she would have to say so.

She handed him the TV remote and headed for her stairs. "I'm sure you can be trusted to stay downstairs while I shower and change." She went up the stairs without waiting for his answer.

Drake punched the remote and couldn't decide if he should have been upset or flattered by her question. But he was a little turned on with the accusation. It would serve her right if he was bold enough to walk in her bedroom unannounced and join her in the shower. Too bad the strength of his headache had increased at least fivefold.

He rubbed his forehead, wishing the pain would just stop. He took out his cell phone and dialed his commanding officer's number. He hadn't wanted to take extra leave, but his headaches weren't getting better, and there was no way he could report to Fort Benning while still nursing these headaches.

"Colonel Stark," the gruff voice stated.

Colonel Mason Stark's bark was always worse than his bite. "Colonel, this is Master Sergeant Drake Harrington." He had to make it sound official, just in case the big brass was listening in on their conversation.

"Yes, Master Sergeant?"

Drake knew the probability of getting additional leave in wartime was probably nil, but he had to try. "I was hoping to get some additional leave, sir."

The colonel sighed. "How much time are we talking? Jump school is set to begin July first."

He was making the refusal sound good, Drake thought. "About a fortnight, sir." Asking for two additional weeks in wartime was just nuts. He was lucky he was able to leave Iraq in the first place without having his tour extended.

"Family problems?"

"No, sir."

"Health problems? How are you feeling since your return from Iraq? Any kind of pain?"

"No, sir." Why would he ask that? "No. I just have some loose ends I'd like to attend to before reporting to Fort Benning."

"I'm sure something can be arranged, Harrington. Take the time, and I'll see you in a few weeks." The colonel ended the call.

Being a career soldier, Drake knew better than to question the good hand that life had just dealt him. He had expected to have to go into a long explanation of why he needed more time. Granted, he had known Mason Stark most of his military career and had covered Mason's ass more times than he wanted to count, but nothing in the military was this easy. Something wasn't right.

Upstairs, Mikerra rushed through her shower, just in case Drake wasn't feeling entirely honorable. Although, she knew that was about as likely as a snowstorm in Texas in July. She was surprised to see him today, and even if he had thrown a monkey wrench in her plans for cleaning her house, she could always initiate plan B—finding out about his headaches.

She slipped into her favorite peach Victoria's Secret bra and panty set and then put on pleated denim shorts and a tank top, complementing her healthy frame. She glanced at herself in the mirror. "You still got it, girl." She shoved her freshly pedicured feet into her sandals, grabbed her purse, and headed downstairs.

Her foot stopped on the bottom stair. Drake wasn't in the living room. Had he changed his mind already? Maybe her crack about him being untrustworthy had been too much. Men's egos were so fragile these days. You couldn't say much to them without them running scared, she reminded herself. In desperate need of an outing, she decided she would go to the diner for lunch with or without Drake. The walls of her house were beginning to get to her. She needed to get out. Perhaps her mother or grandmother would be willing to have lunch with her. She was picking up the cordless phone, ready to hit the speed dial option, when she heard the toilet flush in the downstairs bathroom.

Drake entered the room and stopped. "I didn't realize you'd be dressed so soon. Most females take forever." He stared at her outfit. "You look nice, though."

Mikerra laughed, though she didn't really want to hear about those other females he knew. Why was she feeling jealous? It was just lunch. "Well, Drake, I'm not like most women. I do my own thing in my own time."

He walked toward her. "Hey, chill on the 'I am woman' speech. I'm just stating a fact."

She was overreacting. Mikerra took a deep breath and apologized. "How about that lunch?"

She motioned him to the front door.

"Lead the way, Care Bear."

He wasn't playing fair. He'd used his nickname for her. That nickname brought back all those memories that had haunted her dreams this last year and had most likely brought her back home to Wright City.

Chapter 4

After settling in one of the booths at Jay's Diner, Mikerra studied Drake a little more carefully. He rubbed his forehead constantly, obviously in pain. His beautiful dark brown eyes looked tired.

"I'm sure Jay has some aspirin," she said, waving for the waitress.

"I don't need any aspirin. And I don't need a mother. I already have one," he said in a clipped voice.

Mikerra decided not to argue with him and snatched the plastic menu from its holder. "I am well aware that you do not need another maternal figure in your life. I was merely stating the fact that you look like you are in a great deal of pain and want to ease it."

Drake stared across the table at her. "I guess I'm a little touchy today. Sorry."

"Something wrong?" She placed the menu back in the metal holder and focused her attention on Drake's handsome face.

He smiled. "I probably shouldn't be telling you this, but it's starting to work on my nerves. And I know once I say it aloud, it will seem stupid."

"Share."

"You haven't changed one bit, Care Bear," he teased. "I called my commanding officer to get some additional leave time, and he authorized it without any hesitation."

"Okay, I know I'm military stupid and I don't know a lot of the rules, but isn't that a good thing?"

"Sorry for the delay, guys," the waitress said, interrupting their conversation. "We've been swamped." Her brown eyes immediately went to Drake. "You're Drake Harrington. I've seen you in here before with your mother. I'm Janice Brandt. I graduated with your brother, Dylan. If you need anything, you just let me know."

Drake nodded and looked at Mikerra, silently asking if she was ready to order. It was as if the last twenty years didn't exist and they were back in their senior year in high school and this was the Dairy Queen. "Ready?"

Mikerra nodded. "Yes, I'll have the chicken salad."

Drake shook his head. "No, she'll have the fried pork chops, with mashed potatoes and corn, and I'll have the same." His voice left no room for negotiation.

Janice nodded and left before Mikerra could object.

"How do you know I still eat pork chops?"

"Do you?" he asked.

"Yes." She hated when he was right.

He smiled at her. "Well, I think it's rather a moot point, don't you?"

Mikerra nodded, thinking about the amount of highly fattening food she'd eaten over the last few months. Oddly enough, she'd lost forty pounds in the last three months. "I guess you're right. I'm still stuck in a New York frame of mind."

"Well, you're home, and that salad crap isn't going to work here, girl. Besides, I think you look great."

Of course, he was just trying to make her feel good, she thought. He probably didn't give one thought to what he ate. His metabolism was probably so high, he could eat anything he pleased and not gain a pound. "Thanks, Drake."

"You don't believe me, do you?"

"I didn't say that."

He stared at her with those dark brown eyes. "You didn't have to. I know that look. There must have been a man or two who didn't appreciate you and told you lies."

Mikerra felt exposed. How could he read her so well? "I didn't say that, either."

The waitress returned with their food. She placed the plates on the table all the while looking at Drake. Once she finished, she glanced at Drake again. "If you need anything, don't hesitate to call me." She left them alone again.

"Sounds like you've got an admirer," Mikerra teased, changing the subject. She didn't want to talk about her past anymore.

Drake cut into one of his thick pork chops and glanced up at her. "Sometimes we get attention from everyone but the right one."

"Possibly."

He laughed and started eating his lunch. "You think you can dodge me, but it's not going to happen. And you know exactly what I mean, so don't try to play those word games with me."

He stared at her with those intense eyes, making her feel like she was in trouble and he was about to sentence her to life in jail or something much worse, like a night in his company.

Mikerra sighed. She wanted to get to the bottom of his headaches but knew it was going to cost her something. Would it be a secret of her past?

"Are you going to stare at the food or eat it?" he asked.

Mikerra looked down at her plate and realized she hadn't taken a bite. Drake, on the other hand, had made a considerable dent in his two pork chops. "Sorry. How's your head?"

"Fine."

Mikerra smiled as she picked up her fork. "Now who's playing the avoidance game?"

"Touché." He lifted his glass of tea and toasted her. "To Mikerra. I will know all your secrets inside and out, even the one that chased you all the way back to Wright City." He took a healthy sip.

"I-I don't have any secrets, Drake." She shoveled some food in her mouth before she started confessing about being on the grassy knoll in Dallas on that fateful day in November 1963.

He shrugged and kept eating, as if she hadn't said anything. "You have secrets, CB. Even a thickheaded man like me knows someone like you wouldn't just move back here because you miss your mom. You're hiding, aren't you?"

She didn't want to admit it. Her family didn't even know the real reason she'd come back. They seemed to have bought the old homecoming story, and it was partially right. But the cold, hard truth was staring her in the face in the form of her high school sweetheart. She was running from herself.

Drake watched Mikerra stare past him. He was mostly guessing, but he knew a woman with a secret when he saw one. What or who was Mikerra hiding from? Her light brown eyes became distant; she was in a place far away. How could he pull her back? "Are you going to answer me today, or what?"

She blinked. "Oh, I'm sorry. What were you saying?" She took a quick sip of water.

"I was saying you need to finish your meal." He'd save the cross-examination for later. Mikerra obviously couldn't concentrate on two things at once. "People will think the food isn't any good."

Mikerra nodded and began eating.

When Drake was satisfied she was eating, he paid more attention to the throbbing headache. He needed something for the pain. It seemed to have settled right between his eyes.

She leaned across the table, her cleavage claiming all of Drake's attention. "Okay, Drake. I'll make a deal with you. You tell me about your headaches, and I'll tell you why I left New York."

To the average man, it would seem like a win-win situation, but as a career soldier fresh from a war zone, Drake knew nothing was what it seemed. She continued her meal as he considered her offer. "Okay, you've got a deal."

She smiled at him. "You first."

She had him, he knew. He had to tell her something. So a slight obliteration of the facts was in order. "I've been having some slight headaches since my return to the States."

"How slight? I mean, yesterday you passed out. Was it from the pain?"

He had forgotten about that little episode. "It was a combination of things. This is Texas, it's summer, and it's damn hot."

"Very true. But you passed out, and we had a time reviving you. I just don't want it to be something more serious, especially since you're ignoring it."

"It can't be that serious. I was checked out by the doc before I could come home on leave from Iraq."

"So you believe the doctor?"

"Why wouldn't I? It was a military doctor. If it were something serious, he would have said so. He told me I'd have some slight headaches for a few weeks. I'm sure this is normal."

"How is having splitting headaches normal?"

"Who said they were splitting? I said they were slight."

She waved her hand at his statement. "Oh please! You look like you're two seconds away from crying right now."

Did he really look that bad? Maybe he wasn't as good at hiding his emotions as he thought. "All right, CB. I'll tell you what. I'll go to the doctor tomorrow, and you can even go with me, so you can know for sure."

She wiped her mouth, then dabbed the cloth napkin at the corners of her full lips, thinking about his offer. She probably realized his offer was about as honest as hers. "I take it we're going to have to go to Veterans Administration Medical Center in Waco or to Fort Hood," she said matter-of-factly. As if the options she presented weren't really options at all.

Drake nodded. "Waco is closer, and I could probably get in and out quicker."

She reached her hand across the table for a handshake. He took her hand cautiously, as if it were a snake. Since he didn't think it was poisonous, he shook her hand, sealing the deal.

"Why don't we leave? Janice is starting to stare at us for taking so long," she said, taking her hand back.

Drake knew she'd felt it. He sure had. The mild shock had run from the bottom of his feet to the top of his head, and he wasn't thinking of his headaches anymore. He was thinking about the woman sitting across the table from him. She'd turned him into mush with just a smile. He was so done.

That evening Drake parked in front of Mikerra's house. After the extra long lunch at Jay's, they'd taken a ride to the lake. The time they'd spent at the lake was wonderful and stress-free. Mikerra remembered the boy she'd loved in high school.

As the emotions between them had become too powerful to ignore, both Drake and Mikerra had decided to head to the shelter of the town. Neither had said a word all the way back to Mikerra's, and for that, she was grateful.

Drake Alexander Harrington had a way of getting under a girl's skin. Mikerra couldn't decide if she was against the idea or not. She watched him as he opened her car door for her. "W-would you like to come in?"

Drake looked at her. "Sure." He took her hand and led her up the walkway to her front door. "You better wave at your neighbors, or someone will be calling your parents, telling them I'm trying to force my way in your house."

Mikerra waved at her neighbors, Clyde and Melba Evans. The Evanses sat on their porch every evening and could probably report what time everyone went to bed on her street. Except Mikerra, since she was the youngest home owner on the street by at least thirty years.

"Hello, Mr. and Mrs. Evans," Mikerra called to the couple.

"Hello, Mikerra," Mrs. Evans called back. "And we told you that since we're neighbors, you can call us by our first names. Don't make me have to tell your grandmother."

"Yes, ma'am." Mikerra elbowed Drake in his flat stomach as he snickered.

"You and your man have a nice evening. We were young once, too, you know. We know what goes on at this hour of the night," replied Mrs. Evans.

Mikerra nodded, unlocked her front door, and hurried inside. Once Drake entered the house, he doubled over in laughter. Mikerra closed the door with a thud. She walked to the foyer table and plunked her purse down.

"That was too funny. They're worse than my parents," he joked, chuckling.

Mikerra didn't see this as such a comedic moment. "How is that funny? They think we're going to . . . to . . . you know." She could feel her face become more flushed with each embarrassing word.

"Now, Mikerra, we both know you want me, but I'm not as easy as you think," he teased, walking toward her.

She knew she was in trouble when he stopped directly in front of her. The aroma of his cologne penetrated her nostrils. She couldn't help it; she inhaled deeply and apparently lost all use of the practical side of her brain. "Yes, Drake, I want you. But this time there's no walking away for either of us. Do you think you're ready for that?"

Chapter 5

The next morning Mikerra paced her large kitchen nervously. Drake was supposed to pick her up ten minutes ago for their trip to the Veterans Administration Medical Center in Waco. Maybe after last night he'd decided against her accompanying him to Waco. She placed her breakfast dishes in the sink just as the phone rang.

She snatched up the cordless phone, ready to read him the riot act for being late, and said, "This had better be good, Drake."

"This is better than good, and it's not Drake," Sloan said. "Actually, I'm surprised you're not checking your caller ID before you pick up the phone."

"If I had more sense, I probably would. But I don't, so I didn't. What's up? I know you're not just calling me to pass the time of day."

Sloan sighed. "Well, I've been snooping around, and I really need to talk to you guys in person. So I'm coming home next weekend. This is big, Care Bear."

"Not you, too."

Sloan laughed. "I couldn't resist. It's been ages since I called you that."

Mikerra didn't want to travel down memory lane. She'd done enough of that the night before with Drake, but some things were inevitable. "Drake's been calling me that," she admitted.

"Why are you waiting on Drake, anyway?"

Mikerra walked through her house as she answered her childhood friend. "We made a deal that he'd go to the doctor and I'd tell him about my life in New York."

"You're going to tell him about Seth and his threats?"

Mikerra had known the dangers of telling Sloan her troubles when she was considering breaking off her relationship with the senator, but the man had threatened her job and her life. She'd had no one else to turn to but Sloan. He was a wonderful listener. Almost as good as Terror. "I'm telling him part of the story. I just want him to get those headaches checked out."

"Doesn't he have to go to the VA in Waco?"

"Yes, he does." Mikerra didn't think Drake would get a proper examination, but had little room to voice her opinion. "It was either there or Fort Hood."

"Oh, I see," Sloan said. He was silent for almost a minute before he spoke again. "Hey, can you get the doctor to fax me the report on Drake's exam? Fax it to my house."

That didn't sit well with her. Why would the junior administrative assistant to the Joint Chiefs of Staff need to see Drake's medical results? All he had to do was request the report from his superiors, unless he didn't want them to know he was looking at it. "Sloan, what the heck is going on?"

"Can't talk now. Got a meeting with the big boys. See you next week." He ended the call.

Mikerra shook her head. Sloan was in the perfect job. He knew some of the most powerful secrets in the free world. He'd also leaked to Mikerra some of her best stories, but it was Seth who got her fired. He'd thought being unemployed would make her stay with him, but it had only made her see the person she had become.

She was just about to look for her car keys to drive to Drake's house when the doorbell rang. "About damn time." She stalked to her front door and wrenched it open. "You're late."

Drake smiled and stepped inside. "And you look very nice." He kissed her on the cheek and walked farther inside her house.

Mikerra was stunned into silence. Glancing down at his apparel, she forgot she was upset at him for being late or for the fact that he hadn't apologized for being late. She opened her mouth to voice her protest but immediately closed it when she got a good look at him.

Drake was dressed in cotton shorts that only made that army body look too good to think about. The dark T-shirt molded his muscular upper body like a dream. Mikerra could easily imagine running her hands over that flat stomach and defined chest.

"Hey, are we going, or what?" he asked.

Mikerra snapped back to the conversation. "Sorry. What were you saying?"

Drake walked over to her, a wide smile on that chocolate face. "I said we'd better get going. But I think you need to get your head out of the clouds first. And I know just the thing to do it." He stepped closer to her.

Mikerra took a step back, out of his range, but that only made him move closer to her. "W-what?"

His big hand captured her around the waist. "You keep trying to get away from me, but you'll soon find it's useless." He pulled her closer and kissed her lightly on the lips.

She tasted heat in those lips, which were now nudging hers apart. She was putty in this man's arms. She opened her mouth to protest, but he only pushed his tongue farther into her mouth. As his tongue dueled with hers for control of her brain, Mikerra gave up the fight.

He chuckled against her lips. "That's it, Care Bear." He moved his body against hers, letting her feel how aroused he was.

Mikerra tried valiantly not to let the sensations he was waking in her body overtake her good sense of judgment. She knew they had to stop, but couldn't form the words, especially with his tongue wrapped around hers.

Slowly he ended the kiss. "You're trying to make me miss the doctor's appointment, aren't you?" He caressed her face. "I'd forgotten how good you could kiss."

Mikerra placed a hand over her rapidly beating heart, hoping to slow it down, but it was useless. She hadn't forgotten how good he was, period. She hadn't touched this man in over twenty years, and he still lit her up like a firecracker and just as fast. "Right back at you. Ready?"

"Yeah. We'd better get out of here, or I won't be responsible for your actions." He smiled at her, daring her.

"My actions! Whose tongue was that down my throat?" She walked to the foyer table and snatched up her purse. "You act like I'm doing this on purpose." Mikerra tried to calm her nerves. She'd just had the most intense kiss she'd had in years, and he was trying to take away her moment of near orgasmic proportions. "Drake, you are a jackass." She walked to the front door, brushing past him, not caring if she bumped into him or not.

"And you're sexy when you're mad."

Mikerra stopped dead in her tracks and whipped around to face him. "Just like a man. Always thinking about sex."

"Yeah, like you weren't all into that kiss. Let's go." Drake opened the door and motioned her outside.

She went out and attempted to lock the door, but her shaky, sweaty hands betrayed her. Why did it take so many attempts to lock the door to her own house? "I didn't say the kiss wasn't nice," she said, still fumbling with the key.

"Give me that. We'll be here all day," he joked and chuckled. He took the key ring from her damp hands. He slid the key inside the lock and turned gently. Once the lock slid home, he handed the keys back to her, then kissed her on the lips for all her neighbors to see. "See? That didn't hurt, did it?"

Dazed and confused, she let Drake lead her to the truck and open the door. After she was settled inside, he closed the door and walked to the driver's side and got in.

"Why don't you tell me what happened to you?"

"Why don't you tell me about your headaches?" She shifted in her seat but didn't look in his direction.

It was going to be a long drive to the VA, he mused. Drake knew he had a woman with a guarded past. His best offense was a good defense. If he wanted to know what she'd been up to and how much trouble she was actually in, he'd have to give up a little information.

"Since the trip is about thirty minutes, why don't we both do a little sharing? You like to share, right?"

"What are you talking about?"

She was going to be slipperier than the men in his unit trying to get out of extra duty. "I mean, I tell you something about my headaches, and you tell me who has you scared enough to sell your Manhattan condo and your Benz and has you scooting all the way back to Wright City like a scared rabbit."

She sat up straight. There were only two people who had all the pieces to the puzzle. She knew her friend since childhood Kissa hadn't spilled the beans, so the other choice was her most likely squealer. "I see Sloan still can't hold his liquor."

"No, he can't." Drake hadn't denied it for a second. "He's also my best friend, just like he was yours. He might have mentioned something about you having a pricey condo a time or two in a few e-mails over the years." Drake knew that wasn't the case. He and Sloan had remained friends since graduation and had kept in contact, which also meant that Sloan had given him Mikerra updates on occasion. Unfortunately, this had also brought up some feelings he hadn't felt since high school.

"All right, but I get to go first," she said.

"Done."

"When did the headaches start?"

"The week I was scheduled to go home. In the military, when you're overseas, you have to take a variety of shots when you arrive at your destination and when you're leaving a destination. I mentioned it to the doc at the debriefing, and he told me it was normal."

"Did anyone else in your unit have those headaches?"

"You're limited to only one question."

"Damn."

Drake smiled. "My turn. When did it all fall apart?"

"That's a loaded question and you know it. To answer your one question would take longer than this trip. Try again."

She had him there. "Okay. Why buy the house? You could have just stayed with your parents until you got your head straight."

"Because I needed to do this for me. I'm almost forty, and all I had to show for my life was an award, a man who wanted to kill me, and a job with a company that fired me when he told them to."

Whoa. That was more information than he'd dared hope for, and more than he needed to know right now. He had to find something encouraging to say to her. The mood in the cab of the truck was getting downright dark. "The story on the terrorist attacks was amazing."

"That wasn't a story, Drake. I intruded on people's lives during their time of grief and asked them heartless questions about how it felt to lose someone during America's first terrorist attacks on American soil."

He watched as tears trickled down her face.

"I wanted to write a story about compassion in a city known for its rudeness. My ghoulish managing editor wanted a story about desperation and grief," she added.

"But it got you an award."

"That freaking award doesn't mean crap to me right now. That's why I don't mention it. I have to find me. I lost me somewhere."

"I know you'll find what you're looking for. That's the good thing about being back home. You can take the time you need to get your life in order."

Mikerra sniffled, grabbed the Kleenex Drake's father kept in the console of the truck, and blew her nose. "Thank you, Drake. How do your headaches feel?"

"Sometimes they're slight, sometimes they feel like migraines, and sometimes they're so intense, I have to have complete darkness to ease the pain."

"Surely, you have medication?"

"That's another question," he mocked.

"Damn."

He chuckled, loving the sound of her voice. She was sounding more and more like his old Care Bear with each muttered expletive and less like the big-city woman he'd met a few days ago.

"I think it's my turn," Drake drawled. They were on Highway 6, heading directly to the veterans medical center. "How do you plan on getting Mikerra back?"

"Well, that's where you come in. I shouldn't have left you like that all those years ago. I would like to make amends for that first. I should have handled it better. We should have stayed in touch with each other. Outside of my family, I think I only really kept in touch with Sloan and Markissa over the years."

"How is Kissa? She was always a ball of fun in high school. Last I heard, she'd divorced her husband."

"Are you using that as your next question?" Mikerra smiled at him.

"Yes, I am." He would have done just about anything to see a smile on her face.

She smiled wider. "Well, after Kissa threw that no-good lawyer out on his cheating behind, she moved back here. She started her own practice about two years ago."

"What does she do?"

Mikerra giggled. "Since you've been defending the country and everything, I'll cut you some slack. She's a chiropractor, and her practice has been very successful. She'd originally started it to piss off the ex, but she's pretty busy."

"That's great," Drake commented. And he meant it. "Maybe one evening we can have old friends' night and all catch up."

"Yes, that would be nice. I can spend time with the two people that meant the most to me in high school, and we can share our life stories."

Drake didn't know if he was ready to hear Mikerra's life story, but he knew he had to if he wanted to move forward with her.

After they arrived at the medical center, Drake and Mikerra were directed to the doctors' offices' wing. Drake felt uneasy in the large four-story building. What if it wasn't just headaches and something more serious was going on? How would he handle the news?

He held Mikerra's hand as they searched for Dr. Harry Preston's office. Finally, at the end of the hall, they located the large office.

He handed his military ID to the receptionist. After his insurance was verified, he was directed to the waiting room.

Mikerra plopped down in the seat next to him. "I'm sure this won't take long, Drake."

"You were always the optimist, weren't you?"

She smiled. "You know, I missed this."

"What? We haven't seen each other in a while."

"I miss being able to be me. I just didn't realize it until now. Thank you."

Drake watched her carefully. She'd been so guarded whenever they were alone. Nothing like the woman who broke his heart into a million pieces over twenty years ago. It was hard to tell where the real Mikerra began. "If you want to thank me, take off your clothes."

Mikerra gasped. The elderly lady sitting across the

room gasped. The elderly man sitting next to her looked a bit excited.

"Drake, have you lost your mind?"

He leaned over and kissed her soundly on the mouth. "No. I'm dead serious. We didn't finish playing Twenty Questions in the truck. You owe me."

"I do not."

"Chicken."

Mikerra opened her mouth to retort, but the receptionist halted all verbal foreplay. "Master Sergeant Harrington, Dr. Preston is ready for you."

Drake stared into Mikerra's very expressive face. "Well, looks like this is it." He rose from the chair.

Mikerra nodded. "I'll stay here. I'm sure civilians aren't allowed back there."

He knew she needed time alone and so did he. "Okay. Be back soon."

After he stripped down to his birthday suit and was suitably attired in a paper gown, Drake sat on the examination table, waiting for the doctor. This was the part he hated the most. The waiting. It reminded him of the debriefings he'd endured after returning from Iraq. The waiting. At least they could have allowed him to leave his boxers on.

The metal door opened, and a tall, blond man of about six decades sauntered into the small room, with a clipboard in his hand. He extended his free one to Drake.

"Hello, Master Sergeant. I'm Dr. Preston. According to my notes, you're having some headaches."

Drake nodded. "Yes, sir."

"Tell me, what kind of pain are you experiencing?"

Drake shrugged. "Sometimes it's slight. Sometimes it's a bitch."

Dr. Preston nodded. "Any vomiting? Loss of appetite? Is your vision affected in any way?"

Drake almost said no. "All of the above. When I first got home, a few weeks ago."

The doctor nodded, scribbled something on his clipboard, and continued his barrage of questions. "Tell me how you feel right now. Are you cold?"

"Freezing."

Dr. Preston noted that in his little chart. "Put your clothes back on, and I'll be right back." He left the room.

Drake did as the doctor bade him and then waited for him to return.

A few minutes later Dr. Preston entered the room again and sat on the stool next to the examination table. "Okay, Master Sergeant, you have what we call island headaches. I don't see it much, since I'm at the VA, but other military hospitals see it quite often when soldiers return from a war zone, especially from the desert. Island headaches can last anywhere from one week to six months. I'm going to prescribe you some painkillers for when your headaches are too much to handle."

Drake had never heard of these headaches but trusted the doctor. After all, he was a military doctor. Drake knew Dr. Preston wouldn't tell him anything that wasn't true. "I'm due to report to Fort Benning in a few weeks. I'm an airborne ranger. How's my health going to effect jump school?"

The doctor handed him a paper with his illegible handwriting on it. "I'm sure everything will work out for you."

Which told Drake absolutely nothing. Which meant it was the doctor's little way of saying he had no freaking idea how Drake's headaches were going to effect jump school. Drake took the paper, rose, and shook the man's hand. "Thanks, Doc."

Dr. Preston watched the large man leave his office. He had instantly noticed the Special Forces logo on Drake's medical records when he'd pulled them up on his computer. He'd also noticed three letters on the records that told another story—PPP, Project Perfect Participant. He picked up the phone and dialed the Pentagon.

The phone was answered on the first ring.

Dr. Preston took a deep breath, hoping this wouldn't end his thirty plus years in the military. He'd come to love his cushy job watching over veterans. "Dr. Harold Preston calling." This part he felt really silly saying. "The shepherd has lost a sheep."

"Right away, sir."

"MacArthur," a voice rang out.

"General, this is Preston. I just had a visit from Master Sergeant Drake Alexander Harrington of the Two Hundred Ninetieth Airborne Rangers. He has island headaches."

"How bad?"

"Without the proper care, he could be dead within six months."

"Damn. That's not going to sit well with the big brass."

Dr. Preston cleared his throat. Some days he really hated his job. There went thirty years of his career down the drain. "He seemed to be satisfied with the island headaches theory."

"But when those headaches get worse, he's going to get suspicious. He may even go to a regular doctor.

You have to make sure he doesn't go to a regular doctor."

"He said his next permanent change of station is Fort Benning."

"No, we want control over the experiment. We're rerouting all the test subjects to Fort Hood. We need to keep them isolated until we get those island headaches controlled, and we have to keep this story away from the media at all costs. Although Harrington is only the second test subject to have any side effects, we still need to keep this as quiet as possible."

Dr. Preston cursed silently to himself. He'd known this project would spiral out of control, and now it had. He'd back out of this mess if he knew Senator McCaffrey wouldn't kill him. He was just as dead as the master sergeant.

Chapter 6

After Drake's appointment was over, they decided to have lunch at an Italian restaurant before leaving Waco. Mikerra had heard great things about this very cozy place and wasn't disappointed. The atmosphere was sure to lead her to trouble with Drake. The lighted candles, the singing waiters, and the wine could turn a cynic into a gushing romantic.

She took advantage of a few free minutes while Drake went to the men's room by calling Sloan. At the moment, she felt like strangling her childhood friend if he didn't stop babbling like an idiot. Mikerra rolled her eyes toward the ceiling, praying for divine intervention, or she was going to travel through her cell phone and give Sloan a piece of her mind.

"Sloan, they wouldn't give me a copy of the medical report. The doctor said Drake's commanding officer would have to request it."

"Something doesn't smell right."

Mikerra snorted. "Really, Einstein? What was your first clue?" She kept her eyes on the men's room door. Drake would be back shortly. "Look, Sloan, I don't have much time. What's plan B?"

"Why is it I need a plan B? He's your boyfriend," he taunted.

He went there. "Sloan, I can't believe you said that. Nothing has happened between Drake and me." Okay, it was just a tiny lie, she thought. Besides, Sloan didn't really need to know.

"You *do* know you live next to two of the nosiest people in Wright City? Melba Evans had that story all over town before Drake stuck his tongue down your throat."

Mikerra groaned. Her grandmother. Between her granny and Melba Evans, the entire free world probably knew she and Drake had shared kisses earlier that morning and the night before. "I'm getting some really dark tint on the windows of my house."

"Won't do any good. Melba said you guys were going at it on the porch. Where's Quinn?"

"You're not going to enlist his help, are you?"

Sloan laughed. "Why not? He's one of the best hackers this side of the federal prison system."

"And I would like to keep him on the free side of the federal pen, thank you very much."

"Look, Mikerra, this is serious. I need to see that medical report before I get there, and this is the only way. I don't have time to go through the proper channels. Tell Quinn to call me." He ended the call.

"The next time I see that skinny fool, I'm going to kick his ass," she muttered.

"Who are you talking about?" Drake took his seat across the table from her.

"Nobody," Mikerra answered, avoiding eye contact. The last thing she wanted to do was lie to him, but she also didn't want to be overheard.

Drake took a sip of water. "Sounds like another story to me. If I wanted a story, I'd read the paper."

"Sloan," she admitted. What was it about this man that turned her into a babbling idiot? "He's coming to town for a visit next weekend."

Drake laughed. "Why is Sloan coming home? It's not a holiday. His parents are in perfect health, and I know he's not serious about anyone, so I know there is no engagement party planned."

"He wants to talk to us."

"Us . . . as in you and me?"

Mikerra felt like she was the straight man in a comedy bit. A very bad comedy bit. "Yes."

"Well, well, well. This sounds serious, if Sloan is flying down here to see us."

"Yes, I told you that." She lowered her voice. "It's very serious."

He nodded, then threw his napkin on the table. "Well, I think this is a discussion for the truck." He signaled for the waiter to bring the check.

The young man quickly appeared with the small black folder. Drake pulled some bills from his wallet and handed them to the waiter. The waiter smiled and left the table.

"I might not be ready to go, Drake." Mikerra was ready to go but didn't want Drake thinking he was running things. That was an invitation to disaster, and she couldn't have that. Besides, it was just too much fun battling with him.

"Are you ready to leave, baby?"

He was hitting below the belt with those terms of endearments, and he damn well knew it. "Yes, I'm ready to go, Drake Alexander Harrington."

"Ouch. My whole name. You must really be pissed."

Mikerra wanted to knock the knowing smile off his handsome face, but she knew it would be impossible.

"I'm not pissed, Drake. I just don't want you ordering me around like I'm some child."

He nodded. "The last thing I think of you as is a child. You're all woman in my eyes."

When he said things like that, Mikerra didn't know whether she should be upset or turned on. Most likely a combination of the two. "Now we can leave."

Drake chuckled, rose from his seat, and helped her with her chair. "Care Bear, I can read you like a book. And you should know I am not a toy, so quit tryin' to play me. If you're not careful, I might just have to kiss you right here, in the middle of the restaurant, to show you I mean business. How's that fit in your little game?"

It would fit too well for her taste. Since sharing those kisses that morning, Mikerra hadn't been able to think straight. Any more of those and she'd be in more trouble than her dormant hormones were ready for.

"Mikerra?"

She blinked. She had to quit daydreaming in front of this man. She had to be strong, she reminded herself, and she had to quit thinking about how good his lips felt or how well he could use his tongue.

"Mikerra?"

"What?" *Damn him for interrupting my fantasy,* she thought.

"I said if you're going to look like you want to have sex, I could accommodate you. But I'd rather do it in private versus in the middle of a crowded restaurant, with all these people looking."

"Drake, you're just impossible." She tried to keep her voice stern, but she could feel the giggle trying to slip past her lips.

"Oh, and then some," he drawled. He grabbed her hand and headed for the exit.

Once outside the restaurant, Drake took her in his

arms and kissed her fully on the mouth. At that moment Mikerra stopped trying to control her emotions where this man was concerned. It was a lost cause, much like her heart.

When Drake and Mikerra returned to Wright City, Drake was ready for a nap. All that foreplay on the trip home had begun to wear on him. Not to mention that the shot the doctor gave him had kicked in.

He parked in front of Mikerra's house, determined to keep the game going, but Mikerra had other plans.

"You don't have to walk me to the door, Drake. I'm not a teenager. Besides, you look exhausted. What kind of shot did the doctor give you?"

He shrugged, not wanting to admit he hadn't questioned the doctor's advice. If the military said he needed a shot, then he had it with no questions asked. "I can still walk you to your door. There could be a dangerous person hiding behind those over-grown bushes in your front yard."

"They're not overgrown. They have character," she countered, opening the passenger door. "I let them do their own thing. Who says uniformity is right?"

He opened his door and slid from behind the steering wheel. He walked to her side of his father's truck just as she closed the door.

They headed to her front door, side by side. "Mikerra, you don't have to sell me on the whole yard thing. It's just that the rest of the neighborhood has gone with the uniformity of trimmed hedges, and yours are the only ones doing their own thing. I would hate for Sheriff Johnson to give you a ticket for it."

She laughed. "Okay, you got me." She unlocked

her front door. "I'll get Quinn to cut them when he mows my lawn."

He watched her step inside the entryway. "You mean, you don't do your own lawn? They're going to take away your superwoman card. I can't believe you're letting a mere man work on your lawn."

She smiled at him. "Me either. When I was in the process of moving here permanently, I had dreams of manicuring my own lawn and having a lush garden." She motioned him inside.

He took the invitation and entered the house. "So what happened?" he asked after she closed the front door.

She sat on the couch and sighed. "Well, it seems moving back here only showed me how empty my life really was. Between visits to my grandmothers, aunts, and cousins, I haven't had time to buy a lawn mower."

"I could do the lawn for you tomorrow," Drake said carefully as he sat on the couch beside her. He hadn't planned on offering to work out in the sun, as if twelve months in Iraq hadn't been hot enough. He just wanted to help her any way he could.

"Drake, I couldn't ask you to do that. The hot sun would probably play hell with your headaches."

Well, she definitely had him there. "What's a little pain for a former high school sweetheart?"

"I don't want you to experience pain on my behalf. Quinn doesn't mind."

"Is this the same guy who pulled up all the grass in his front yard and put down artificial turf when he moved into his house a few years ago?"

She sighed. "The same."

"I'll be over by nine in the morning."

* * *

An hour later, after extracting about as many kisses as his body could take from Mikerra, without the promise of penetration, Drake went home. And not a moment too soon, for his taste. One more kiss and they would have both gone up in flames. They needed more time together as friends before they headed toward intimacy. But Drake didn't know if he had that kind of willpower.

He parked in front of his parents' home. He stared at the house. It seemed so far away and was getting farther away by the second. He didn't know if he had the strength to walk to the front door. Where had all his strength gone?

"Drake, wake up."

He heard the muffled voice. It was a feminine voice. It sounded like Mikerra's voice. What was Mikerra doing in his dreams?

"Drake Harrington, open this damn door!"

Now that *was* his Care Bear. Drake struggled to open his eyes. What was he still doing in the truck? He stared at her as she frantically yelled his name and jiggled the door handle. Why was she trying to get inside the truck? Why was it so damn hot?

Mikerra was glad she'd followed her instincts. Drake hadn't looked well when he left her house. After thirty minutes of constantly calling his cell phone and not getting an answer, she'd gone to his house. She'd found him sitting in the truck, dead to the world, with the windows up.

"Drake! Drake! Wake up!"

He stared at her as if she were a stranger and made no move to unlock the door.

Taking matters into her own hands, Mikerra went

to her brand-new SUV and extracted the tire iron to break a window on his truck. How long had Drake been sitting in the truck?

She hurried back to the truck, and he was still in the same position. His head lolled against the leather headrest. Clearly, he was out of it. She was going to need some help.

She muttered a silent prayer that Drake's father wouldn't be too upset with her for what she was about to do. She planted her feet in the soft grass, shoulder-width apart. Not wanting to see the look on Drake's face, she slammed her eyes shut and swung the tire iron in the direction of the driver's side window.

Crack!

Mikerra opened her eyes and viewed her handi-work. Pieces of glass were everywhere, on the driveway, on Drake, and some had landed around her feet. Drake was unfazed. She reached inside the truck and unlocked the door. Drake's handsome face was drenched in sweat. Acting on some emotions she thought she had a handle on, she unbuckled Drake and helped him out of the truck. But he was too large for her to handle him for long. They both fell down on the grass, with Mikerra landing on top of Drake. Even that didn't wake him. Breathing hard, she scram-bled up and headed back to her SUV, reached for her cell phone, and called her mother.

"Mom, I think something is wrong with Drake. The doctor gave him a shot, and I think he's having a really bad reaction to it."

Carolina Stone gasped. "Mikerra, you must be mis-taken. The military wouldn't do that."

"Mom, I found him in his truck with the windows up. He was sweating a river. He looks like he's taking drugs. His eyes are glassy, and his responses are slow."

Mikerra sat down on the ground by Drake. "He's out cold right now. What can I do?"

"Throw some water on his face, and call the paramedics."

"I thought he had to go to a military doctor," Mikerra said. She leaned over him and tapped his face. Nothing.

"Mikerra, just do what I say. They can go to regular doctors. Get the garden hose and water him down. Most likely he just fell asleep and is dehydrated. But you need to get him conscious. Now do it." She ended the call.

Mikerra pushed the end button on her phone and did as her mother said. She glanced around the neighborhood, hoping to find someone to help her, but the only person she laid eyes on was Mrs. Flagstone, Wright City's oldest citizen at ninety-five years old, who was watching her. Not the most likely person to help.

Mikerra turned on the hose at the side of the house, rushed over to Drake, and sprayed him with water. Slowly, he came to, spitting out water and struggling to sit up.

"Mikerra, what the hell?"

Chapter 7

She watched as Drake huffed and puffed and threat-ened to knock her straight to the devil. "Dammit, Care Bear, why you wanna get me all wet like that? My dad is going to kick your ass for breaking his window. He really loves that truck."

At that point, Mikerra really didn't care. The only thing she cared about was this man with the look of murder in his dark eyes. She stood, walked to the garden hose spigot, turned off the water, and stomped back to him. How dare he question her like she was crazy? "I had a hard time waking you. What did you expect me to do? Let you suffocate? This is Texas, you know, and it's summer."

She walked over to her car and returned with her purse. She scribbled out a check and shoved it at Drake. "This should cover it." When he made no move to accept the small piece of paper, it fell to the ground, but at this point Mikerra could have cared less. "If not, tell Mr. Harrington to call me." She stomped off to her car, determined not to shed a tear. She wasn't mad; she was furious.

She opened her SUV door, threw her purse to the

side, but Drake closed it quickly. He grabbed her by the hand and all but pulled her onto the porch. "Sit down."

Since there were no chairs, Mikerra plopped her behind on the cement porch.

Drake sat down beside her. "Look, I didn't mean to hurt your feelings or anything. I'm glad you came by, actually. I don't know what happened. The last thing I remember is pulling up in the driveway and thinking how tired I was."

Mikerra looked at him. He did look tired—and wet. Little droplets of water still clung to his forehead. "When I couldn't get your attention, I guess I panicked."

"Well, I do appreciate you breaking my father's window to help. I don't know how Dad will take it, but it's very appreciated." He kissed her on her cheek. "Sorry for getting a little crazy there."

She didn't want to ask, but the reporter in her had to. "Did my spraying you with water remind you of being in the war?"

His dark eyes searched hers. She didn't know what he was looking for, but something told her she had it. "Yes, it did. About a month before I came home, I got real sick and had a really high fever. My commanding officer had the guys in my unit throw water on me. I almost drowned."

Mikerra gasped. "How could you?"

"Easy. It caught me off guard and I got scared. My friend Josh died in the shower."

Mikerra could count the times her brothers had admitted they were scared on one hand. Drake, the big, bad army ranger, had just admitted it, as if it were nothing. "That's understandable, Drake. You were probably delirious with fever."

"Possibly. But a soldier is only as good as the men he's commanding."

"Soldier or not, you're still human. You're allowed to be scared."

"Well, I guess you *have* changed, Mikerra. The Mikerra I knew didn't like it when men were weak."

Mikerra grabbed his hand. "I was in high school. I was supposed to have high expectations of the man I love."

The Pentagon, Washington, D.C.

General Horace MacArthur slammed the phone down on his desk. All he wanted was to succeed in one damn experiment, but people kept bringing him more problems with it. He knew success would depend upon the confidentiality of PP 192, and now that definitely had been breached.

One phone call from one scared doctor with a cushy setup in Texas and his whole plan could fall apart. His side door opened, and William Harris, his assistant, entered the room. "Wasn't that the VA on the phone?"

"Yes, we found the variable in the experiment. One of the soldiers just showed up at the VA in Waco, Texas, with island headaches. You know what this means?"

Harris stared at him with those cold blue eyes. "I know that means something is wrong. Symptoms shouldn't have shown up for another year. If he's got island headaches already, the tumor will start to grow in less than a month. What are you going to do?"

"What are *we* going to do?" MacArthur corrected. "Well, I got a few options at this point. If it comes down to it, we can kill him."

"Isn't that a little drastic? How are we going to explain his death if he's not in the war zone? If the doctor is telling him it's island headaches, then he'll believe him. He's a career soldier, after all. Isn't that what this experiment is all about? The perfect soldier?"

Drake stared at Mikerra. Did she really just say the word *love* like it didn't mean anything? Granted, she was talking about what she felt two decades ago, but still.

He looked down at their joined hands. It brought back so many memories. He should have chased her down all those years ago and married her. But hindsight was everything.

"Drake?"

"What is it, Care Bear?"

She wiggled her hand free from his. "I think you should go to the emergency room."

Of course she did. "I'm fine. Maybe it was just a bad reaction to the meds. It's happened before."

"When?"

"In Iraq."

"What happened?" She grabbed his hand again. "I mean, what led up to you having a bad reaction?"

He knew what she was asking. He had been asking himself the same question these last few weeks. "When you are deployed, there is a series of shots you take before you can leave the country. I had a bad reaction to one of the shots. The medic there told me I'd have a fever, but I'd be okay. But it was kinda like today. My motor skills couldn't catch up with my brain."

"Oh," she whispered and moved closer to him.

"I know it sounds crazy. I wanted to open the truck door, but my hands wouldn't move. They felt like lead."

She hastily wiped a tear away. "You should go change

out of those wet clothes. It will only make your fever worse."

"Who said I have a fever?"

She cocked a brow. "I guessed."

He had her in a place that he didn't want her. She was pitying him. "How about I change clothes if you promise to stay here?"

"All right. I can't stay long. I have to pick up Terror later today. My mom's been keeping him while I've been getting settled."

Drake knew the fake when he saw it. He was the master of it. He'd been faking being happy for so long, he didn't know much else. But he'd be damned if this woman was going to do it to him. "Then we'll go pick up your mutt together." He stood and started to walk to the front door.

"Drake Harrington, don't you dare call my baby a mutt!"

Well, at least, she didn't feel sorry for him anymore. Now she was pissed.

"Terror is a very sweet, high-spirited dog. And I hope he bites you on the ankle!"

He turned around and found she was right on his heels. "Hey, you named him." He searched his pockets for the house keys and realized they were still in the truck. Before he could form a thought, Mikerra was way ahead of him.

"I'll get them." She hurried down the few steps and was back in a flash. "Here."

Drake took the keys out of her outstretched hand and muttered, "Thanks, but I could have gotten them." He unlocked the front door and motioned her inside.

She smiled smugly at him as she walked past him. "I know that. I was just trying to help." She sat down on the couch. "I'll stay right here while you change."

Drake sighed and went upstairs. He peeled off his wet clothes and headed for the shower, smiling. Even with the medication making things hazy, apparently he still had enough of a hunger for Mikerra to have an erection.

Mikerra sat patiently on the couch while Drake was upstairs. Nothing was making sense. If all soldiers had to take those shots when they were deployed, maybe there would be something in the news about Drake's entire unit getting sick. Perhaps he'd just had a bad reaction to the medication, as he said.

She reached for her purse and remembered it was outside, in her SUV. She was about to open the front door when Drake's voice stopped her.

"Trying to sneak out, huh?"

"No," she said quickly. "I need my cell phone, and it's in the truck. I was going to get it." She took a deep breath as she glanced at his attire. Drake looked like a vision of chocolate, all six feet three of him. He was dressed in Bermuda shorts and a bright yellow shirt. Water glistened in his dark hair as he made it down the stairs. *Steady, girl,* she warned herself. But it was about as good as saying she just wanted one piece of cheese-cake. Good in theory, but impossible to actually do.

"I guess you looking at me like I'm a piece of meat means I meet your approval," he said as he closed the distance between them.

She could deny it, but what good would it do? "I have no idea what you're talking about. Do all military men have an ego the size of yours?" She saw the flaw in that question, but again, it was too late.

"Not many men are my size. Period." He kissed her on the lips.

She felt the warmth of his lips and melted. She offered her open mouth to him for the taking, and that was exactly what he did. He pulled her body closer to his and deepened the kiss. Her breasts were pressed against the hard planes of his chiseled chest. She thought she would die if he didn't make love to her soon. *Whoa!* That little thought brought her back to life with a jolt. She pried their heated bodies apart.

"Drake, you're sick. We shouldn't be doing this." She tried to catch her breath.

Drake shook his head. "Damn, girl! I don't know what you're doing to me, but I can't take much more of this teasing." He pulled her body flush against his. "Next time there will be no stopping." He kissed her hard, letting her feel his hunger. "I might not be one hundred percent right now, but I can still get you there."

Mikerra didn't need a house of bricks or condoms falling on her. Good sense had to prevail, or they both would regret it later.

As if he were a condemned man on the last day of his life, Mikerra kissed him with total abandon, not giving one thought to the consequences of her actions. She teased his mouth open, which didn't take too much effort, and showed him who was boss. Or at least that was the theory in her mind until Drake joined in the kiss.

Drake's tongue dueled with hers, and he guided her to the wall with a thud. "I told you," he teased between kisses. "You started the game, but I'm going to finish it."

Mikerra moaned as he bit her bottom lip. Trying to gain the upper hand had been a stupid idea, and now she was paying the highest price. There was no way she could stop him. Hell, she couldn't even stop herself.

Drake slid his hands under her shirt and raised it. Mikerra held her breath as his hot fingers fumbled with the back clasp on her bra. He expertly unhooked her bra and held her bare breasts in his hands. He squeezed gently, and Mikerra gasped and collapsed in his arms, willing him to do what he pleased.

Chapter 8

"Can I take you here?" Drake whispered against Mikerra's ear.

Mikerra's passion-driven haze cleared for just a moment. She had to get a hold of her hormones. "Yes."

He chuckled and moved away from her. He grabbed her hand and led her upstairs. He stopped at the doorway to his bedroom and turned to her. "You sure?"

"Just open the door," Mikerra said. Only one thing was on her mind at the time, and she'd worry about the consequences later. Right now she knew only that she wanted Drake.

Drake did as she asked, and Mikerra walked inside his room. Drake closed and locked the door. "Not that I think you'd try to get away, but I don't know where Mom is, and who knows when she'll be back."

Mikerra nodded and sat on his bed. She started to take off her T-shirt, but Drake's powerful hands stopped her. "Let me, Care Bear. Let me look at you."

He tugged off her shirt and kissed her as he pulled her bra off and threw both items on the floor. Drake laid her down on the bed and kissed her with a hunger that was ready to be satisfied.

Mikerra ended the kiss. "Your turn." She kissed him and pointed at his shirt. "I want you naked."

"Well, I like to please my woman when I can." He took off his shirt, shorts, and was down to his boxers before he stopped. "This is all you're getting for now."

Mikerra laughed as he dove onto the bed and took her in his arms. He kissed her on the lips, then gently forced them apart and let his tongue slide inside. Mikerra liked the feeling of being on top of him. It had been ages since she'd been in this position, and it felt great.

"Did you ever think we'd be here like this again?" Mikerra lowered her head and kissed him.

Drake smiled. "No more talk." His large hands went directly to the button of her shorts, and in a move she was totally not contemplating, he rolled her over on her back. He stretched out on top of her and kissed her. His kisses moved lower as her shorts did the same. Before she could even think about that move, she felt his hot hands inside her red lace panties, and he was pushing them down.

Mikerra moaned, groaned, and thought she'd lost her mind from the heat his hands were creating.

"No, I didn't think I'd ever be here again, but I'm so glad I am." Drake kissed her forehead, her cheeks, and nuzzled her neck. "I don't want to think about anything but you."

Mikerra couldn't resist the urge to tease, since he was doing the same to her. "I thought you said no more talking."

"My body is going to do all my talking from now on." Drake kicked off his boxers, and finally they were skin to skin.

"Condom."

He stopped cold. "You mean you're not on the Pill?"

She shook her head. Hoping against hope. Surely he had something. What moron would go this far and not have some kind of protection at home? He rolled off her body, and she got her answer. Drake reached for his shorts.

"Sorry, Mikerra."

Mikerra rolled her head from side to side, not believing her bad luck. "You don't have a secret stash somewhere?"

He pulled on his shorts and grabbed his shirt before sitting on the bed. "I've been home three weeks. Sex kinda hasn't been high on my list of things to do."

Mikerra sighed and sat up in the bed. "Oh, I better get to my mom's. Got any aspirin?" All this sexual frustration was killing her head.

"In my nightstand." He finally looked at her. "I'm really sorry about this."

"Yeah, yeah." Mikerra opened the nightstand drawer and started laughing. She couldn't believe it. "When was the last time you looked in this drawer?"

"I don't know. A few days ago. I think Mom said she bought some aspirin yesterday."

"Looks like your mom bought more than aspirin." She shook the gold box at him.

He stared at her, grinning like a schoolboy who had just discovered sex. "Mom put condoms in my room?" he muttered. "I can't believe that woman."

Mikerra looked sideways at him. He was clearly missing the point. "You do realize that now we can have sex."

Drake took the box out of her hand. "Yes, I do. Now." He rose and slipped out of his clothes faster than any bullet. He moved onto the bed and wrapped Mikerra in his arms. "Last call."

"Just put on the condom, already." Mikerra smiled

as a challenge rose to her mind. "Or would you like me to do that for you?"

Drake forced himself to breathe. "Yes, I would like that very much."

Mikerra pushed him gently on his back and straddled his lower torso. She leaned down and kissed him. "When I finish, remember you agreed."

Drake nodded and closed his eyes. This was probably going to be the sweetest torture he had ever endured. He expected to hear the condom packet opening, but instead he felt her soft lips against his.

Not that he didn't enjoy the feeling of her thick body stretched out on top of his, but he needed her. Now. "Baby, are you going to put it on, or what?"

She didn't answer him. Her kisses descended down his body. She nipped at his collarbone before sucking on his hard nipples. Drake sucked in a breath. If she didn't hurry, he was going to have to stop this silly game. He let his hands roam to her waist as her kisses moved farther southward. Was she really going to do that? He felt her take him in her hand and stroke him gently. Finally he heard the tearing of the packet. *Thank God!*

Mikerra slid the condom on, and they both sighed with relief. Drake's control finally snapped, and he quickly rolled her over on her back and took over. He kissed her as he entered her body. He hadn't expected her to feel so good. She wasn't supposed to feel so good and tight.

He pulled back and looked at her face. Her eyes were lightly closed. She looked like she was having a dream. He knew he was. He leaned down and kissed those closed eyelids. "Open your eyes, baby. I want to see your beautiful brown eyes."

Mikerra's eyes fluttered open, and she smiled at him.

She licked her lips and raised her head for another kiss. Drake couldn't disappoint her. He kissed her again and moved farther inside her body.

He swallowed her moan and began moving inside her. He noticed her eyes had become moist, and he instantly stopped. "Am I hurting you?"

Mikerra shook her head and wrapped her long legs around him, urging him to continue. When he didn't, she kissed him hard, letting him taste her hunger, and moved her body against his. Needing her for so long and not having her had taken a toll on his psyche. His willpower shattered; he couldn't hold back. He moved against her, each stroke longer and harder than the last. When he felt her grab his waist he knew she was close to a release.

Drake watched the woman beneath him reach for the stars. She slammed her eyes shut as the intense pleasure washed over her. "Oh, Drake!" Her body betrayed whatever she thought she was holding back. She whispered fragments of gibberish in his ear as her body calmed down.

He felt his own orgasm as it made its way through his body. He held on to her as tightly as he could as he came. Mikerra didn't seem to mind; she caressed his back as his body twitched and jerked against hers. Nothing in all his adult years of making love could compare to the sensations he had just experienced. Thank goodness his parents weren't home; it would have been quite embarrassing for them.

Drake eased off of Mikerra but pulled her to him. "That was excellent, Mikerra." He couldn't admit it was even better than he could have ever imagined.

Mikerra didn't answer him. She sighed audibly. "You know, I don't think I can move right now."

He pulled the sheet over them. His body was

demanding relaxation, too. "Right now we don't have to."

He didn't know if she answered him or not, because he fell asleep with the woman he loved in his arms.

A few hours later Shirley Harrington pulled up in her driveway, not liking the scene before her. It looked like something in one of those crime reality shows. Mikerra's SUV was parked in her driveway, the driver's side door not quite closed.

Not used to seeing such a bizarre scene, Shirley extracted her cell phone from her leather purse. Although her husband was in Austin on business and couldn't do much from there, it wouldn't hurt to hear his calm voice of reason. She speed dialed her husband as she got out of her car.

"Daniel Harrington."

"Honey, it's me." Shirley walked past Mikerra's SUV and noticed Mikerra's purse lying open on the passenger seat. "I think something is wrong. I just got home, and things don't look right. Did Drake call you?"

"No, I haven't heard from my son since yesterday. Have you called the police?"

"No. Mikerra's SUV is also parked in the driveway. What if it's nothing?"

"You can laugh about it later. Now call the police. Then call me back. I'm getting ready to board the plane for home. I'll get one of the guys to bring me home."

"Okay. I love you, Danny."

"Right back at you. Now call."

Shirley ended the call. Now, if her brain had been working, she would have dialed the police like her husband of forty-three years had advised. But something told her to investigate further before calling the authorities. She walked farther up the drive and noticed the broken glass on the ground and the damage to her husband's truck. Daniel would have a fit when he set eyes on his truck. "What on earth happened?" She ventured into her home and searched the downstairs.

Everything appeared to be in order. Nothing was out of place. No droplets of blood on her hardwood floors. What would Jessica Fletcher of *Murder, She Wrote* fame do at a time like this? She'd check upstairs for more clues, Shirley thought.

Shirley walked upstairs and checked the rooms. The rooms at one end of the hall looked fine, and nothing had been disturbed. Drake's room was at the other end of the hall. She knew he'd had a doctor's appointment earlier that day. She also knew that Mikerra had gone with him. So why was Mikerra's SUV outside? Drake would have picked her up and driven them to Waco. Could those two have mended fences that quickly? Shirley hoped so. She wanted Drake to see where he'd gone wrong all those years ago and to marry Mikerra. But that was just a mother's dream. She tried to turn Drake's doorknob, but the door was locked. Her baby never locked the door. She smiled, hoping against hope.

But as a mom, she had to know for sure, especially with Drake not being himself lately. She stood on her tiptoes and ran her finger along the door ledge and grinned when she felt the spare key to his room. She unlocked the door and stepped inside, surveyed the picture before her, and closed the door. Maybe her pigheaded son had finally started listening to his mother. After she made sure the door was locked, she walked downstairs to enjoy a cup of tea.

As she prepared her favorite Darjeeling tea, the doorbell rang. She hurried to the front door, hoping the noise wouldn't wake Drake. She opened the door and gasped. "Sheriff Johnson, what are you doing here?"

Sheriff Kevin Johnson smiled shyly at her. His tall, lean frame filled her doorway. He respectfully tipped his black Stetson at her. "Mrs. Harrington, your husband called me and asked me to stop by. You having some kind of trouble? I noticed the broken glass in the driveway."

Leave it to Daniel, she thought. He always took care of her, no matter where he was. "Oh no, Sheriff. I thought something was wrong, but everything is fine. Drake is upstairs, asleep."

Sheriff Johnson nodded. "Isn't that Mikerra Stone's Chevy TrailBlazer in your driveway? Mrs. Porter said it's been there for at least four hours. Is she also inside?"

"Yes, she is."

Again, the sheriff nodded. "I see. So there's nothing to report?"

"Nothing criminal, no. Everything is just fine."

"You're sure everything is fine?"

"Yes, Sheriff. I'll call Daniel right now."

"No need. I have him on the phone right now." He handed her his cell phone. "He'd like to speak with you before the plane takes off."

Shirley could easily imagine them holding the plane until Daniel knew all was well at home. "Hey, baby. Everything is just fine."

"I'm glad, honey," replied Daniel.

"I'll explain everything to you when you get home tonight."

"I can't wait to hear this," he said. "Talk to you later." He ended the call.

After stepping out on the porch and watching the

sheriff leave, Shirley went back inside the house and waited. It should be fun.

Drake woke from the most restful sleep he'd had since arriving home three weeks ago. Mikerra was nestled against him, naked and smiling in her sleep. How long had they been asleep?

He glanced at his bedside clock and did a double take. Had they really been asleep for over three hours? Surely, his mother was back by now. Thank goodness he'd locked the bedroom door. Talk about embarrassing. He eased out of bed, gathered his clothes, and headed for the shower.

After he was suitably attired, he ventured downstairs. It was exactly as he had feared. His mother was sitting in the living room, reading a paperback mystery novel. How long had she been in the house?

"Hey, Mom." He sat beside her on the couch.

"How did the doctor go? Did he give you something for those headaches?" She continued reading, not making eye contact with him.

Drake took the book out of her slender brown hands. "Now, Mom, I know you don't want to talk about that."

She finally looked at him, smiling big as you please. "Yes, I do, baby. But first, I need to know what happened this afternoon. I saw Mikerra in your bed. You guys looked so cute."

Drake knew his reflexes were slow because of the medicine the doctor gave him earlier, but his mother was speaking as if they were in the middle of a conversation. "Are you telling me you walked into a locked bedroom?"

"Don't you raise your voice at me. What did you expect? I come home and find something right out of

CSI in my front yard, the house unlocked, and your father's truck window broken. He's going to kill you."

"Mom, can you please put it in neutral? I know you mean well, but how on earth can you enter a locked bedroom?"

His mother's brown eyes searched his face. "Well, I had a spare key made a few weeks ago."

"What?"

"Honey, when you first came back home, you were so distant. The slightest noise had you jumping, and your father and I had just seen this show on TV about the war and how some of the soldiers were having a hard time adjusting."

Drake hated to think of his very own parents being afraid of him. "Did I do something to frighten you guys?"

Her hesitation was his answer. "The first few nights you were screaming something about shooting someone. It was like you were still there, in the war zone. We started locking your room from the outside so you wouldn't hurt yourself or us."

"I'm sorry, Mom. I didn't mean to frighten you."

"I know that, baby. I didn't want you hurting yourself, either."

Drake took a deep breath. His very predictable life was getting way too complicated. The headaches he could manage, but this nightmare stuff was going to be hard to deal with. "Thanks, Mom." He hugged his mother. "Have I had these nightmares lately?"

"Not for the last week. I guess when you reconnected with Mikerra, your mind had something else to focus on."

"Yeah, I guess she still pushes all the right buttons."

Chapter 9

Mikerra came awake slowly. Nothing about her surroundings seemed familiar. Where was she? The bedside clock was right, but it wasn't her clock. She'd just bought a retro-looking clock for her bedroom but hadn't plugged it in yet. Where was she, and why didn't she have on any clothes?

She attempted to sit up and winced in pain. Her body felt like she'd just run five miles at top speed. What could she have been doing? She noticed the pillow next to her; then she saw it. An opened box of condoms. Then she knew.

She'd had sex with Drake that afternoon. What had she been thinking? As the memories came crashing down on her, she knew exactly what she had been thinking. Twenty years later and the man could still make her holla. She sat up, gathered the bedsheet around her tired body, and stood up. Her legs were a little wobbly, but she managed to gather up her clothes. She opened the nearest door and found Drake's closet. The next door revealed the bathroom. Yes, a nice hot shower would clear her head.

After she showered and dressed, she headed downstairs. Drake immediately stood when she entered the living room. "Hey, I was wondering when you were going to wake up," he said.

"I guess I was really tired," Mikerra whispered.

He grabbed her hand and led her to the couch. "I think we should discuss what happened between us."

She nodded, because her mouth refused to work. Her brain was buzzing with plenty of thoughts. Most of them were about what had happened earlier and her wanting an instant replay.

They sat down and Drake began speaking. "Care Bear, I don't regret what happened this afternoon. Okay, maybe the effects of the medicine, but not the final outcome. I think there's something between us, and it has been hanging over us for the last week, and we just didn't realize it. I would like to see what there is between us."

Okay, now she had her voice. "Drake, I'm sure that was just adrenaline talking. We haven't seen each other since high school. Why don't you concentrate on getting rid of your headaches first? That should be your top priority. You really should go to the doctor."

"I went to a military doctor."

She knew he was a career soldier, and if the military said boo, that was good enough for him. "All right. Let's see if the medication the doctor gave you will take effect soon." She glanced at the grandfather clock in the hallway. "It can't be almost six o'clock."

He smiled and leaned back on the couch. "Yes, it can. We went upstairs about two."

"My mom is probably having a fit. I was supposed to pick up Terror two hours ago." She looked around for her purse. "Where is my purse?"

Drake shrugged. "Mom brought it in earlier. Why don't you calm down? Just call your mom, and we can go pick up your dog right now."

"We?"

"Yes. We." He handed her a cordless phone. "Call."

Carolina Stone tried not to stare at the couple sitting across from her. Mikerra and Drake sat on the couch, smiling at each other like two schoolchildren who knew a naughty secret.

Terror jumped into Mikerra's lap, but not before barking at Drake for some twenty minutes. Drake took one look at the hyperactive dog and snapped his large fingers. The dog immediately stopped barking.

"Thank you, Drake," Carolina said. "He's been yipping for days. I know it was because he missed Mikerra." She met her daughter's gaze, and Mikerra only shrugged, but Carolina had to know what was going on with her and Drake. She opened her mouth to start the inquisition, but her daughter beat her to the draw.

"Mom, I was telling Drake he should go to a regular doctor about his headaches." She placed the tiny dog on the floor.

Carolina smiled at her daughter and knew she was fighting her resolve not to get involved with Drake again. From the looks of the smiles on both their faces, Mikerra was losing the battle. "I'm sure Drake is a grown man and knows when he needs to see a doctor, dear." She turned her attention to Drake. "Don't you, Drake? My daughter is trying to steer my attention away from the fact that she called me earlier, when you passed out. I take it you're feeling better."

He nodded. "Yes, Mrs. Stone, I feel much better. I guess it was a bad reaction to the meds." He picked up Mikerra's hand and kissed it. "Thank goodness for Mikerra, or I probably would have died in the truck."

Carolina watched her daughter blush. "Yes, thank goodness she had the sense to go by your house," she teased. "I know it would just break her heart if something happened to you."

Drake laughed. "Really? I mean, I haven't seen her since high school. I wouldn't think she would have cared one way or the other."

"Surely, you remember the care packages you received while you were in Iraq?" said Carolina.

Drake nodded. "Sure. My mom sent most of them. All but a few from some women's group in New York, but they sent them to all the guys in my unit."

"Mother," Mikerra warned, "I'm sure Drake doesn't care about the packages those women sent."

Carolina loved getting her daughter in an awkward position. It happened so seldom, she rather liked savoring the moment. "Why wouldn't he care if you were on the committee of the Manhattan Women Journalists League?"

Drake's dark, chiseled face lit up with recognition. "You're a member of the MWJL? You mean, you knew I was there and you never said a damn word?"

Mikerra shot her mother a glance. "It wasn't that big a deal, Drake. I saw your name on the list of soldiers and sent you a few packages. It was no big deal."

"I got packages from someone calling herself Cathy Hardcastle. I can only assume it was an alias."

Mikerra nodded. "I didn't want you to know it was me."

He chuckled. "Well, you lost. I knew it was you after about the third package."

"How?" both mother and daughter asked in unison.

"Well, my packages weren't like the other guys'. Mine were a bit more personal. When I was in high school, I ate macadamia nut cookies by the truckload, but I developed an allergic reaction to them as an adult. I mean, the norm is chocolate chip, peanut butter, sugar. Chocolate macadamia nut is a bit out of the usual for a care package."

Mikerra was busted, thanks to her mother mostly, and she knew it. But she refused to acknowledge it. "Maybe they just felt like making those kinds of cookies."

"How did you know they were homemade?" Drake laughed. "Anyway, I had to give them away, and the guys said they were dry."

"I'll have you know I made those with the finest ingredients, Drake Alexander Harrington!" Mikerra wished she could have taken those words back the minute she'd said them, but it was too late.

Drake pulled her in his arms and kissed her on the lips right in front of her mother. "Gotcha!"

Terror barked and jumped on Mikerra's lap, breaking the kiss.

"All right. So it was me," Mikerra confessed.

"Why didn't you say something?" Drake's dark brown eyes stared at her, demanding the truth.

"I was afraid," Mikerra admitted as Terror leaped off her lap.

"Well, we're both here now, so that has to mean something," Drake said.

Later that night Mikerra sat at her kitchen table, working on her laptop. Terror was so happy to be at home with her, he was at her feet, begging to be picked up.

"No, Terror. Mommy is working." She continued to search the Internet for more information. This was the one time she wished she had Quinn's computer-hacking skills. Quinn could get through almost any firewall.

She decided to take a little break and make some tea. As the teakettle whistled, the doorbell rang. "This had better not be Drake," she muttered, walking to the front door.

She opened the front door and yelled, "Kissa, what are you doing here?"

Markissa Phillips stood in Mikerra's doorway, laughing. "I was taking my evening walk, and I thought I'd drop by. How was Drake's doctor's appointment?"

Mikerra waved her friend inside. "How do you know about that?"

Kissa sat down on the couch as Mikerra closed the front door. "Girl, this is Wright City, not New York City. People here know when you blow your nose. You know that."

Mikerra sat by her friend on the couch. "I know. It would be nice if I could actually *tell* someone something. I like that little outfit."

Kissa glanced down at her workout outfit. "Present from my dear ex-husband when he found out I was getting half of all his crap. He thought if he bought me clothes, I would let him have his precious stock options back with no fuss. Not."

Mikerra laughed. "Where is the lying, cheating waste of space?"

"The last time I spoke with him, he was in Houston. He called me about three months ago, begging me to give him another chance. He claimed he couldn't live without me. Apparently, he forgot I caught him in our king-size bed with not one woman, but two."

They could laugh about it now, but a year ago Kissa had been a wreck mentally and physically. She'd gained a hundred pounds due to all the stress she was going through with her now ex-husband. But now Kissa had already lost sixty of those pounds and was much happier being back home in Wright City.

"What's going on in your head, Care Bear?"

"Why is everyone using my old nickname all of a

sudden? First Drake, then Sloan, and now you. Are we back in high school?"

Kissa snickered. "Why are you fighting this? You know you like it. Sloan called me earlier. He wanted me to try to get a copy of Drake's medical report from the VA."

"Have you been able to get it?"

"Well, yes and no," Kissa said.

"What do you mean?" Mikerra knew it wouldn't be easy to get her hands on a military document, but this was ridiculous.

"I mean that I may have doctor's credentials, but to get that report, I'm going to need a miracle. I've gotten copies of medical reports from the military before without this much trouble. Dr. Preston told me I had to get the approval of either Drake's superior or a General MacArthur to get a copy of the report."

"H-Horace MacArthur?" Mikerra's blood chilled at the thought of who else could be involved in this mess.

"Yeah. How did you know?"

"He's on the Joint Chiefs of Staff. Why would he have to grant his approval, unless . . . ," Mikerra thought out loud.

"Unless what?"

"Nothing," Mikerra whispered. "If they call you back, tell them you directed Drake to return to the VA."

"Mikerra Stone, what have you gotten me into?"

"Nothing," Mikerra lied.

"Well, it's too late. I'm already involved, so share."

Mikerra looked her dear friend in the eye and had to make a decision that she hoped would not get her killed.

Chapter 10

"You have exactly ten seconds to tell me what the hell is going on," Kissa said calmly. "Or I'm calling Drake."

They were sitting in Mikerra's spacious kitchen, with Terror lying between them. Mikerra got up and fixed them both a cup of tea as she weighed her options. She didn't want to involve her friend, but it was already too late, anyway. The wheels had been set in motion when Drake left the war zone.

She set one cup in front of Kissa and the other on her own place mat. "Okay, Kissa. I'm going to trust my instincts and let you in on what I think is going on. I won't have any proof until Sloan gets here next weekend."

Kissa took the lid off the sugar canister and spooned several teaspoons into her cup. "Why on earth is Sloan coming home? I didn't think the boys at the Pentagon would let him out of D.C. since the war is still going on full force."

Mikerra squeezed the juice of a lemon wedge in her cup of tea. "Well, he said this was important."

"Will you just spit it out, already? I'd like to know what I'm up against."

Mikerra took a deep breath. "Remember when I came home three months ago?"

"After you got fired," Kissa noted. "Yes, I remember. Do your parents know what happened?"

"No. And they're not going to know if I can help it. The reason I got fired is that I stumbled onto a military secret."

"I remember something about the perfect soldier."

"Yeah, that's it in a nutshell. Drake has been complaining of headaches, and the doc at the VA gave him some medicine that only made him worse."

Kissa sipped her tea. "When I called and identified myself, the doctor got very nervous."

Mikerra could see the details of the intricate plan like it was the plot of a too-complicated mystery novel. What did Drake have to do with all this?

"You're going to have to call Quinn. He could hack into the military's system, get the information we need, and no one would be the wiser," Kissa suggested. "Then we could see what we are up against."

"I'd rather not involve another person in this right now. Although he is a great computer hacker, I don't want my younger brother in federal prison for doing me a favor."

Quinn didn't need another complication in his life. Over the last year he'd worked hard on piecing his life back together after his marriage fell apart. Mikerra didn't want to be responsible for the fall of Quentin Stone.

Boston, Massachusetts

The phone rang, shattering the quiet of the master bedroom. Senator Seth McCaffrey didn't bother with the bedside lamp. He knew exactly who would be calling at two in the morning.

"McCaffrey."

"We got a problem," MacArthur grumbled.

"Now what?" Seth rose from the bed, careful not to wake his wife of thirty years. He walked down the hall to the guest bedroom and closed the door.

MacArthur took a deep breath and told him the bad news. "Just this evening some doctor called, requesting that same file. I don't know how long I'll be able to stall. Eventually, a nonmilitary doctor is going to examine that soldier and tell him what he's really got, and then what? How many people are you planning on killing to keep this a secret?"

Seth wanted only one person dead, and that person was Karen Mills. "You just keep up your end of the bargain, and I'll keep up mine. Just send the doctor a different file. Harrington is a career soldier. He's not going to do anything we don't want him to."

"So what's the next step?"

"Where's this doctor located?"

"She has an office in Houston. That's the address she gave to mail the copy. The fax number is also a Houston number."

Seth hated people who weren't thorough. "Think about it, Horace. Harrington's hometown is some Podunk town in Central Texas, and he was at the VA in Waco, so it would be normal to assume that they are near there, or he would have gone to the base hospital near Houston."

"He could have just been in the area," MacArthur countered.

"Yes, this is also true. Since he's already showing the symptoms, he'll be returning to the doctor soon. Preston told me he injected him with the serum to bring the brain tumor on sooner. He should be back to the doctor very soon."

"Soon isn't soon enough. I want all this to be over."

Seth hated whiners, too. "Yeah, all you big boys want just the results, not the details. You want me to take all the risks with the project, and you boys want all the glory."

"You said you'd back Project Perfect and help us get funding for it. Everyone has kept their end of the bargain. No one said anything about the subjects getting brain tumors."

Wimp. "What did you think would happen when you injected perfectly healthy soldiers with a variety of drugs? The human body can take only so much before it begins to break down. The experiment has been going on for over twelve months, and he's showing symptoms only now. I say this is good."

"But . . ."

"Don't give me problems, Horace. Give me results."

"Mikerra Stone knocked out my truck window?" Daniel Harrington stared up at his son. Although his father was over six feet tall, Drake still towered over him at six-three. "Might I inquire as to why a perfectly normal person would do such a thing?"

Drake stood in the kitchen, preparing a glass of iced tea. His father was positioned near the kitchen sink, pouring his version of relaxation, which was an imported beer, into a glass. Drake poured some lemon juice in the glass and faced his father. "Well, I kind of blacked out and would have suffocated if she hadn't come along when she did. The truck's doors were locked. She didn't really have a choice, Dad. I'll get the window fixed tomorrow."

Daniel took a long drink of the beer and then sat at the kitchen table. "Son, you know it's not the window I'm concerned about. It's you. Your mother thought something awful had happened to you. You haven't been yourself since you've been home. I fought in Vietnam, so I know how the war can mess with your mind. Don't ever be afraid to talk to me about it. I understand."

Drake took his glass of iced tea and sat by his father at the table. How could he reassure his father if he wasn't sure what was going on himself? "I'm not real sure what's going on with me right now. I do know these headaches have been constant since I got home. The doc said they were island headaches."

"What is that?"

"They're severe migraines. Doc said they are common among soldiers coming back from the desert."

Daniel looked at his son. "I work with plenty of soldiers with my volunteering at the VA in Waco, and I have never heard of such a thing. Maybe you should go to a doctor that Uncle Sam isn't paying for."

Drake didn't feel up to being poked and prodded by another doctor. He wanted only to reflect on his afternoon with Mikerra. Those thoughts made the headaches go away. "Maybe in a day or two. Right now I think I'm heading to bed."

His father smiled. "Oh yeah, your mother told me about you and Mikerra. Was that before or after she broke my window?"

"After," Drake said, smiling. "I can't believe Mom ratted me out."

"Well, you know I have my ways of making that woman talk." His father rose and took his empty beer glass to the sink. "I think we're turning in early, too.

She hasn't talked to me since yesterday." He walked out of the kitchen, smiling.

Drake knew his parents still loved each other, which was saying a lot these days. They'd been married over forty years, but to think of them actually loving each other in the biblical sense was more than he could tolerate at the moment. He had to get out of the house.

Drake grabbed his cell phone and headed out the back door. Maybe a little reconnecting with his hometown would clear the thought of his parents making love out of his head. Plus, he could always visit his younger brother, Dylan. He lived just a few blocks away.

Drake walked down the street, taking in the quiet surroundings. Wright City hadn't changed much since his last trip home almost two years ago. It was still the small town he loved. But would he come back here to live when he retired? He'd traveled the world on the military's dime. Could he be content living in a town of five thousand?

He thought of Mikerra. She'd lived in the ultimate big city for almost twenty years, and she'd returned to Wright City. Was she the reason his thoughts had turned to retirement in Wright City? Once around the block with her should have been enough, he thought. But when he was with her that afternoon, once hadn't been enough, and twice definitely hadn't been, either. It was like he had just discovered sex. What was he thinking?

"You look like a man wrestling with love." Dylan jogged up beside him. "Heard you and Mikerra hit the sheets today."

Drake tried to control his temper. "You will not talk about her like that. We had an encounter this afternoon."

Dylan laughed. "Well, well. It seems my big brother

is in love with his high school sweetie. Oh, I'm gonna have to call Romantics Anonymous."

"Oh, you got jokes."

Dylan smirked. His slender frame finally stopped shaking with laughter. "Of course I do. Why do you think you've never married? You have never brought a woman home to meet the family?"

"I just didn't want my women knowing what kind of idiot I have for a brother," Drake countered, knowing where his brother was going with this and hating Dylan for knowing him so well.

"That wasn't the only reason," Dylan said. "Remember when you were stationed in Massachusetts? That woman was beautiful. She adored you, but she wasn't what you needed."

Drake remembered Tonia well. But she wasn't the one. He knew that. "So maybe I'm not meant to have a wife. Look at you. You've been married twice, and you're four years younger than me."

"Okay, so it took me two tries to get it right. But I'm happy now. I want you to find that happiness, whether it's with Mikerra or not."

"Has everybody discussed us?"

Dylan stood in front of his brother. "Are you new here, or what? It's all over town that you guys were arguing in the furniture store a few days ago. Then Mom finds you in bed with her. So what do you expect?"

When faced with the facts, Drake couldn't help but smile. "Okay, you got me."

"It's about time," Dylan drawled. "Okay, so what was this afternoon? I know Mikerra has been tackling her own set of issues the past few years, according to Quinn. I just don't want to see either of you guys settling for something that feels good right now but isn't what you want."

Drake stared at his brother. "Spit it out, Dylan. What are you really saying?"

"I'm saying that just 'cause it feels good to you doesn't mean it's good for you."

"I've been with enough women to know what and who I want," Drake said. "Mikerra is an itch, and I just scratched it. That's all." Drake knew it was a lie and hoped those very words didn't come back to haunt him.

"What do you mean? You and Drake had sex today?" Kissa asked as she prepared to leave Mikerra's house. They were standing on the porch, enjoying the quiet of the night. Mikerra decided to drop the bomb about sleeping with Drake just as Kissa said good night.

"Would you keep your voice down? I don't want my neighbors knowing." Mikerra couldn't stop the small smile from forming on her mouth.

Kissa laughed. "It's after ten. They're asleep by now. I need some details. You know, it's been ages since I've gotten some, so it's nice to hear someone is."

"Yours is by choice," Mikerra commented. "Mine was a slip in judgment. He started kissing me, and my brain melted."

"So, is he as sexy as he looks? I mean, he was a cutie in high school, but now with all those muscles, he must have the stamina of a racehorse."

"That's not the only thing," Mikerra said. "Did I say that out loud?"

Kissa grabbed Mikerra's arm and led her back inside the house and closed the door. "Oh, you got to tell me all the dirt."

The friends sat on the couch, giggling like school-girls, and Mikerra recounted her afternoon with Drake Harrington.

Chapter 11

"Was he really that good?" Kissa asked, sipping her tea. She and Mikerra were still settled on the couch, enjoying some good old-fashioned girl talk. "Sounds like you guys were rocking that house."

Mikerra nodded. She couldn't actually believe it, but she was spilling the contents of her soul to another human being. It felt good to voice her concerns about getting involved with Drake again. "Even though he had an episode earlier this afternoon, he still knocked me out. What a difference twenty years make."

Kissa fanned herself, mocking Mikerra's words. "Oh, to have a man make love to me all afternoon, and then to fall asleep in his big, strong arms. Poor Mikerra. She got some," Kissa teased.

"Okay, okay. I get it. I'm whining. But you gotta admit, that's pretty amazing. It was like he just blocked out the pain and just concentrated on the sex."

Kissa suddenly rose. "On that note, I'm going home. I think you have some feelings you're not exactly ready to share with Drake or me. I will try my best to get a copy of that medical report, but if it's Project Perfect, you can forget it. You're going to have to call in the big guns, which in this case is Quinn. The military isn't going to willingly admit that they have pumped Drake full of an untested drug. That's why he could make love to you so passionately after just suffering a black-out episode."

With all that had passed between her and Drake, Mikerra hadn't been thinking clearly. Yes, she should have realized that something was helping Drake perform, not that she was complaining. She should have been more aware. "I didn't realize, Kissa. You really think that the government has been giving him that kind of medication without his knowledge?"

"From what you've told me, yes, I do. His slow responses and then passing out tell me that he's been exposed to some inhibitors."

Mikerra nodded, her mind slowly coming up to speed. "Well, from what I understand about the project, it concerns a certain group of soldiers. What I'm not sure of is what any of that has to do with Drake. Maybe Sloan can provide some answers."

"And maybe you can get Drake to go to a regular, nonmilitary doctor before then."

Mikerra laughed. "And maybe I can get donkeys to fly out of my big butt."

Kissa shook her head. "You have a lot more power over him than you realize. I bet if you suggested he go to the doctor, he'd go. 'Cause he wants to please you."

"Then you'd lose. I already asked him to see an emergency room doctor, and he refused. Claimed the military doctor was good enough for him."

"Was that pre-sex?"

"Yes, Perry Mason," Mikerra shot back.

"Well," Kissa said in her most annoying urban voice, "since you and Drake have done the deed, I say ask again. You might be surprised at his answer."

* * *

After Drake left his brother, he continued his walk down the street. Somehow he ended up on Mikerra's street. Now how did he end up there? He knew exactly how: his feet led him there because that was where his heart wanted to go.

He noticed that the lights at her house were still on and that she was standing on her front porch, talking to someone. He was too far away to see who it was, but he was definitely going to find out. He could be as quiet as a mouse when he needed to be. He stayed in the shadows and neared her house.

He didn't realize his heart was beating rapidly until he relaxed when he heard Kissa's voice. He grinned as he realized they were talking about him.

"Mikerra, I think you're nuts. Just ask him."

Mikerra shrugged her shoulders. "I don't know, Kissa. I just want to take a hot bath and sleep for about ten hours. I'll think about all this tomorrow." She took a deep breath. "I can't believe I'm sore."

Kissa laughed. "Just think if he'd been up to par."

Mikerra groaned. "I probably wouldn't be able to walk right now. But I think I will talk to Quinn tomorrow. Why don't we have dinner or something tomorrow night? That way we'll have a game plan for next weekend."

"Are you going to ask Drake?" Kissa stood directly in front of Mikerra in a game of stare.

"Do I have a choice?"

Kissa started down the steps leading to the sidewalk. "No, you don't. I'll talk to you later." She headed down the sidewalk. Luckily, she went in the opposite direction of Drake.

Drake breathed a sigh of relief until he heard a voice.

"Okay, Drake, you can come out now."

He stepped from behind one of her overgrown hedges and grinned. "How long did you know?" He walked over to her.

She smiled at him, then led him inside the house. "I didn't know until I heard you laughing."

"I wasn't laughing that loud," Drake said.

"I know, but I could tell it was you." She closed her front door and joined him on the couch. "Now, what brings you by at this late hour?"

He reached for her hand. "I came by to see you. I know we talked about what happened between us, but I want to make sure you're okay with it."

She glanced sideways at him. "D-Drake, I don't know what you mean. I thought we agreed to take this one step at a time." She cleared her throat. "I do think your first priority is going to the doctor to see about your headaches."

He wanted to kiss her. That was his priority. "I've already been to the doctor. I think your priority should be to take a long hot bath, since you're so sore. Did I hurt you?"

She shook her head. "No, it's just been a while, and the last thing I was expecting was you to be so, you know, large."

He liked the way her face was tinged red with embarrassment. It gave him a perverse sense of satisfaction knowing he was getting under her skin, because she was definitely having the same effect on him. "I can't apologize for being who I am."

"I didn't ask you to." She wiggled her hand free. "I really hate that you heard that part of my conversation with Kissa. Now you're going to start thinking you're all that."

Drake didn't have to start thinking that. He already

knew that. But something about Mikerra Stone made his being a career soldier pale in comparison. "I would never think that. I don't have to."

"So what are you trying to tell me? There's competition out there?"

He had her. Was she actually jealous? "No, you don't have any competition." He leaned forward and kissed her gently on the lips. "The only competition you have is me."

Mikerra stared at him. "W-what?"

He kissed her again. He hadn't meant to, but he couldn't stop himself. Her lips were like nectar from the gods. "I'm trying to give you the space you need to think about us. But with you looking at me like that, I'm going to forget all my good intentions."

She smiled and leaned forward, her lips a kiss away from his. "Maybe I want you to forget about all those good intentions." She closed the distance between them and kissed him. This time their kisses quickly escalated into a total make-out session. Drake eased them or Mikerra pushed them—he couldn't be certain which—down on the couch, with her on top of him.

Drake tried to fight the little voice telling him to take over. He wanted Mikerra to take the lead. He had to see how far she'd go.

Drake was getting lost in the kisses when she stopped abruptly and stood. His body felt bereft without her on top of him, creating warmth. He knew his erection had already given him away. "Baby, what happened?"

She sighed. "Open your eyes and you'll see."

If he had to look at her, it would just make the fact that they weren't making love that more painful. He opened them, anyway, and couldn't believe his eyes. "Are you sure?"

Mikerra was holding out her hand. In her hand was

a gold packet. "If I wasn't sure, I wouldn't have let you in my house. And then I wouldn't have let you kiss me. And then I wouldn't have let you kiss me again. And again, and again. The only thing I ask is that we carry on this conversation upstairs. I don't want Terror to see us."

This woman was full of surprises, he realized. One day he hoped to know all her secrets, but getting there would be half the fun. He took her hand, and they walked hand in hand to her bedroom.

To say he was surprised would be an understatement. Her king-size bed was the one thing she hadn't bought at Wright City's only furniture store. An Edwardian four poster bed had to be special ordered from Dallas.

"A present from Gram. She loves Thomas Pinckney furniture and believes it's a good investment." She closed the door and walked to the bed.

Drake followed her and sat next to her. "Look, Care Bear, if you've changed your mind, I understand."

Mikerra stood and pulled her T-shirt over her head and let it fall carelessly to the floor. "Drake Harrington, if I didn't want you here, you wouldn't be here. Period."

He nodded. "I know that, Mikerra. I just don't want you regretting anything that we do together, baby."

"Well, I'm glad that's settled." Mikerra leaned down and kissed him gently on the lips. "Last week you were the last person I had expected to see." She motioned for him to take his shirt off.

Drake didn't need to be asked twice. He whipped the T-shirt over his head and threw it on the floor. "You knew I wasn't in Iraq anymore, so why would you be surprised that I came home?"

"It just didn't occur to me." She slipped out of

her shorts and stood in front of him in just a lacy peach-colored bra and matching barely there panties. "Now, are we going to talk all night, or what?"

Drake laughed, pulled her in his arms, and kissed her. He unhooked her bra, and it slid from her shoulders. "I think you know the answer to that question. Or at least you should be able to feel it."

She wiggled her hips under him. "I think I feel something," she teased as she unzipped his shorts and reached inside his boxers, stroking him gently. "Yes, I think I feel something. Is that a lead pipe in your shorts, or are you just glad to see me?"

He struggled out of his shorts and boxers and kicked them aside. Where had he put the condom? He glanced around the bed and didn't see the packet anywhere.

Mikerra laughed as she reached under a pillow. "Are you looking for this?" She handed him a black packet with bright gold letters.

"How many different kinds of condoms do you have?"

She grinned seductively at him. "Do you really want to have this conversation now?"

Drake was too excited and turned on to answer.

"If you must know, the gold ones I bought, but Quinn left these as a housewarming present. He gave me a condom tree."

Drake laughed. "Sounds like Quinn. He has always marched to a different drummer." He opened the packet and slipped on the condom. "Now, no more talking, teasing, or asking questions."

He expected an argument, but she only shimmied out of her panties and sent them sailing across the room. She gave him a challenging look as she relaxed against the pillows, looking exactly like a seductress.

"You were saying something," Mikerra whispered.

Drake moved on top of her. He kissed her gently on the mouth before devouring her. Something about kissing this woman sent his hormones into overdrive. She moved against him, trying to hint to him to get the show on the road, but Drake wanted to prolong their agony as much as possible.

His kisses moved slowly downward. He paid homage to her full breasts and smooth skin. He licked the valley between her breasts before taking a turgid nipple in his mouth. He loved the way she smelled and tasted.

Mikerra thought the ceiling in her bedroom was spinning out of control. She caressed his face and head as he continued his journey downward. He gently bit her rounded stomach as his long fingers invaded her.

"Drake!"

He raised his head and smiled. "I just want to make you feel good. Want me to stop?"

Mikerra couldn't form a coherent sentence. She shook her head and flopped back against the pillows and closed her eyes. This felt too good, and she didn't want the feeling to end.

Drake's tongue soon replaced his nimble fingers. Mikerra gasped at the powerful feeling. She was in a free fall from the highest cliff and was helpless to do anything but hit the ground with anticipation.

He put his hands under her derriere and raised her body closer to his mouth, and that was when Mikerra couldn't take one more thrust of his tongue. She tried to warn him she was about to climax, but that was at the exact moment. It was too late. Her entire body shook with excitement, exhilaration, and not one ounce of embarrassment.

Before she could recover from that, Drake filled her to the hilt with one strong stroke. He kissed her as they found a comfortable rhythm. Mikerra didn't think she could hang on to her sanity for many more delicious strokes, but she would definitely try. She wrapped her legs around his very muscular behind as he continued driving his thrusts home. He wrapped his strong arms around her, bringing her closer, as he increased his tempo.

"Drake, Drake, oh, Drake," she panted.

"I know, baby. Just hold on," he whispered in her ear.

She did as he asked, and one thrust later they both exploded. Drake lay atop her, exhausted and spent. Mikerra didn't mind the extra weight. It felt good to hold him.

When he didn't move in the next few minutes, she began to get nervous. She felt his forehead. He was burning up. She tried to rouse him, but it proved difficult.

Horrid thoughts started tumbling through her mind. Had she killed him in her quest for a replay of that afternoon? She should have known something like this would happen? This was the price she paid for not telling her family the truth about her job.

She pushed at Drake's naked torso, and he finally moved enough for her to slide out of bed. She grabbed her bathrobe from the bathroom and paced the room, wondering what to do. *Kissa!*

Mikerra picked up her cordless phone and called her childhood friend. Kissa would know what to do. After all, she was a doctor. The phone rang once, twice, three times. Mikerra was about to give up when she heard her best friend's sleepy voice answer the phone.

"Kissa, I need your help," Mikerra said frantically.

"That's rich. What happened? Drake came over and you guys had amazing sex and now he's passed out?"

"Yes."

"Please tell me you're kidding."

Mikerra looked at Drake's still form. "Well, maybe he's not passed out, but I can't seem to wake him. What should I do?"

"Get him dressed, and take him to the emergency room. I'll meet you guys at the hospital." Kissa ended the call.

Mikerra pushed the end button on the phone and sat it on the table. "Well, how am I supposed to get this big man up and dressed?"

Drake finally moved and opened his eyes. They were glassy, but at least he was alert. "What are you doing?"

Mikerra sat next to him on the bed. "Baby, we need to get you to the ER. You passed out again."

He picked up Mikerra's hand. "You called me baby." He smiled and closed his eyes.

Chapter 12

By some miracle, Mikerra managed to get Drake dressed and into her SUV without causing him any injuries. As she sped to the hospital, she called Quinn for a little support, just in case. Although her younger brother didn't like being interrupted in the middle of the night, he agreed to meet her at the hospital.

"Be there in ten," he promised while stifling a yawn.

Mikerra thanked him and snapped her cell phone shut. She pulled up to the emergency-room entrance and ran inside to get help.

Two transporters followed her outside to her SUV. Drake had that cute dazed look on his face. Mikerra opened the passenger door. "Drake, these men are going to take you inside to see the doctor."

"I'm tired, not stupid, Mikerra. I know Trey and Earnest." He nodded to the two young African American men standing behind the wheelchair. "And I can walk inside just fine." The tone in his voice left no room for bartering.

Trey and Earnest looked at Drake, then at each other, before taking the wheelchair inside the hospital without their patient. Mikerra was not so easily frightened. "Okay, Drake. Now that you scared the transporters off, show me what you got."

He eased out of the SUV in slow motion. "I think that's how we got in this little predicament, isn't it?" He closed the door and headed inside.

Mikerra stood in the ER driveway, wondering what the heck had just happened. She didn't have time to reflect on that, because someone was blowing their horn, insisting that she move her vehicle quickly.

Luckily, she was able to park close by. She marched inside the hospital, ready to give Drake a piece of her mind, but didn't get the chance. She saw another face from the past. "Oh my gosh! David?"

A tall African American man walked toward her, smiling. "Yes, Mikerra. It's me. I bet you thought you'd never see me working here, didn't you?"

Mikerra shook her head. Although David Johnson was a few years older than she, he was easy to remember, being one of the handsome Johnson men. David had three brothers, and they were all gorgeous and had the manners of true Southern gentlemen. "No, I didn't. The last I heard, you were living in Houston and working at Sam Houston Memorial."

He nodded. "Yeah, I moved back recently, after my divorce was final. I have three boys, and Mom is spoiling them like crazy." He looked around the room. "What brings you to the ER?"

"I brought Drake Harrington in. He's been having some headaches." She stepped closer to David. "Is there somewhere I could talk to you privately?"

He nodded. "Actually, I was paged to the ER. I bet Drake is the reason. I specialized in neurological disorders when I worked in Houston. Why don't you tell me what's going on while we walk?"

David didn't give her a real option, since he started

walking down the hall without her. Mikerra picked up her pace and began telling David about Drake's headaches.

"Well, I'll give him a thorough examination. I might need you to calm him down, so be prepared." He pointed to the waiting room. "But right now I'm going to need you to wait."

Mikerra nodded and headed to the small room. Kissa and Quinn were already there, waiting for her. Quinn ran to his sister as she entered the room. "Is Drake okay? You weren't supposed to use all the condoms at one time. I thought that they would last you guys the entire summer."

Any other time Mikerra would have been able to shoot back with something sarcastically funny, but it was too much. Mikerra burst into tears and wrapped her arms around her brother. "I think I killed Drake, Quinn!"

"No, you didn't." Quinn comforted his sister. "You just get a hold of yourself. It was probably just the sex. It was so good, he passed out or something."

"I don't know."

Quinn shook her. "Now, you listen to me, Mikerra. You wouldn't do anything to hurt Drake. We all know that. Maybe it's like that thing the Vietnam vets had. So get it together, girl. You're going to have to be strong enough for both of you. And besides, you'll have to call his mama and tell her you put her baby in the hospital."

That took her mind off Drake taking ill in her bed. "But I don't want to call his mama," Mikerra whined. "After what happened this afternoon, she's going to swear I'm trying to kill him!"

Kissa laughed. "Stop it."

Quinn looked at Mikerra. "Thank you," he told

Kissa. "Finally, someone I can relate to. Tell her to quit being such a drama queen. Drake is a big, bad army dude. There's no way one, two, or five times with Mikerra could clean his clock."

Kissa waved his comment away and took a seat. "She's your sister. I'm only her best friend. I don't think she's listening to either of us right now."

Mikerra placed her hands on her hips. Glaring at Quinn and Kissa, she couldn't decide which one to be mad at first. She decided on both. "You guys, I'm standing right here. How many times I had s-e-x with Drake doesn't matter."

Quinn took a seat next to Kissa. "Who is she spelling for? Maybe Drake sucked out her brain when they were kissing."

Kissa nodded. "I know. It's like I'm talking to some blonde named Buffy or Tiffany."

At that comment Mikerra gave up her martyr stance and took a seat by her brother. "Thanks, you guys, for bringing me back to earth."

Kissa threw her hands up in the air. "Finally. Quinn, I think your sister has seen the light!"

Mikerra opened her mouth to retort but noticed David standing in the doorway. He was not smiling. This wasn't going to be good. She stood and walked over to David. "How is he?"

"Sit down, Mikerra."

Mikerra walked back to the seat next to Quinn and sat down. Whatever David was going to tell her was going to alter her life one way or another. "What is it?"

David sat down next to her and opened the chart. "I should be discussing this with a family member, but since you brought him in, you could possibly connect a few dots for me."

"You couldn't get his medical records?"

David shook his head. "I was told to send him home and some general would be in touch with me in the morning."

"It's like I told you," Mikerra said. "The doctor at the VA told him he had island headaches and gave him some more medication yesterday."

"Island headaches?" repeated David.

Mikerra nodded. "The doctor said that they were common among soldiers returning from the war zone and that they would level off in a few weeks."

"That's a load of rubbish," David said. "Just because he is a military doctor doesn't mean he's telling the truth. The only symptom associated with being in 'the trap,' as the soldiers call it, is a rash that lasts about two days."

Mikerra was beginning to feel like a witness in a high-profile case whose testimony had just been ripped to shreds by the prosecuting attorney. "I'm sorry, David, but that's what the doctor said, and you know Drake. Whatever the military says is good enough for him."

David took a sheet a paper and handed it to Mikerra. "Not in this case. I've run a few prelim tests on a hunch. I don't like what I'm finding."

She knew he was leading up to something, and that this something was huge, but she just wanted him to get it over with. "What did you find?" She held Quinn's hand for support.

David looked at her with sadness in those light brown eyes. "Mikerra, I've found the beginnings of a brain tumor."

"What?" Mikerra cried.

David placed a hand on her shoulder. "Now, don't get alarmed yet. The headaches are one of the biggest symptoms. Now I want to run some more tests, but Drake is refusing at the moment. I gave him a medicine that will neutralize the drugs already in his system and will relieve the headaches temporarily."

Mikerra nodded. "So you want me to convince him to stay here, don't you?"

"No, I want you to call his mother, and she can convince him to stay here," he said sarcastically. "Of course, I want you to convince him to stay. If he did, we could run the tests now with a minimum of fuss. I bet I can even get you a bed for the night in his room." David smiled as he noted Drake's chart.

Mikerra really hated being manipulated like this. But did she really have a choice? She looked at Quinn and Kissa for guidance. "What about Terror?"

"I'll go by your house and pick him up," Quinn told his older sister. "You know you want to stay with Drake in his time of need."

"David, save that speech for somebody else. You just don't want Drake's mama up here." Mikerra laughed at the thought of Shirley Harrington storming through the halls of Wright City Memorial when she found out Drake was sick.

"True. My plan is to run the tests, get him stabilized and we'll go from there," replied David.

Mikerra looked at David. "Okay, David, tell me exactly what's going on, and I'll see if I want to get between you and Drake's mama."

"Damn, girl. You haven't changed one bit." David passed her a very small picture. It was actually a picture of Drake's brain. "You see that area circled in red?"

Mikerra nodded.

"Well, that is a brain tumor," David explained. "See how the tumor cells are larger than the other cells?"

Mikerra studied the picture and noticed the tumor cells were at least twice the size of the other cells. "Yes."

"This is what we call a grade three brain tumor. Actually, it's called an anaplastic astrocytoma. It's common in people around his age, but he didn't get his as a result of the aging process. He has this because of the medicines he's been injected with. It accelerates the brain tissue at an alarming rate. When I was in Houston, there were some mumblings about a drug that would make the body stronger, but the one side effect was it caused brain tumors."

"It's called the Project Perfect serum," Mikerra said dryly. "I didn't know about the side effects. It's supposed to heal the body, not kill the person."

"So they're testing the soldiers and not telling them? No wonder they were so nervous on the phone when I called about his charts. I'm still going to need to do more tests. If it is PP One-ninety-two, we're all dead."

She knew that, too. "I know."

Drake didn't want to open his eyes. For the first time in three weeks, he didn't have a headache or piercing pain. Actually, he had no pain at all. Then the smell in the room hit him. He was in a hospital.

He opened his eyes and focused his blurry vision on the overhead light. It finally became clear. He gazed around the room and smiled. Mikerra was sitting in a chair, reading a magazine.

"Hey, what are you doing here?" He struggled to sit upright, a feat easier said than done. Finally he gave up. Damn, he felt so weak.

Mikerra stood and sat down on the bed, facing him. "I'm here because you need to be here."

"That only means David blabbed. I'm not taking any more tests."

Mikerra picked up his hand and rubbed it against her face. "Drake, it would mean a lot to me if you did."

She was playing hardball, he realized. *Let the games begin!* "Okay, Care Bear, I will take the tests on one condition."

"What?" She kissed his hand and moved closer to him. "Like I don't know where this is going."

He was thinking along those lines, but he also knew something was seriously wrong with his body. He didn't want to go through this alone. "Please stay with me tonight."

She scooted off the bed and pushed the button for the nurse. "I'll stay if you take the tests."

Drake didn't think he'd won, but it felt like he had. He had the woman he'd always wanted at his side in his time of need. Maybe he *had* won.

David walked in the room, smiling. "I knew you could do it, Mikerra. We got a nice private room at the end of the hall. We'll run the tests in a few hours and go from there." He glanced in Mikerra's direction. "Mikerra, I need to speak with Drake privately."

Mikerra nodded. "Sure, David. I'll be right outside."

But Drake didn't want to hear the bad news alone. "No, David. I would like for her to stay."

David glanced at him. "Okay." He pulled the chair near the bed and sat down.

Drake motioned for Mikerra to sit next to him. He saw her hesitate and glance at David. She shrugged away her worries, walked to the bed, and sat next to him.

Drake accepted the victory for what it was. That one simple gesture was more than Mikerra Stone wanted to give at the moment, but still she gave in. Because of him. He reached for her hand. "Okay, David. I'm ready." And he wasn't talking about the doom his friend was about to bestow on him.

David opened the chart and handed him a picture.

"I'm not going to beat around the bush with you, Drake. The area I've circled is a brain tumor. It looks like the beginning stages, but I want to be sure. Have your headaches stopped yet?"

Drake nodded. "I can't believe this. I've been suffering for months, and the medic kept telling me they'd go away. I told Mikerra it had only been going on a couple of weeks. I didn't think it was this serious."

"I understand. How long have you been getting shots?"

"How did you know I've been getting shots?"

David shifted in his chair. "I know because the drug is in your system. You've been injected with an experimental drug called PP One-ninety-two serum, and you can only get it one way. My guess is you've been getting injected about three times a year. I know you probably got some shots when you left for Iraq and when you returned stateside, but do you remember another time?"

Drake shrugged. "The only other shots I got were when I had a sinus infection about eight months ago."

"Shots?"

Drake nodded. "Yeah, I had a real bad sinus infection, and they gave me something to kill the infection." He felt like an idiot for not questioning the military doctors. Those quacks were playing with his life!

"That answered my next question," David mumbled. "Did any other men in your unit have a sinus infection?"

Drake shook his head. "No, not in my unit, but a buddy of mine had a really bad infection, like I did." He'd only given the military the last twenty years of his life, and this was how they repaid him.

"What happened to him?"

"Killed last year in a freak accident." Now that Drake thought about it, drowning in the shower didn't sound so realistic.

"He would have been the first variable," David mumbled. "Were there any witnesses to this death?"

"No. It was the middle of the night," Drake said quietly. "The commander found him the next day."

David nodded, but Drake knew he wasn't really listening. The first clue was that David was tapping his gold pen against the metal chart. The second clue was that he was being paged for a phone call, but he didn't move.

Finally, Drake couldn't take it anymore. "David, man, you're being paged."

"Oh, sorry." David took a cell phone out of his coat pocket and pushed a button. "David Johnson."

Drake listened to the one-sided conversation and knew instantly David was talking to someone of great importance, but he wasn't expecting the chairman of the Joint Chiefs of Staff.

"Of course, General MacArthur, I can understand your position in this matter, but as I told your aide earlier, he's just in for some headaches."

Okay, why was David lying to one of the most powerful men in Washington? Drake wondered. He continued listening.

"No, I didn't run any kind of tests. I merely gave him some aspirin and sent him on his way. Yes, I will keep you informed should he return." He pushed a button on the phone and placed it back in his pocket.

Mikerra cleared her throat. "Please tell me that wasn't General Horace MacArthur on the phone," she said in a quiet voice.

"I'm afraid so," David said. "Even though I'm just a mere civilian, I do know generals don't call hicktown doctors in the middle of the night. Which tells me my guess is right, and we're all in a shitload of trouble."

Chapter 13

The three high school friends stared at each other. Mikerra thought the silence was nerve-wracking and had to say something. "Did MacArthur say he was coming to town?"

David shook his head. "No, he didn't. He just told me to run any changes by him first. And to let him know if Drake comes back for any medication." He glanced at Mikerra. "He wanted to know if anyone accompanied him to the hospital." David closed the chart and sat it on the bed, beside Drake. "Now, Mikerra," he said in a very calm voice, "I think I've been pretty patient about not asking the details of your involvement in all this. I think I have a right to know what really happened between you and Senator Seth McCaffrey."

"I'm not sure what you mean, David?" She hated lying to her friend, but too many people were becoming involved, and she didn't want to see anyone else get hurt.

"Mikerra, you knew the drug by name. Most members of the Joint Chiefs don't know that. There's only one way you obtained this inside information."

Mikerra looked at David, then at Drake. Yes, everyone had a right to know, since she'd practically just signed all their death sentences. They had a right to know why they were going to be killed. She took a deep breath. "You're right, David. You do have a right to know, and so do Drake, Kissa, and Quinn."

David nodded as if he knew how big a deal this really was. "We'll do this in Drake's private room. No use getting anyone else involved in this." He stood, then pushed the button for the transporters. "I need a patient transported immediately."

"Yes, Dr. Johnson," a voice called. "Right away."

"I'll get Kissa and Quinn, and we'll meet you in the room," David announced.

Mikerra nodded. "David, why is this so important to you? I know I'm in it up to my neck, but you could have just turned us over."

"Because I don't like what's going on here. My father always told me and my brothers to fight for what we believe in, and I believe in you and Drake." David walked out of the room.

Mikerra turned her gaze to Drake. He was staring at her with a look of indifference. Either he was extremely ticked off or he empathized with her. "I really did have your best interest in my heart, Drake. I wasn't trying to get you involved in all this."

He shrugged those broad shoulders. "I know that, Care Bear, but trouble does seem to be following you at the moment. You think the military pumped me full of something, and I guess now that I'm faced with the bad news, I do, too. I wish I had listened to you a week ago. Maybe something could have been done."

She sat on the bed and grabbed his hand. "Drake, we aren't sure about anything yet, so save the pity party for later." She kissed him on the forehead. "I don't want you worried about anything but how many times we can make love once you're well."

"I think I like that idea."

The transporters came with a wheelchair to take Drake to his new room, but Drake was already shaking his head. "I'm not getting in that chair. I can walk down the hall under my own steam."

Trey, one of the young men who had tried to transport Drake earlier, nodded his head in agreement. "I told Dr. Johnson you ain't no punk, but he said if I value my job, you will ride in this chair. And I really need my job, Mr. Harrington."

It would be a standoff, Mikerra knew. Drake had this macho soldier head game going on, and the poor transporter was just trying to keep his job. It was time for Mikerra to work some of those powers of persuasion Kissa kept telling her she had. "If you want those other activities we talked about earlier to take place, Drake, you'd better sit in that chair," she said only loud enough for his ears.

Drake didn't have to be asked twice. He quickly eased out of bed and sat in the wheelchair. "Want to ride in my lap?"

Mikerra knew her hazelnut complexion had a definite rosy hue to it now. "No, thank you. I'll walk with you."

Drake shrugged. "I think my way would be more fun."

An hour later, with Mikerra's help, Drake was settled in the private room. Quinn, Kissa, and David had joined them. Mikerra prepared to tell her saga of Seth McCaffrey. She sat on the bed, holding Drake's hand, and began her own process of soul cleansing.

"About six years ago I met Senator McCaffrey at a

journalists' award dinner. It was right after September eleventh, and my piece had just run in *The New York Times* and had gotten picked up by the wire service. The city of New York threw a dinner for the journalists who wrote stories about the terrorist attacks." Mikerra sighed. It seemed so long ago, and she should have seen the warning signs, but hindsight was everything. "Anyway, a few days later, he sent me flowers, candy, and started to woo me. I'd never had anyone do that for me before, and odd things I should have questioned went unnoticed."

"Like what?" Drake asked, caressing her hand.

Mikerra felt hot tears betraying her and sliding down her cheeks. "Like him not being able to take me certain places. At first he said he was tired of always eating out, and I was, too." She knew she had to explain that statement. "When I wrote the piece about September eleventh, I was being wined and dined by most of the major newspapers so that I would leave my job. Anyway, fast-forward to a year later, and I found myself in an affair with a married man. Yes, Seth was married, and I was stupid enough to believe that he actually loved me and would leave his Barbie clone of a wife. You do stupid things when you think you're in love."

Kissa nodded. "I can attest to that."

Mikerra smiled at her friend and continued her story. "I found myself willing to accept whatever morsel of affection Seth threw my way. That's when he started getting careless. He left all kinds of high-level security documents at my apartment. Top secret documents. So I decided to use Seth like he was using me."

"Oh, baby," Drake said.

There was so much emotion in those two words, Mikerra almost started blubbering, but something in those dark brown eyes made her continue. "About two years ago, after one of his visits, I found a file folder marked PP in my living room. I was going to call Seth and tell him he'd left it, but something in the back part of my brain told me to read it. I did, and that's when everything went crazy."

"How so?" Kissa asked.

"Well, a few days later, Seth asked me about the file, and if I'd read it or not. Of course, I lied and said I hadn't read it." She took a deep breath. "There was information in that file that needed to get out to the public, but if I spilled the beans, I knew Seth would realize where the information had come from."

"So you wrote a story about the proposed bill about the testing," Kissa said. "I remember seeing something about all military testing being halted."

"Yes, I know, and that was the first and last time Seth hit me. That was when I realized that wasn't the way I wanted to live my life. It took three months to cover my tracks, but I did with some help from a good friend."

Mikerra looked at four somber faces. "Now, don't feel sorry for me. It took that little episode in my life to make me change."

"I don't know if I can take much more, honey," said Drake.

Mikerra had to get it all out into the open, or she'd never be able to move on. "There's not much more. Promise."

Drake nodded.

"The last straw was when I discovered I wasn't Seth's only extra woman. I mean, I had tried to end it several times before, but Seth can be very persuasive, especially when he kept threatening me with my job. In the end Seth got me fired from my job. I decided to make a clean break and come back here. Not many people knew I was from Wright City. I had never used my legal name. I'd kept that part out of my bio, so I felt relatively safe. I mean, I figured that if I kept a low profile and worked on my memoirs, it would be a while before he tracked me down."

"But, Mikerra, why does Seth want to track you down? I just don't understand. If it was the end of an affair, he'd just move on to the next one. Not try to track you like it was hunting season," Kissa said, stating the obvious.

Mikerra nodded. "Well, he told my bosses that I took something of his and wouldn't return it, but I gave him back everything he ever gave me. When he drafted Project Perfect, he wrote two versions. The one the president signed and the real one. I have a copy of the real one in a very safe place. Any mail coming from New York goes through ten states before I get it. Carter, my friend at the Justice Department, worked out all the diversions. I couldn't go to the police, with Seth being so high profile. Besides, would they believe the black editor or the white senator from Massachusetts with a Moral Majority platform?"

"But what does one have to do with the other?" Quinn asked.

"Seth and Horace are buddies. Same alma mater, you know," replied Mikerra. "And Seth is chairman of the defense committee. That's how all this perfect soldier stuff started. I don't know how Drake figures in all this yet, but I will."

David took a deep breath. "So that's why no one can get at Drake's file. And from what I've heard about the senator, I know you're in a lot more trouble than you know."

It was Mikerra's turn to look surprised. "What do you mean?"

David stood and paced the room. "I mean, my ex has some friends in D.C., and the running gag is how many women the senator has had eliminated when they tried to end the relationship. Oddly enough, he's never been charged with anything. The authorities always claim there was not enough evidence to make the case stick."

"What?" Mikerra swallowed hard.

"You're not the first woman he's put a hit on. And that's what is going on," David explained.

Mikerra felt the blood rush from her face. Sure Seth was mad, but was he actually paying someone else to make her disappear in a million tiny pieces?

David nodded, instantly following her thought process. "When I was making arrangements for Drake's tests, my ex called me with the latest gossip and told me the news. There's a price on your head. McCaffrey just doesn't know exactly where you are. He thinks you're here, but no one can verify it, 'cause he's looking for Karen Mills. The reason he put a hit out is that he can't find you. It's nationwide."

Mikerra sighed. Thank God she'd had the good sense not to use her real name in New York. Her reason might have been off the mark, but now it literally had saved her life. All those years ago, she'd thought that her name sounded too much like a country hick name and that she needed something more cosmopolitan. Carter had told her that Seth would eventually find her, and boy, was he correct. "What does Drake have to do with this?"

"I think I know," Drake said ruefully. "I've been mentally putting the pieces of my tour of duty together in my mind. Some big chunks are still missing, but here goes. When my unit was deployed to Iraq, a ranger unit was already there. When we were lined up for shots, I noticed a friend of mine and I got an extra series of immunization shots, but I really didn't think anything of it. It's the military, for chrissakes."

"I know, Drake, but that's just the problem. You got a few choice idiots thinking they can take a few medical shortcuts and a few more idiots too afraid to say no. I hate that this is happening to you, but hopefully you're not too far along. I take it your friend wasn't the same one who died in the shower," Mikerra said.

Drake shook his head. "No, this guy was in my unit."

Mikerra could see the handiwork of a master plan, and that plan was playing with the lives of innocent soldiers. She watched Drake closely as he leaned against the pillows and closed his eyes. This time this story would see the light of day no matter what it cost her. Even if that meant her life.

6:00 A.M. the following morning, Danbury, Connecticut

"What do you mean, you couldn't get confirmation? How hard is it to find one overweight black woman?" he needlessly barked. With the invention of wireless headsets, Seth could have whispered and still have been heard. But raising his voice eased his frustration.

"She's currently off the grid, sir. It's like she doesn't exist."

"I don't need your belligerent tone right now, either. I need some damn answers. She dropped off the face of the earth four months ago."

"Sir, Karen Mills didn't exist until about fifteen years ago. We're assuming she was using an alias and no one ever called her on it. We have been searching the database for her true identity and can't make a connection."

"How could she use an alias? You have to have real ID to open bank accounts, pay income taxes, buy property," replied Seth.

"She did all that under the assumed name."

"How do you know Karen Mills is an assumed name?" Seth continued jogging down the isolated country road. "I mean, how do you know that's not her real name?"

"We don't exactly," the young man hedged. "We're just going on the evidence presented. Karen Mills has ceased to exist. Once she was dismissed from *New York* magazine, she sold her condo and her Mercedes. Those are the last transactions she completed. She closed out her bank accounts."

Seth smiled. "Surely, she had the funds forwarded to another bank! Don't tell me she didn't have money. I know she did. I put enough money into her account to know better."

"Yes, but her accounts were closed by a third party, which we can't identify. The funds were converted to cashier's checks, and those were converted to money orders."

"Monitor them," Seth demanded.

"Money orders are hard to monitor, sir. It's the red tape of cash transactions, sir. Yes, two of the cashier's checks were cashed about three months ago. One was in Washington state, and the other one was in South Dakota."

"Dammit!" Seth didn't like this. Karen was proving more cunning than he'd given her credit for. He should have known better than to get involved with a reporter; now he was paying for not following his gut instincts.

"We could put out an alert with a BOLO."

"Yes, and every government agency hot dog will be out looking for her. The last thing I need is more people in on this fiasco. Find that woman and don't call me back until you can give me something I can use."

* * *

7:00 A.M., Wright City, Texas

Mikerra woke from one of the most peaceful nights of slumber since returning to Wright City. Although her position in the hard plastic chair next to Drake's hospital bed should have been uncomfortable, it wasn't.

They'd fallen asleep holding hands. Something about it made her feel safe and told her that this mess could be fixed. It might take a miracle, but it could and would be fixed.

After her confession the previous night, Drake had been wheeled away for an MRI. Mikerra had had lots of time to reflect on her life as she waited for Drake's return.

With a price on her head, she knew her options were few until it could be sorted out. No one but her friends knew of her alias, and as long as no one thought to pass around a picture of her in her hometown, she would be safe. Besides, she'd lost about fifty pounds since the last time Seth had actually seen her. Had she really dropped that much in weight in such a short amount of time?

"Hey. How'd you sleep?" Drake asked. He was resting on his side and staring at her.

Mikerra stretched and yawned. "Fine. The big question is, how do you feel?"

He struggled to sit up. "You know that will depend on David. I'm eager to know the results of the tests. I hope Mom isn't freaking out 'cause I didn't come home last night."

"No, she's fine. I told her that we were together and not to worry. I just didn't tell her you were in here taking tests."

Drake laughed. "Mom is going to have your ass for lying."

Mikerra knew that. "I'll just tell her you made me do it."

"Mom knows you probably seduced me, and I'm too tired to move," he joked.

"About that, Drake," Mikerra hedged. "I would never have let you in my house if I knew you were going to pass out. I promise I'm going to make all this right."

"Mikerra."

"No, Drake. I have to do this, and this time I'm not going to back down from Seth. He's the reason the magazine fired me, but in a way I'm glad it happened, or I would never have come back here. But the scope of the Project Perfect program is unbelievable." She fumed at the idea of her own government killing innocent servicemen.

Drake scooted over in the hospital bed and motioned for her to lie beside him. As inviting as the bed looked, Mikerra knew that was a definite no-no. She could envision some busybody nurse walking in at just the precise moment and getting an eyeful.

"Oh, come on, Care Bear," he chided. "Who's going to care if you try to seduce me in the hospital bed?"

She decided not to lie beside him, but to just sit on the bed. "The same people who will have it all over town. You're going to get to leave. I do live here now, you know."

"Well, if David brings me bad news, I might be out of the military permanently, so I might be here with you."

Mikerra had been so focused on her own troubles, she had forgotten about Drake's. If he did in fact have a brain tumor, he would more than likely be given a medical discharge from the military. Mikerra knew that would break his career soldier's heart.

Chapter 14

Dr. David Johnson sat in his quiet office and contemplated life's big questions. The first and foremost one was, how did you tell your old friend from high school that the military he'd been serving in for over twenty years was killing him? The second one was, how did you bring up the question of trying an experimental drug on him and possibly doing the same thing to him that the military had been doing all these years.

He had a few options. But to exercise any of those options would mean involving more people and endangering their lives. He had to keep this quiet for the hospital's sake. And the last thing their little town needed was a scandal. He had to get Drake out of the hospital as quickly and quietly as possible. He had intended to discharge Drake right away, but complications with the tests had gotten in the way.

A soft knock interrupted his thought process. Surely, his senior charge nurse wasn't already at work. He watched as the door slid open and Mariel Harvey walked into the room, with his traditional cup of morning coffee. She sat the large plastic cup, three sugar packs, and two French vanilla creamers on his desk.

"Mariel, you didn't have to do this," David lied. He was very glad she'd taken the time. Usually, they spoke of her two boys and how they were adapting to life in Wright City. Mariel was a recent widow, thanks to the former president and his wars.

She sat in the chair facing him, ignoring his usual protest. "I know that, David, but I wanted to, so I did. Aren't you on night duty this week? Shouldn't you be going home to the boys? Looks like you've settled in for the day."

David knew he'd have to tell her. She knew him too well for him to hide anything from her. But for the moment he just gazed at her smooth cocoa brown complexion.

His life was complicated enough, and having a schoolboy crush on his nurse would only make matters worse. Mariel was everything he wanted in his second wife, but that was jumping the gun.

"David, why are you gawking at me? Do I have a milk mustache or something? I was racing with the boys this morning, but I'm sure I wiped my mouth before I left the house." Mariel pulled out the handy compact that she kept in her scrub pocket to check her flawless face. "There's not a speck on my face, David. What's going on?"

He took a deep breath. "Something big and I don't want to get you involved."

Mariel curled an errant strand of her black hair behind her ear, revealing small gold stud earrings. Her round face usually held a smile, but now she had the most serious look on her face. "David, when I moved to this town a few months ago, you hired me without checking my references or credentials. You have been a dear friend to me. You've been a rock to me and helped me adapt to living in a town without a Starbucks. There's nothing you could do or say that would make me turn my back on you."

David smiled. He remembered the day Mariel Harvey entered his life. He hadn't regretted it once. It was nice for someone to have his back for a change. "Thanks, Mariel. But this is huge, life threatening, and career ending."

She waved away his remark. "David, quit trying to make this a man thang, and tell me who you're hiding the patient in room three-twenty-one from."

Totally busted. "Okay. It's Drake Harrington. But this is strictly a need-to-know situation. I don't want any other nurse, or anyone else for that matter, going in that room."

She nodded. "Got it." She noticed the reports on his desk. "You're giving him Demerol for swelling?"

"Yes. It's helping his headaches."

"This is a tumor, David."

"I know. I have one option and it's kryptonite."

Mariel's brown eyes widened in surprise. "That hasn't been approved by our wonderful government. I think he would be an excellent candidate to try it on, but isn't he in the military?"

"And there's the problem." He handed her Drake's brain scans. "See how fast the cancer is growing?" He motioned to both scans.

Again Mariel nodded. "Looks like about ten percent growth." She examined the time of the scans. "In about thirty minutes. Was that before or after the Demerol?"

"Before. Since Demerol decreases the swelling, I had a scan taken about an hour ago, and it's decreased about half the amount."

Mariel stared at him and studied him carefully. "I'm in."

David laughed. "I hope you know what you're doing."

"Yes, this is why I'm a nurse. I want to save a life. When my husband was killed in Iraq last year, I picked up my two very young sons and picked a place on the map and moved here. I haven't regretted coming to Wright City, and I sure don't regret working for you."

"Thanks, Mariel." He rose, grabbed the reports, and headed for his door. He opened the door and motioned for her to precede him. "Come on. Let's go tell Drake the good news."

Mikerra held her breath as she watched David and a nurse walk into the room, with solemn looks on their faces. She'd seen the slender woman occasionally when she ate dinner at Jay's Diner, usually with two small boys in tow.

"Drake, Mikerra, this is my senior nurse, Mariel Harvey. She is going to be assisting me with your case and knows we're keeping this on the down low."

Drake nodded. "Come on, David," he said shortly. "Just spit it out."

"Okay, Drake. I know you guys want to know where we stand, and I'm going to explain it to you," said David. "Mariel will act as my assistant. No other personnel will come in this room."

Mikerra didn't like the sound of that. "Isn't Drake getting out of the hospital today?"

David cleared his throat and took a seat in the chair she'd vacated hours earlier. "Well, yes and no."

"Look, David, I know this is serious business, but if you don't tell us what's going on and fast, I'm going to have to hurt you." Mikerra grabbed Drake's hand. She hoped she didn't faint at the news.

"I guess I'm going about this the wrong way." David looked from Mikerra to Drake. "Sorry, guys." He shifted in his seat as he opened the metal chart. "I just received the reports from the MRI and the brain scans. The reason it took me so long is that I'm trying to keep your identity hidden, because if the military gets wind of this, we could all end up in the shredder."

Mikerra knew the danger they were in and didn't want innocent people to get killed because of her or what she knew about PP 192. "David, you don't have to do this."

He smiled that gorgeous smile that all those Johnson men were famous for. "Yes, I do. No one tells me how to run this hospital or what kind of care I should prescribe to a patient needing medical attention." He turned his attention to Drake. "Now, Drake, if you don't understand anything, just let me know."

Mikerra really didn't like the sound of that. That meant complicated mumbo jumbo. She took a deep breath and said, "Just start."

David nodded. "Okay, I've already told you what my suspicions were, and they were correct. The tumor, or cancer, you have is anaplastic astrocytoma, and it grows rapidly. From what you told me about your tour of duty and the severity of the headaches you had, I believe it's a grade three."

Mikerra felt the room spin counterclockwise. It was all too real now. Before, when it was just a possibility, she could fool herself into thinking it was all just a big mistake. But now, as David rambled on about symptoms and experimental drugs, it was real life. "What did you say?"

"I was saying there aren't many options available

unless we want to alert the Joint Chiefs of it. I've been giving Drake Demerol to stop the growth of the tumor. Usually, it's administered to those suffering from head injuries to reduce the swelling of the brain tissue. But because of the PP One-ninety-two serum, I can't administer it to Drake for much longer. The side effects could be worse than the headaches you've had."

"So what's left?" Mikerra wanted to spare Drake the bad news, but he was the person who would have to make the decision, no matter how much it was going to hurt them both.

David sighed. "We have one and only one option. It's kryptonite."

Drake actually laughed. "Like Superman?"

David laughed as well. "In a real, roundabout way, yes. It is an experimental drug and hasn't been approved in the United States. It's been used in the UK on car accident victims with severe head trauma and on people with brain tumors. It has a ninety-eight percent success rate. Before I subject you to this drug, I need to run some more tests."

"What are you leaving out?" Drake asked, suspicion evident in his deep voice.

"Not much. I'm going to discharge you for now. But I need you back here on Sunday night, and we can complete the tests by Monday morning. After that I can start giving you the medication. Drake, if this medicine is in your system and the military gives you another shot of PP One-ninety-two, it will cause a seizure. Once this happens, it will most likely end your military career with a medical discharge."

Mikerra didn't see any other way out for Drake. She moved closer to Drake and kissed his cheek. His cheek was moist and tasted salty, and she realized he was crying. Mikerra wiped the tears away and hugged him. "We're in this together, baby. No matter what. I'm right here for you, and I'm going to expose those bastards for what they did to you."

Drake was trying his manly best not to lose it in front of David, but this was his life they were discussing so casually. He listened to Mikerra sob uncontrollably and wanted to join her, but what good would that do either of them?

So like any good career soldier, he sucked in his emotions and turned his attention to the one man who could actually help him. "Okay, David. This is your show."

David breathed a sigh of relief. "Does this mean I'll have total cooperation?"

"As much as I can," replied Drake.

"Well, first we'll administer the tests, and then we'll get you started on the kryptonite," David explained. "When are you due at your next post?"

"About three weeks. I just arranged for a little extra time off."

David looked puzzled. "According to my military buds, that's like asking for your walking papers. I hear it takes almost an act of God to get time off approved."

"Man, I must have had my head up my ass," Drake murmured. "I called my commanding officer, and he approved it with no hesitation and no red tape and over the phone. I should have known something was going on." At the time he'd been too intent on taking Mikerra to bed to wonder about how easy it was to get extra leave in wartime.

"Don't worry yourself, Drake. When you get home, I want you to take it easy. I'll give you a three-day supply of Demerol. That will keep your headaches at bay. Now, here's the hard part. Kryptonite, medically known as Krypatonical, is just as the name states. It's a tonic, given intravenously. That way it gets into the bloodstream quicker, and it will shrink the tumor without surgery."

"How long will it take to shrink it?"

"That will depend on you." David sized him up. "You look to be in excellent health. I'd say it won't take over a month to get rid of all the tumor. However, I must caution you that this is an experimental drug and could have side effects."

Drake nodded. "Such as?"

"Mostly mood swings, anxiety, depression, and maybe some performance problems," David said slowly. "The end does justify the means."

Drake knew that. He hadn't had any headaches in the last few hours and felt almost human again. "Okay. What do you need from me?"

"Just your cooperation," said David.

Hours later Mikerra pulled into Drake's driveway. His dad's truck was missing, but his mother's black Lincoln Navigator was there. She looked over at Drake and smiled.

For the first time since she'd laid eyes on him seven days ago, he looked rested. No lines around those dark, sensual eyes, and he was smiling back at her.

They'd discussed this very scene all the way from the hospital. Drake thought it would be best if he talked to his mom one-on-one. Lying to her was out of the question. He respected his mother too much not to be one hundred percent honest with her. Besides, if the military called, she'd run great interference.

Mikerra cut the engine and turned to him. How

could she already feel so much love for a man she hadn't seen in over twenty years? She didn't know, but somehow she'd done it. She'd complicated the life she was trying to uncomplicate. "Drake, I know you said you could face your mother alone, but I think I should go in with you."

"I'd like that." He unfastened his seat belt, opened the door, and slid out of the SUV.

Mikerra sat there dumbfounded. She'd been ready to argue her point, but instead, Drake had turned the tables on her again. He'd agreed before she could formulate a thought. And by the time she did formulate that thought, he was at her door, helping her out of the SUV.

"Drake!" Mikerra yelped as he pulled her in his arms, kissing the stuffing out of her in front of all the neighbors.

He let go, grabbed her hand, and led her up the walkway to the front door. "What? I can't show my gratitude? I'm very grateful we ended up in the ER last night."

"You were where last night?" Drake's mother stood in the doorway, her perfectly manicured hands planted on her slender hips.

Mikerra knew they were both in the soup now. "Mrs. Harrington, Drake had a little accident last night, and we had to go to the ER." Mikerra took a deep breath. "We probably should talk inside."

"Of course." Shirley motioned them both inside. "I don't want all the neighbors to know my son has a tumor."

Mikerra stopped dead in her tracks. They had thought they were being so careful. "How on earth did you know?"

Shirley walked to the couch and took a seat. "You

think you invented investigative reporting? Honey, the minute you called me last night, I knew where my boy was. I have spies, too."

Drake cleared his throat. "Are you trying to tell me that you have had me followed?"

"Not followed," his mother quietly clarified. "Discreetly observed. You were having such a time adjusting to being home and not in combat, I feared for your mental health. Some days I was afraid to let you out of my sight."

Drake shook his head. "That would explain all the shopping expeditions."

His mother bowed her head. "Yes. I didn't want you getting hurt or hurting someone else."

Mikerra wiped her eyes as she listened to Drake's mother's confession. It was too much. Her emotions had already been on one roller-coaster ride with Drake. She didn't know if she had one more cry left in her body. "I think I'd better go home," she told her audience, rose, and headed for the door.

"Mikerra, you've already weathered the worst part," Shirley said. "Sit down. You need to hear what I'm about to say."

Oh, that did not sit well with Mikerra. What else could go wrong? "What is it, Mrs. Harrington?"

"First, you're going to call me Shirley. Second is that someone from the army called a few hours ago, wanting to know if Drake was in the hospital."

Mikerra shook her head. She wondered how long it would take the military to figure all this out. They were a day ahead of her. "What did they say?"

Shirley took a deep breath. "Well, it wasn't what he said. It was what he didn't say. My baby has been in the armed forces for quite a while, and I know how military people talk on the phone. This idiot was asking all the wrong questions. Instead of inquiring about Drake's health, he proceeded to tell me the effects of being in a combat zone, like I'm stupid or something. I told him Drake was fine."

Mikerra wanted to laugh. The big brass hadn't known what they were getting themselves into when they picked Drake to be a participant in the Project Perfect experiment. Shirley was going to be a very worthy adversary. Osama bin Laden had nothing on Shirley Harrington when she was pissed.

Chapter 15

"What I want to know is, how does my baby figure in all this? Why are those men wanting to know about his health?" asked Shirley.

Mikerra looked from Drake to his mother. Neither one of them knew the entire story. It was time she shared the truth. "Well, about two years ago, I came across some information about some unauthorized drug testing on soldiers. At first I couldn't tell how they were chosen, but now I think I know. Sloan will be able to confirm my theory when he arrives next weekend, but I believe it's because these soldiers are the best of the best."

"What?" Drake sat up. "Are you telling me that because I'm a ranger, I got picked for this mess?"

Mikerra nodded. "Yes. From what I've learned from you in the last few days, that's exactly what I'm telling you. A hundred soldiers have been given the serum since the beginning of the conflict in Iraq."

Drake stood abruptly and began to pace the room. "So for the last four years, these idiots have been giving me injections they know will eventually kill me and have not said one damn thing!" His voice grew louder with each word he uttered and each step he took.

Mikerra noticed the frightened look on his mother's face. Shirley had been here emotionally with him before. Mikerra said softly, "Drake, I know you're upset, but you're scaring your mother. David said he could eradicate the tumor, so you are lucky in that respect. And we're finally going to expose the drug testing to the world, so the other soldiers can get help."

Drake stopped his frenzied pace and studied her. "Why are you so concerned about this? Are you trying to make up for something else? Is this your idea of penance for breaking my heart on graduation night?"

Mikerra hated the fact that he could read her so well and so quickly. "Yes," she admitted. "I'm trying to make up for what I did to you, to myself, and for what could have been. But mostly I want to fulfill a promise I made to myself when I left New York. I should have said something when I found out about Project Perfect One-ninety-two, but I buried my head in the sand and hoped that it would go away or that someone else would realize what was happening."

"So what's this got to do with me?" he asked.

She picked up Drake's hand. "It has everything to do with you. Because I love you."

Drake stared at her, probably trying to figure out if she was lying or not. "So what is this? You need me to get the rest of the details? You want quotes from me to humanize your story? You can have all the info you want without spinning me some kind of yarn. You don't have to say you love me if you don't feel it. I've been on that side of the coin, and I didn't like it. Don't play with me."

That was the last thing she wanted to do. "Drake, this is about you, true. But it's also about the other ninety-eight men that are still involved in the testing, whom we can save. When this gets out, they will have to kill the testing."

"If they don't kill us in the process," Drake said. "I'm all for getting the bad guys, but I'm not going to die just so you can have your name on a byline again."

Mikerra fought back her retort. "Drake, I understand your point," she began in a calm voice. "But this thing is bigger than you can imagine. Yes, I want to do the story and expose the higher-ups, but I wouldn't knowingly put you or your mom in danger. When I left New York a few months ago, Project Perfect was the last thing on my mind. In fact, I didn't think about it again until the afternoon you passed out at my house. Your symptoms set warning bells off in my head. I had asked God for a chance to make this right, and now that I have the chance, I'm going to take it."

"Where do I figure in all this? I can't believe you're doing all this just because you're trying to do a good deed," replied Drake.

Of course, he'd push the envelope to the bitter end. "I already told you that I love you. You made me fall in love with you again, and I swore that I wouldn't."

He smiled at her admission. "You loved me in high school?"

Were men really this thickheaded? "Yes. Telling you good-bye on graduation night was the hardest thing I've ever done, but I knew I couldn't stay here. I kept expecting you to show up at college, but you never did. Did you love me in high school?"

Drake pulled her in his arms and kissed her. "I probably shouldn't say this, especially with Mom sitting within hitting range of me. Do you honestly think I would have waited an entire year to have sex with you if I hadn't?"

She really hadn't given it much thought. Mikerra shrugged. "No, I thought you had some bet with the guys or something."

"Well, that explains why you wouldn't talk about it. You thought I was that underhanded? I would never bet or talk to anyone about what we did together," he replied.

"I know that, and I feel like the biggest fool. I guess it just took me twenty years to realize it," Mikerra confessed.

Shirley cleared her throat and rose from her comfortable seat on the couch. "I see you two have a lot to work out. And I'm not talking about this military mess. But that does figure in somehow." She walked to the kitchen counter and grabbed her shoulder bag. "I am going to the store and should be gone about two hours. So that should give you guys plenty of time to sort all this out." She walked to the front door and left.

Mikerra and Drake stared at each other in disbelief. "Well, I guess your mama sure told us, huh?"

Drake eased her onto his lap and kissed her. "Yes, she sure did." He kissed her long and hard. "Race you upstairs."

"I just don't understand it, Kissa," Mikerra complained that evening. After a very passionate afternoon with Drake, Mikerra sat with her best friend in her living room for a little girl talk. "Drake didn't perform like a man with a tumor. He was like a teenager. He didn't even perform like a man who had just gotten out of the hospital this morning. In fact, if I hadn't begged and pleaded for him to stop, I'd still be in his bed right now."

Kissa sipped her wine thoughtfully. "Let me see if I

have this correctly. You're complaining because Drake is ringing your chimes constantly? Excuse me if I don't have any sympathy for you."

"You know it's not that. I just figured he'd either be too tired, in too much pain, or too something. He was excellent. He should have been showing some of the effects of the medicine. You know, he shouldn't have been able to perform."

Kissa shook her head. "Not necessarily. Each time he's had an intense episode, you guys have had amazing sex, and you're bitching. Can you even count how many times you and Drake have made love in the last forty-eight hours? Remember, David did say this was a side effect, as well as mood swings, depression, and anxiety."

Mikerra felt the lightbulb as it snapped on in her head. "That's why he was so defensive earlier." She remembered the discussion she had with Drake about breaking the story and how he was so against it.

Kissa sighed. "Mikerra, I can only brainstorm with you if you give me all the information. So I take it, Drake was against the whole story idea?"

Mikerra nodded. "I really needed his take on the situation, but the more I talked about it, the more he assumed I was just using him and his circumstances for a story. He said I was using him to humanize the story. Can you believe he could think I'd be that heartless and cold?" Mikerra tried to keep the hurt out of her voice, but it was useless. Drake's accusations had made her heart ache.

Kissa placed her glass on the table. "Oh, Mikerra, he hurt your feelings," she said softly.

Mikerra couldn't hold back the tears any longer. They fell of their own accord. "Yes." She wiped the tears away. "I felt like he'd cut my heart into a million tiny pieces with a machete."

"You love him, don't you?" Kissa wasn't accusing her, just stating a fact. "You really love him."

"Yes, I do. Despite how hard I fought it, it still happened. We're not good for each other, Kissa."

"Why not?"

"Kissa, this isn't high school. I live here in Wright City, and he's in the military, bound for Georgia in a few weeks. Please explain how any of this could possibly work. Providing we all survive this little fiasco!"

"Mikerra, you're just scared. That's normal. It shows you care. It can work if you guys want it to. Distance is just a detail to work out. A tiny, unimportant detail. Just because you love him doesn't mean you have to marry him. Big deal. He's going to Georgia. You can fly there, and he can come here. Now quit whining about something you can't control, and focus on your task. You have a story to write, and we have some government ass to kick."

Mikerra laughed at Kissa's serious tone. "You always did know what to say to keep me going." She took a deep breath. "First thing we need to do is get Quinn to get to those medical records. I can't believe I'm even suggesting my own brother break the law, but this is an extreme situation. We also need to get in touch with Sloan."

Kissa picked up her glass and drained the last of the wine. "That's my girl. You'll see. Tomorrow Drake will have forgotten all about you trying to sell his story to the highest bidder."

"That's so not funny."

Kissa nodded. "I know, but what kind of friend would I be if I didn't take a dig at your expense every now and then. Plus, it happens so seldom. I couldn't resist. Now call Quinn."

Mikerra reached for her cell phone just as she heard a strange noise coming from her front door. She looked at Kissa. "Are you expecting anyone?"

Kissa shook her head. "No," she whispered. "You think it's Drake?"

Mikerra shook her head. Then she noticed a silhouette, courtesy of the streetlight. It was too slight to be Drake. "I have a gun in the desk drawer upstairs," she whispered to Kissa.

"We'd be dead by then. You got a baseball bat?"

"Be serious." Mikerra rose from the couch and walked quietly to the front door, with Kissa right behind her. "Kissa, you should stay back, just in case."

"Hell no," Kissa said just above a whisper. "We're in this together."

Mikerra should have known Kissa would be with her to the end. Hopefully, that wasn't tonight. She noticed the umbrella stand and grabbed the oversize umbrella her father had given her just weeks before. She had thought she'd never have a use for it. Boy, was she wrong.

She noticed that the figure was searching for something. Her spare key! Soon he or she found it in her secret hiding place of the flowerpot and inserted the key into the lock. Mikerra took a deep breath, hoped for the best, wrenched the front door open, and gasped. "Quinn?"

"What?" He dropped the key on the porch, then reached to pick it up. "Why is Ethel behind you, Lucy?" It took a few minutes for the scene to register in his brain. "Oh, so you thought I was coming to get you, huh?"

Mikerra wanted to strangle her younger brother.

Quinn had the irritating habit of making himself at home. It didn't matter whose home it was.

Quinn walked inside the house and closed the front door. He pried the umbrella out of his sister's hand and put it back in the umbrella stand. "I thought I'd come by and try to get those medical records."

Kissa laughed. "We were just getting ready to call you."

Quinn winked at Kissa. "Telepathy. I sensed there were two beautiful women who needed my help."

Mikerra stared at Quinn. When exactly had he started flirting with her friends? "Well, since you're here, let's go to the kitchen."

Quinn nodded and headed for the kitchen, but not before he let a remark past his lips. "I heard you and Drake are cornering the condom market. Mom said she saw his mom at Wal-Mart, buying some condoms."

Mikerra should have been used to this by now. She shook her head as her best friend and Quinn laughed boisterously at her expense. "One of these days, Quentin, I'm going to get you back for this."

Quinn walked over to her and gave her a big bear hug. "Hey, don't blame me if Shirley was telling your business in Wal-Mart. I did, however, suggest she buy the magnum size when I saw her there today." He scampered off to the kitchen before Mikerra could react.

"Just forget it, Mikerra. Remember you do need Quinn's expertise right now," Kissa advised, slightly nudging Mikerra to the kitchen. "We really can't afford to make him mad by ridiculing his non-dating habits."

It was commonly known that Quinn Stone didn't date, didn't want to date, and had had no intentions of dating since his divorce. He didn't have a problem with a booty call now and then, but anything beyond that wasn't going to happen.

"I know I'm not in a position to piss him off, but one day," Mikerra promised. "As for people not dating who should be, when are you going to get on the party train?"

Kissa laughed. "Right after you and Drake get married."

Mikerra snorted her response and walked into the kitchen, where Quinn had already booted up her laptop and was happily surfing the Net.

"'Bout time you and Ethel got in here. I thought I was going to have to get a cattle prod after you two." Quinn continued to enter information into the computer. "Got any food?"

Mikerra hated to admit it, especially being an amateur gourmet chef, but her cupboard was bare. "No. I need to go shopping tomorrow, and I didn't have time to cook today."

"We could always order pizza," Kissa said, taking a seat at the table.

"All right," Mikerra said. "I'll order it. A large with everything? Is that doable?"

Quinn nodded and continued his task. "What day did Drake originally go to the doctor?"

It seemed so long ago, Mikerra thought as she reached for her cordless phone. "Thursday. Two days ago." She dialed the number of Wright City's only pizza establishment and ordered. She ended the call and sat at the table. "Should be about thirty minutes."

Quinn grunted, not taking his light brown eyes off the computer screen. He smiled as the symbol for the Veterans Administration Medical Center filled the screen. "Amateurs."

Mikerra sat in amazement. "You're already in?"

Quinn smiled at his sister. "Of course. Mind you, this

is just the home page to the patients' files. Getting to Drake's records will take a little more of my expertise."

"Why?" Mikerra asked.

"Because he's Special Forces, in the first place, and because of the testing, in the second," Quinn explained. "You wouldn't happen to know his social, would you?"

"No," Mikerra said. "Why would I know that? I just slept with him. I didn't exchange vital information."

Quinn laughed. "No problem. I can get that info, too."

A few hours later, after Quinn devoured the pizza, he printed the information he'd collected from his computer hacking. Mikerra now had Drake's entire military and medical history in her hands.

"I don't see anything about island headaches in these records," Mikerra announced. "In fact, I don't see anything relating to the visit to the military doctor. Nothing about the medicine the doctor prescribed or the shot he gave Drake."

Quinn nodded. "This just shows you how big this thing actually is, Mikerra. They gave him a shot that put him in the emergency room, and there's not one mention of it."

Mikerra's head swam with all the new information. If she blew the lid on this, heads would definitely roll. She just hoped it wasn't her head, Drake's, Kissa's, or Quinn's.

She glanced at her tablemates and sighed. This would probably kill them all. "If you guys want to bail, now would be a good time to say so."

Quinn grabbed her hand. "There's no way I'd let

you face this alone, and you know that. We're all in this together. Got it?"

Mikerra looked from Quinn to Kissa.

Kissa smiled and nodded in agreement.

"Got it," Mikerra said.

Now all she had to do was to convince Drake that she was doing this for his own good. He probably wouldn't believe her once they kicked him out of the military. He'd definitely blame her for ruining his career, his livelihood, and his chance for an honorable discharge.

Sunday evening Mikerra parked in front of Drake's house. She'd kept her side of the bargain: she'd drive Drake to the hospital for the tests. She only hoped he was still in the mood for the tests. They hadn't spoken since Friday.

Mikerra thought they both needed a little breathing room. Plus, every time she saw him, her thoughts seemed to stray to the bedroom. She had to stop that.

She walked up to the front door and knocked.

His mother answered the door, dressed casually in jeans and a T-shirt. "Hello, Mikerra. Drake will be right down. I do appreciate you going with him. I know if I went to the hospital, the entire town would know what's going on. I can't believe the military has done this to him." She took a deep breath. "It's okay. I'm calm." She motioned Mikerra inside the house.

Mikerra sat on the couch. "I know how you feel, Shirley. It just doesn't seem fair, does it? Drake gives the last twenty-one years of his life to the military, and they're trying to kill him in their quest for the perfect soldier."

Shirley sat down beside her. "Don't get me going

again. My husband had to convince me not to go to the hospital. He didn't want me yelling at David for what the military did."

Mikerra hid her smile, easily imagining Shirley Harrington raising all kinds of trouble for David while he was risking his own life and career by treating Drake. "I'll take really good care of him for you."

"I already know that." Shirley heard the unmistakable sound of Drake coming downstairs. "Here he comes," she said, rising.

Mikerra nodded. Drake walked into the living room, with an overnight bag. Shirley rushed to her son and gave him a hug. "Baby, you make sure you call me the minute you know something."

"Mom, it's just a few tests." He kissed his mother on the cheek. "But I promise I will let you know." He reached for Mikerra's hand. "We'd better go, or Mom's going to start crying again. I'll be back in a few hours, Mom."

Mikerra took his hand, not wanting to leave his mother in such a worried state. "I'll call the minute the testing is done."

"Thank you, Mikerra. Now you better get going, or my son will be right. I'm going to start crying again."

Mikerra was pretty close to tearing up herself, so she and Drake left the house before his mother could shed another tear.

The ride to the hospital was somber. Once Drake was wheeled off to the testing, Mikerra had nothing but time on her hands as she sat in his room. She had time to figure out her life, or what was left of it. She had to get started on that story, for one. And there was the matter of her memoirs, which she hadn't started, either. She dug into her shoulder bag and retrieved a pen and notepad. *No time like the present.* She started writing down the facts she did know about the Project Perfect 192 serum.

A few hours later Drake was wheeled back to the room. He was wide awake and ticked off. She instantly knew why. They'd shaved some of his hair off.

"Hey, Drake. How do you feel?" She didn't dare mention anything about the plug missing in his head.

"They cut my head," he said shortly. "I'm going to have to shave my whole head now. I'm going to kill David."

The object of Drake's anger walked in the door, smiling as he closed it soundly behind him. "Sorry about that, Drake. We couldn't get a good reading, and it was the only way. Besides, I thought all the military cats were shaving their heads, anyway."

"Yeah, because they are going bald and are trying to hide the fact. I'm not." Drake was getting more upset by the minute.

"Drake, you need to calm down. It will grow back," said Mikerra.

Drake stared at Mikerra as if she were insane for saying such a crazy thing. "Hopefully."

David laughed, taking a seat near the bed. "How about I tell you what I found out so you guys can leave?"

Mikerra needed something else to focus on. "Please."

David opened the metal chart. "The kryptonite did slow down the growth of the tumor, but there is still some real growth that will have to be extracted. I know you're still having headaches, so I'm going to give you five more pills. Take them only when the pain is intense. That should hold you until surgery."

"What's the OOC?" asked Drake.

David stared blankly at him. "Pardon me?"

Drake laughed. "Sorry, man. Still in military mode.

What's the out-of-commission time? How long will I be laid up?"

David nodded. "Oh, this is the tricky part. The OOC will be about six months. A month to heal from the surgery. The other five you will be in rehabilitation. We will have to test your motor skills on a weekly basis. You may have some coordination issues, and we'll need to test for that."

Drake struggled to sit up. "So you're telling me that I'm going to be a freaking vegetable for the next six months? David, this doesn't sound like a win-win for me."

David closed the chart. "Okay, Drake. How about this? If you have the surgery, you won't have headaches anymore, your body will be back to normal, and the tumor will be gone."

Drake nodded. "Okay, you got me. They're going to kick me out of the service for this, aren't they?"

David nodded. "They can't have any links to Project Perfect. I'd say a medical discharge. Disability will be the bigger question."

Mikerra reached for Drake's hand. His hand engulfed hers. "What do you mean, David?" she asked.

"Well, usually in cases like these, they hate giving a hundred percent disability, which is what I will recommend. That way the army has to pick up the tab for the medical bills and for any other bills, such as rehabilitation, speech therapy, etc."

Mikerra looked to Drake, but he was quiet. She knew he was thinking. She turned her attention back to David. "What does he need to do to get ready for surgery?"

David rose and walked to the door. "The only thing I ask is that you guys try to refrain from sex until after surgery. It will help his recovery time." David opened the door and left without another word.

Mikerra couldn't believe her ears. By the time she opened her mouth to retort to her friend, he was already out of the door. "Damn."

Drake looked at her. "My sentiments exactly."

Chapter 16

Monday

Drake awoke at the invasion of noise into his quiet room. His mother was carrying a breakfast tray. He struggled to sit up as she neared the bed. "Mom, you don't have to do this. I was coming downstairs to eat."

Shirley placed the tray across his lap and sat at the edge of the bed. "Honey, I know. But since your tests went so well, I wanted to celebrate. I fixed you a celebratory breakfast with all your favorites, bacon, scrambled eggs, hash browns, and pancakes. I know your body is probably tired from the stress of all those tests last night. When I think of what might have happened to you if you hadn't gone to the ER, I get so upset with the military." She wiped imaginary tears from her face.

"Mom, I don't really know the whole story of what's happening to me, and I can't lie to you and tell you everything is going to be fine, 'cause most likely it won't be, but I don't want you thinking my career in the military has been a mistake. There is something good about being in the military."

"But, honey, look at you. You've been asleep ever

since Mikerra brought you back from the hospital last night, and you still look tired. You look like you could use a nap right now. Is this one of the effects of the medicines?"

Drake thought carefully about how to answer his mother. After David's little bombshell before he left the hospital, he'd been preoccupied. "I'm just tired, Mom."

Shirley sighed. "I know what you've been thinking about. Mikerra told me what David said. The surgery is necessary, Drake. And as much as I hate to admit it, the thought of you having to undergo brain surgery has me scared, too. But it's something else, isn't it?"

Maybe it was time for him to put his feeling into words. "Yes, it is, but it's something I can't control, so I will just have to adapt." He couldn't fight the aroma of the eggs, bacon, hash browns, and pancakes any longer. He picked up the fork and started eating.

"Well, I can see nothing has deterred your appetite." She chuckled. "I made plenty. I thought you might be extra hungry since you didn't eat dinner last night."

She was hedging, he knew. But one could never rush Shirley Harrington when she had something on her mind, or there would be hell to pay. He took a couple more bites of food, waiting for his mom to cultivate her thoughts.

He had almost finished when she finally spoke again. "Drake, if you need to go anywhere today, I would feel better if I or your father drove you where you need to go."

So that was it. She didn't want him driving. "Mom, after this breakfast you fixed, I don't think I can move, anyway. But I promise to let you know if I need to go anywhere."

She nodded, thinking she'd actually won the battle. "Thanks, son." She rose from the bed and headed for the door. "I'll get you some more food," she said in a voice much too gentle. "And just in case you're thinking about sneaking out of this house, I have spies all over this neighborhood. So the minute you step out of this house, I will know it."

Drake was sunk and he knew it. She was smarter than any commanding officer he'd ever had. He gave his mother a mock salute. "Got it."

"Don't you get sassy with me. I'm still your mama. It's my job to look after you." She smiled and left the room.

Drake laughed and finished his first helping of breakfast, eagerly awaiting the second.

Shirley was busy fixing Drake's second helping when the phone rang. It was the same military idiot that had called her before.

"Mrs. Harrington, I need to speak with the master sergeant."

"Well, he's not here," she answered. "May I take a message?"

He hesitated, sighed, and then said, "No, ma'am. I will try later."

Shirley hung up the phone, not liking the man's tone. He wouldn't give up until he talked to Drake. But he wouldn't get to talk to Drake today. Not on her watch. Those men had already done enough to her baby to last her a lifetime. She didn't care if the military ever spoke to Drake again.

She took the plate upstairs, but Drake was sound asleep. She decided he probably did need his rest. She closed his door and went to the home office to look up brain tumors on her new personal computer. Maybe there was something she could be doing to help.

Shirley dialed a familiar number and waited for someone to pick up. "Hi, Carolina. It's Shirley. We gotta problem."

Washington, D.C.

Seth paced the length of his large corner office. He had a make on her, and now he was going to take care of the one loose thread that could unravel everything he'd worked so hard for. If he could prove the Project Perfect serum was a viable product, it would mean billions. His phone rang, interrupting his thoughts. He stalked to his desk, snatched the phone from the cradle, and pulled it to his ear. This call was too important for the speakerphone function. Not only did the walls have ears, but so did his secretary.

"McCaffrey."

"I heard you are looking for someone," a voice stated.

"Maybe." He wasn't a fool and knew his little endeavor was slowly leaking all over Washington via the underground.

"How much is it worth to you?"

Seth gritted his teeth. He wanted to say "Nothing," but that would be a lie, and obviously, the caller would know that. "I'd be willing to negotiate a price if the information is good."

"Oh, it's better than good, and I know it is."

Seth rolled his eyes toward the ceiling. He could initiate a trace, but that would mean that he needed to keep the caller on the phone for at least thirty more seconds and signal his secretary at the same time without putting the caller on hold.

"Tomorrow at the Grotto, for brunch." The call ended.

"Dammit!" Seth slammed the receiver down and uttered a barrage of expletives.

Jonelle Hartson rushed into the office. "Is there a problem, Senator?" she asked in a nasal tone.

"Yes, there's a problem, and no, you can't help me. Go back to your desk."

She looked at him with hatred in those blue eyes. If Seth hadn't known better, he'd think that hatred was directed at him. But Jonelle had been his secretary for the last six months, and an excellent one at that. Too bad she was married and loved her husband.

Any other time those deterrents wouldn't have stopped him.

It was going to be one of those days, Sloan realized as he sat in the Joint Chiefs of Staff weekly meeting. He glanced around the table at the men representing each branch of military service. Little did the men they commanded know that their lives had been traded like a common piece of meat and with about as much regard.

He usually enjoyed his job as the Joint Chiefs of Staff's junior administrative assistant. But today was a different story. Something has gotten General MacArthur very upset, or perhaps he hadn't been getting any. He kept conferring with Seth McCaffrey, and they were all but disrupting the meeting. Twice, Admiral Cambridge had to reprimand them.

"Gentlemen, maybe we can table our discussion if you think yours is more important than the war on terror," growled the admiral.

That, and the fact that every word that came out of the admiral's mouth sounded like a direct order, made the two men stop talking.

As the meeting continued, Sloan took notes on what he could actually tell America in the press release. "Yes, we're still at war. Yes, everything is going fine. Yes, we do feel that we are justified." He jotted down what he couldn't tell America. "Yes, many young men and women have died in a needless war. Yes, more and more innocent Iraqis are also dying due to the violent acts of the last supporters of their outted dictator and because the Americans are on their soil. We have no earthly idea when or if this war will ever be over." But the really big news he couldn't tell America was that there were a hundred soldiers that would die at their own country's hand.

Some days the burden felt too heavy for him to carry. But by the end of this weekend, he would be relieved of that burden. If his suspicions were correct, the lid would be blown on the actions of about four of the eleven gentlemen seated at this conference table.

"Sloan, when is the next briefing?" asked General MacArthur.

"Tomorrow at ten, sir." The same time it had been every week for the last four years, Sloan thought. "I can lead with how great America is doing in the war and give them some stats on the body count."

General MacArthur glanced in Sloan's direction and nodded. "Is everything ready?"

"Yes, sir. Would you like to proofread the speech for tomorrow? I can e-mail it to your office as soon as the meeting adjourns."

"No, no. I was just wondering if there had been any noncombat deaths reported recently by the troops."

"Well, there are always freak accidents happening

in the war zone. Being a career soldier, you know that, sir." Sloan knew exactly what the general wanted to know, but wasn't going to give him any information until he asked for it directly.

General MacArthur nodded. "Good. Don't need another shower incident happening. The boy's mother finally quit threatening to sue the army."

"The Hughes incident," Sloan said. "The one where the soldier drowned in the shower in Iraq. Yes, I remember that well. His mother swore up and down he was killed. She said he'd been complaining of being sick to his stomach when he talked to her on the phone. She demanded an investigation."

"Luckily, she finally gave up, or we'd be in a world of trouble," General MacArthur said. "What ever happened to her, anyway?"

Sloan shrugged. "I don't know, sir. The complaints stopped suddenly, and the lawsuit was dropped."

"All right. Now, is everything set for your absence this week?" The general looked directly at Sloan.

Sloan had anticipated this little maneuver. General MacArthur would try his best to make sure there was some loose end that Sloan had to attend to, ruining his trip home, but not this time. There was too much at stake. Drake's life hung in the balance. "Everything has been taken care of, unless you guys decide to end the war while I'm away." He laughed, knowing that was impossible.

Wright City

Shirley walked inside Jay's Diner, glancing around for Carolina Stone. She spotted her friend gabbing with Jay at a corner table. Jay's slender frame leaned against the table, and she nodded at whatever Carolina was saying. Shirley walked to the table with purpose.

"Hello, Carolina. Hi, Jay." Shirley sat down in the plastic chair and let out a sigh.

Jay stood up straight and took out her trusty pad. "Well, ladies, since it is Monday, it's meat loaf day. How about it?"

Carolina shook her head. "No, Jay. Today I'd like your famous pork chops with a salad."

Jay smiled at Carolina. "Now, Carolina, I'll bring you pork chops, but you can forget the salad. You're getting mashed potatoes and corn, like always. What did your husband tell you about trying to diet?"

"What does he know? He's been thin as a rail since I met him. I keep waiting for him to start gaining weight," Carolina joked.

Jay laughed. "I don't think that's going to happen anytime soon. Especially now that he's retired. I've seen him jogging in the mornings, when I'm out running." She looked in Shirley's direction. "And for you, Shirley?"

"I'll have the same."

Jay winked an eye at her. "Good choice. I'll bring you some sweet tea." She left the table.

"Well, Shirley, what do you think about all this?" Carolina asked, placing the cloth napkin in her lap. "Do you think there is any way out of all this alive?"

"I think there is, but I need to discuss some things with Daniel first, but I think we can save them."

Carolina shook her head. "This is just awful. I can't believe the army has done all this. I just hate this."

"If my plans work out, we're going to get those bastards, and the kids will be fine. I'm glad they found each other again," Shirley said.

Jay returned with their oversize glasses of tea. After she left, Carolina sighed and reached for the sugar container, but Shirley stopped her. "Don't you dare! You know Jay's already put enough sugar in this tea to rot out all your teeth."

Carolina laughed. "I guess I was preoccupied."

Shirley nodded, knowing that was just the mother in her friend. "We both are worried and frightened. I wanted to talk about Mikerra."

"What about my daughter?"

"Don't get your back up, Carolina Stone. You know I love Mikerra. Drake should have married her years ago. He was just being stupid. But now they're here together again, and it seems the magic between them is still there."

Jay returned with their plates. *Platters* would have been a better word. Each was laden with two thick fried pork chops, a mountain of mashed potatoes, and corn on the cob. The meal was accompanied by a cup of brown gravy.

Shirley could feel her arteries clogging up already from the cholesterol in the meal, but this was the best food in the area.

Carolina took a few bites of her pork chops and sighed. "You know, I'm so glad Jay made me get this. That woman's hands have been blessed by God." She took another bite before pouring gravy over the pork chops. "What is your idea?"

Shirley would need her help in getting Mikerra to cooperate. "Do you still own that cabin by the lake?"

Carolina nodded between bites.

"Well, I'm thinking if we could get them to go up there alone, they could rekindle their love and hide from the bad guys all at the same time."

"How are we supposed to get my headstrong daughter and your stubborn son to go along with this?"

Shirley took a bite of her pork chop. "Well, that's where Daniel will come in. I'll have to fix a special dinner tonight to butter him up." Shirley also knew that the favor she needed from her husband of over forty years would probably cost her a night of passion. Or at least she hoped.

"Just take him some of these pork chops," Carolina mumbled, finishing off her meal. "And he will be putty in your hands."

Shirley agreed. "How about some dessert to celebrate?"

Drake awoke that afternoon to the sound of the phone ringing constantly. Where was his mother? Why wasn't she answering the phone? Usually, his mother answered the phone on the second ring. After the fourth ring, he pushed back the covers and walked down the hall to his parents' room and grabbed the phone. "Yes."

"Drake?"

He instantly recognized the voice at the other end of the line. "Mason?"

"Yeah, man, it's me. How are you feeling?"

Tiny hairs rose on the back of Drake's neck. He was suspicious. Was his friend in on this fiasco, too? "I'm fine, Colonel."

"Oh, so we're back to colonel. You know we go back a long way, Drake. I'm calling you off the record."

"Why?"

"Drake, I'm your friend as well as your commanding officer. I just got a memo from HQ about you."

Drake really didn't like the sound of that. "What?"

Mason took a deep breath. "Drake, this is direct from the Pentagon. They want me to reassign you to Fort Hood, Texas. They wanted me to cancel your extra leave and force you to report there immediately. I told them you were unreachable. I tried calling you a few times, but your mom isn't the easiest person to get past."

Drake laughed, imagining his mother giving Mason the business end of her temper. "Yeah, Mom can be harsh. Now, can we please quit playing this silly game? Tell me what the hell is going on."

"All right, man. First of all, Horace MacArthur is changing the orders of quite a few men. But he's separating you from your unit, which is rare, especially in wartime. I didn't like this crap from the beginning, and now that I'm getting the whole picture, I really don't like it. I'm going against every military rule I can think of by telling you this, but, Drake, they're trying to kill you."

Tell me something I don't know, Drake thought. "I'm on it, Mason. I don't want you getting involved. Tell them you tried to reach me but couldn't. How are you calling me, anyway?"

"You wouldn't believe me if I told you."

"After the last few days I've had, try me."

"I went to Savannah and bought a prepaid cell phone, just in case they're watching me. Which I think they are. I'm in Roswell right now, making the call in my car. I know this is big, Drake. This is 'heads will roll' kind of big. This is 'Senate committee hearing' big."

"No, Mason. This is 'get your ass killed' kind of big."

Chapter 17

Mikerra sat on her couch, with Terror nestled in her arms, that evening. She gently stroked his dark brown fur as she gathered her courage to go see Drake. They had a lot to talk about. And he wasn't going to like what she had to say.

How could she confront him with all the information Quinn had retrieved for her illegally? But he had a right to know how much danger they were actually in, and she didn't want anyone else getting killed on her behalf.

Terror growled and jumped out of her lap, heading for the front door. Since returning to Wright City, she hadn't been as diligent about locking her door as she'd been in New York. Not the brightest move on her part, since Seth was looking for her. The knob turned silently, and the door opened just as quietly.

Drake peeked his head around the door, smiling. "Hey, Care Bear." He stepped inside, closed the door behind him, and walked toward her.

She had to admire his build. It was June, so the weather was stifling, and Drake was showing off those muscular legs of his in a pair of baggy knit shorts. His dark blue T-shirt was molded to his muscular chest and showcased his six-pack abs. Good Lord, what that man did to a regular T-shirt was downright shameful.

"I've heard how temperamental you artist types can be. I didn't interrupt your creative flow or anything, did I?" He sat beside her on the couch.

"No, of course not. I was just thinking, that's all," she said casually.

"Were you thinking about kissing me? That's what I'm thinking about." He leaned closer to her.

"You're a man. You are probably thinking about more than just a kiss," she teased.

"Well, yeah. But you could start with a kiss." He moved closer to her and wrapped his arms around her and kissed her softly on the lips.

Mikerra couldn't think straight when she was within kissing distance of this man. Like right now. He teased her mouth open with that tongue and made her do all the things she swore she wouldn't. She remembered why she wanted to see him. "Drake, we need to talk."

He pulled back instantly. "Why does my blood curdle every time I hear that phrase from a woman's lips?" he muttered against her lips.

"I promise it's worth the detour." She placed a hand on his chest, forcing some space between them.

He kissed her quickly on the lips and took a deep breath. "Okay, Mikerra."

Satisfied he wouldn't try to seduce her at least for the next few minutes, she began. "Last night Quinn retrieved your medical and military records."

"So? If you needed them, I could have gotten them. Is this for your story?"

She knew he'd get defensive and he did. She clasped his hand with hers, hoping to soften the blow. "No, baby. This is for you. Remember when we went to the VA and the doctor gave you that shot, and later I found you passed out in your dad's truck?"

"I remember we had some amazing sex that afternoon. I bet the whole neighborhood heard you."

Focus, girl, she told herself. Mikerra ignored his remark, or at least she tried to. "Besides that. I told Kissa about your headaches, and she tried to get your files using her doctor's credentials, but the guy told her she had to talk to General MacArthur. The same thing happened with David. It's like there's an invisible seal around your medical and military history."

He snatched his hand away from hers. "So how'd you get them? Call the ex who's trying to kill you?"

"No. Quinn hacked into the government files and got them. He's just as concerned about you as Kissa and I are."

Drake sighed. "All right. What's the big news?"

"Remember when I was telling you guys about the information on Project Perfect that Seth left at my house?"

"Yes."

"Well, there are still a few more dots to connect, but it is just as I feared. You were chosen because you are the best of the best. I need a little more information on your friend that died, but if I'm right, he was the first variable, and you're most likely the second."

He reached for her hand. "Baby, you're going to have to slow down. Remember, my brain is functioning a little slower than usual. Now, why are you talking about variables?"

Okay, she had his attention. "Well, the way the testing had worked is that they chose a select group of soldiers and they've injected them with the serum a few times a year. Any side effects are noted. Like your friend's."

"Josh?"

"Yes. See when he got sick, that became a problem. The whole idea is to have the perfect soldier. One that can withstand substantial abuse to his body. Once a soldier gets sick, he's not any good to the experiment."

Drake sucked in a breath. "Well, that explains a whole lot."

Mikerra stared at him. "What do you mean?"

"I mean when Josh first complained of headaches last year, he was in the infirmary and no one could see him. He was sequestered like a prisoner. When I started getting headaches, the same thing happened to me. But I got better and was released back to my unit."

She let her brain digest the information. "That sounds pretty strange. Did they give you any shots while you were in the infirmary? You know, like in an attempt to lower your fever or something?"

Drake thought for a moment, then snapped his large fingers. "Hey, you know, the night before my fever broke, the doc gave me like two shots. But the strange thing was he did it late at night, when no one was around. The next morning my fever was gone. I mentioned it to the nurse, and there was no record of any shots on that night. I just figured the doc forgot to write it down in my chart."

"I don't think he forgot, baby," Mikerra said needlessly.

"I know that, Mikerra. I just have a brain tumor. I'm not stupid," he said shortly.

"Drake, I wasn't trying to imply anything. Just merely thinking out loud. It's like the pieces of a puzzle."

He turned toward her. "I have a bigger piece."

"I think I know where this is going." She knew he'd reference sex somehow. "You promised to be good."

He smiled. "Well, you're wrong. I wasn't thinking

about sex. I was thinking about my CO calling me and giving me a heads-up."

Mikerra really didn't like the sound of that. "What did he say?"

"Well, he wanted to know how I was doing and to inform me that they, meaning the big brass, want me to report to Fort Hood instead of Fort Benning."

"Is that normal?"

"Not really," Drake admitted. "I mean, Mason and I go way back, but he told me some other stuff that let me know that you're probably right and this thing is huge. They also wanted him to call me back in."

Mikerra moved closer to him. "You don't have to leave now, do you?" Concern for him made her forget what happened when she got too close to him.

Drake pulled her in his arms. "Try to pry me away from you right now." He pulled her onto his lap and kissed the breath out of her.

"But what about . . . ?"

Drake lowered her on the couch. Terror jumped off the couch and began to bark at them for interrupting his snoozing. "Hey, what do you do with the dog?"

Mikerra laughed as Drake's nimble hands traveled under her blouse and headed directly for her breasts. "He usually sleeps with me."

"Well, not tonight he's not." Drake slipped the blouse over her head. "Any objections?"

Mikerra shook her head. Like she could deny this man anything. "No, not a one." She slipped his T-shirt over his head and threw it on the floor. "Any objections?"

"Only that you're doing too much talking." He stood and reached to help her up.

Mikerra looked up at him. "I thought you liked hearing me talk?"

He took her hand and rubbed it across his erection. "That is my only concern at the moment. Well, that and making you scream."

She knew when she was licked. And she hoped it was soon.

Mikerra led Drake into her bedroom and closed the door. "So Terror will leave us alone." She walked to the bed and sat down. "Drake, are you sure you feel up to this?" She didn't want to relive the last time he was in this room.

He walked over to the bed and sat beside her. "Mikerra, I know what you're thinking. The last time I was here, we ended up in the emergency room. But I'm better now. I feel fine. I rested all day." He moved toward her and nibbled at her bottom lip before engulfing her in a kiss that warmed every part of her body.

There's nothing wrong with this man, she thought.

Drake eased her down on the bed. He unsnapped her bra and flung it on the floor. He kissed her throat and gently bit her collarbone. He moved to her breasts, taking one in his mouth and massaging its mate with his hand.

Mikerra couldn't fight all the sensations running through her body. Her hands glided over his muscular back. She was as helpless as a newborn. But she needed more. She needed her lips on his. She tried to pull him back up for a kiss, but he shook his head. "No, this is what I want," he said against her breast.

His kisses descended to her tummy and lower. She felt his hands inside her shorts. He pulled them down in one easy motion. She kicked them off, and they flew across the room. The same happened to her undies. He kissed her lower abdomen, and then it happened. He kissed her center. Mikerra thought she'd jump off the bed, but the sensations were too strong. The increased intensity of his kiss on her core had her seeing stars. He tasted her gently at first. He positioned her legs over his shoulders, and he loved her thoroughly. She had to hold on to the bed, or she just knew she would fly away.

"Oh, Drake," she moaned, giving in to total abandon.

He continued exploring her and giving her the ultimate pleasure. She felt his hands move under her bottom and lift her closer to his mouth. He gave her a kiss she'd never forget. Her orgasm flowed through her body like a forest fire, not stopping until she screamed out his name.

Drake stood, took off his remaining clothes, and slid back in bed with her. She watched him slip on the condom and pull her into his arms. As he kissed her slowly, his hands slid over her body and pulled her on top of him.

Mikerra, liking her new position, straddled his waist and guided him inside her. They both moaned as he filled her quickly. She moved against him, and he made a sound that echoed her sentiments. "Damn." He put his hands on either side of her waist and guided her so that she moved slower. When they matched each other's stride, he exhaled. "Damn, baby. Don't stop."

She didn't stop, not that she had the chance to. Passion took over, and all she could think about was how good he made her feel. Mikerra's orgasm peaked first; Drake soon followed.

Mikerra glanced sideways at him as she eased off his body. "Well, so much for David's suggestion to refrain from sex."

Drake chuckled. "Yeah, wait till I tell Mom that you

threw yourself at me and I had to oblige you by having sex."

"If I wasn't so tired, I would kick you out of my house for lying." She snuggled against him, and he wrapped his arms around her. Contented and satiated for the moment, they soon fell asleep.

Tuesday morning

Quinn woke up to a ringing phone. Who had the nerve to call him this early in the morning? It wasn't even ten. He grabbed the phone and mumbled a hello.

"Quinn, what are you still doing in bed?" Kissa asked.

"Sleeping."

"Well, you need to get to Mikerra's pronto."

"Why?"

Kissa sucked in a breath. "Why are men so dense? I think Drake stayed over last night. According to my mom, she saw Drake walking in Mikerra's neighborhood last night but didn't see him go home."

Quinn smiled. He liked Kissa's playful side. They both loved giving Mikerra a hard time about Drake. "So you want me to go to her house and interrupt the morning-after breakfast?"

"Well, of course."

Quinn laughed as he pushed back the covers and rose from his king-size bed. He liked a woman with a sense of humor. "Well, what if I interrupt something else?"

"Then we'll really have something to talk about later, won't we? Hurry."

Quinn looked at his clock, knowing that he just had to go and harass his sister, but he had to at least shower first. After he was dressed in cargo shorts and his favorite Jimi Hendrix T-shirt, he headed for Mikerra's. In less than five minutes, he was at his sister's house. He parked his truck and ventured inside her unlocked domain. The kitchen was empty, to his dismay. He was hoping for at least a gourmet breakfast that morning.

Terror met him as he entered the living room. "Hey, boy. Where's your mommy?" He rubbed the dog's fur. "I bet you're hungry." He scooped up the tiny dog and headed back to the kitchen. He located the dog's food and fed him.

While Terror was munching on breakfast, Quinn headed up the stairs quietly. He walked toward Mikerra's bedroom, listening for sounds of morning activity. The only sound he heard was snoring coming from the other side of the bedroom door. He opened the door slowly and smiled when he saw Drake and Mikerra sound asleep and cuddled in each other's arms. It was a Kodak moment. He couldn't wait to tell their mother.

He went back downstairs without uttering a word. Since he was there, he thought he might as well fix breakfast. From the way the clothes were scattered around Mikerra's room, he figured she and Drake could probably use some sustenance about right now.

Someone was in her house. Mikerra heard distant noises downstairs. Slowly she came awake, smiling at Drake. He was in a deep sleep and was holding her against him. It felt different sleeping with him all through the night.

Their lovemaking had been just as intense as the other times, but something else had been there. Love. She really did love him, with all her heart and then some. She didn't know what Drake felt for her. But now wasn't the time to find out. Drake wasn't quite himself yet.

She pushed back the covers and reached for her robe. She quickly wrapped it around her tired body and headed downstairs. When she reached the living room, her nose told her that whoever was in her house was fixing breakfast. So it wasn't a burglar.

She walked into the kitchen and stopped cold. "Quinn?"

He looked up from the stove top, where he was cooking scrambled eggs, and smiled at her. "Well, I see you're finally up. I thought I'd make some breakfast while I was here waiting for you guys to come up for air."

"Who ratted me out?" Mikerra knew exactly who the rodent was. "I'm going to kill Kissa."

Quinn chuckled, holding the heavy skillet at an angle so the scrambled eggs slid easily onto the platter. "I'll never tell. So is he going to be up soon?"

Mikerra poured a cup of coffee and took a seat at the table. "I guess so."

He sat beside her. "So did he have any bad dreams last night?"

For Drake to have had dreams last night, they would have actually had to have gone to sleep at some point in the night. And that hadn't happened until early this morning. "I don't think so."

"Well, I called a neurologist I know in Boston, and he told me that the stuff David is using on Drake is for severe cases of brain tumors in the UK, but it's cured everyone who's used it."

"So why isn't it in every hospital in the world? It could save lives."

"The same reason there's not a fat-free cooking oil for consumer use, or lightbulbs that never burn out, or cars that never need maintenance. It's not good business."

Sometimes she really hated the government.

Washington, D.C.

Seth glanced at the small clock on his desk. It was almost time for his appointment. He hated waiting. He checked to make sure he had all the necessary items: a small tape recorder, ten grand, and a gun. The only item he planned on using was the gun. Nobody, but nobody, would ever have him in this position again.

He left his office and closed the door. His secretary stared at him. "Jonelle, I'm going for lunch. I should be back by two."

"Yes, Senator. I hope you enjoy your lunch."

"That makes two of us," he mumbled as he left the office.

The Grotto was located in the heart of D.C., and it attracted a large crowd, so nothing could go wrong. Just a little information sharing between strangers for a generous fee. He walked inside the restaurant and glanced around the room. How was he supposed to know who he was to meet?

A waiter approached him and handed him a folded piece of paper. Seth felt like he was in a spy movie with this setup. He read the note and headed to the bar.

"McCaffrey," a man's voice called.

Seth stopped and turned in the direction of the voice. The man was an amateur. He was dressed like a spy on TV. A bad spy on TV. He was dressed casually in a Hawaiian shirt and jeans, which were out of place at the Grotto, where everyone was dressed in business suits. He motioned for Seth to take the seat across from him in a booth.

Seth sat down in the booth. It was hard to make out anything but the man's blonde hair. His facial features were cast in shadows by the baseball cap adorning his head. The lighting in this area of the restaurant was dark for a reason. This very reason. The Grotto was known for not telling secrets. "I hope you got something for me."

The man nodded. "Yeah, if you got something for me."

"Are we going to dance, or are you going to tell me what this is about?"

"I like a man who cuts to the chase. You're looking for Karen Mills, the former senior editor of *New York* magazine."

Seth nodded. "I haven't heard anything worth my while."

"Well, I haven't seen any money cross the table, either."

Well, he had Seth there. "Keep talking."

The man continued. "She left New York about six months ago. Sold her condo, her car, and most of her furniture and left without so much as a good-bye party from the job you had her fired from."

Frustration was beginning to wear on Seth. He tried to be patient, but it was hard, especially while this guy talked as slow as molasses. Maybe he was a Texan? "I know all this, guy. Where's she now?"

"That will cost you fifty thousand dollars."

"Are you nuts?" Seth was furious. "I can hire someone to find her for less."

"And let even more people in on your little problem? You're trying to find her because she knows about Project Perfect and she was your mistress for over five years."

How did this man know about the project? It was supposed to be a secret. This was the most known secret he'd ever seen in his political career. Seth knew at that moment this man would have to be eliminated. He knew too much. "Okay. Meet me tomorrow, and I'll have your money."

Chapter 18

Drake woke up feeling contented and rested, but very, very spent. He opened his tired eyes and glanced at the empty space beside him. Mikerra was already up and out of bed. She was probably downstairs fixing one of her gourmet breakfasts. Drake wondered where she found the strength; his body simply refused to move. He closed his eyes and went back to sleep.

But his sleep was short-lived, because he heard Mikerra scream at the top of her lungs. His tired body now reacted instinctively. Years in the military had taught him to dress fast and ask questions later. He located his clothes and struggled into them as he headed downstairs.

He ran into the kitchen and stopped in his tracks. She wasn't screaming. Well, at least not in fright. She was laughing. At Quinn. He was on the floor, flat on his back, with Terror on top of him, barking like he was an intruder.

Drake took a deep breath, hoping his heart would stop racing soon. "You guys scared the crap out of me. I think my heart stopped."

Mikerra, dressed in her bathrobe, was seated at the table. She rose to meet Drake as he walked farther into the kitchen. "Sorry, Drake. We didn't mean to wake you. Quinn is trying to make Terror an attack dog, just in case."

"Just in case what?" Drake didn't find anything comical at the moment. "He thinks I'm too slow-witted to protect you?" He knew that wasn't the case, but still her comment was a hit to the male ego.

Quinn quickly rose and stalked over to Drake. "Now, Drake, don't start trippin' like that. No one ever said you couldn't do your duty, so save the he-man crap for somebody else. You know for yourself that this is huge, and it's bigger than even you, a big, bad army ranger, can handle."

Drake nodded. Quinn could be stern when he had to, especially if Mikerra was involved. "Okay, Quinn. I had forgotten how protective you can be." He extended his hand to Quinn. "We cool?"

Quinn grinned as he took Drake's hand. "Yeah, man. We cool. Just remember we love Mikerra, too, and don't want anything to happen to her."

Mikerra sighed. "Now that he-man hour is over, Drake, why don't you join us for breakfast?" She hugged Quinn and then hugged and kissed Drake. She let go quickly. "Oh, why don't you take a shower first?"

Drake knew that during a night of intense passion, he might have worked up a sweat a time or three, so she was probably right. "Right back at you, Care Bear. Why don't you join me?"

Quinn walked back to the stove and started fiddling with some pots and pans, clanging them loudly. "My tender ears cannot hear such things so early in the morning. You guys have thirty minutes, or breakfast will be fed to Terror."

Mikerra laughed, took Drake's hand, and led him back upstairs to the bathroom. She turned on the water in the shower and untied her bathrobe. He watched as she stood before him in her birthday suit.

Drake quickly shed his clothes, and they stepped inside the shower stall and closed the door. He pulled her in his arms and kissed her under the stream of warm water. "I'm sorry, baby. I didn't mean to go off like that."

Mikerra nodded. "How did you mean to go off?"

He knew what she was doing and had the feeling that they were definitely going to miss breakfast, and probably lunch as well.

Two hours later Quinn finished cleaning up the kitchen. His prizewinning breakfast had been delicious. Too bad he and Terror were the only ones who had eaten it. Drake and Mikerra had never made it back downstairs for breakfast.

He dialed Kissa's office number and reported in. "Hey, I think it's the real thing between Mikerra and Drake. He got all defensive about me thinking he couldn't protect Mikerra. I think he would have kicked my ass if I'd baited him any longer."

Kissa laughed. "Okay, I guess I owe you lunch. Why don't I meet you at Jay's about one?"

Quinn loved food. And Jay's was the next best thing to his mother's cooking. "Sure. See you there. Hey, I'll leave a note for the lovebirds. Maybe they'll be hungry by then."

* * *

A few hours later, Kissa arrived at Jay's Diner, knowing that in all likelihood Quinn Stone would be late. Quinn was late for everything. Even the day his divorce was finalized, Quinn was late for court and almost got thrown in jail for contempt for being tardy.

So when she entered the restaurant and found him already sitting at a table and waving at her, she was shocked, to say the least. Markissa Jackson Phillips's world was knocked a little off center. Quinn was on time and was actually dressed like an adult. He had on a knit polo shirt and walking shorts. The soft green color of his attire was accented by his hazelnut skin. Okay, his hair was still fashioned into short twists, but for Quinn, two out of three things wasn't bad.

She walked to the table and sat down. "Quentin Stone, what are you doing here so early?"

"You said one."

"I know that. But you can't get anywhere on time."

He shrugged those broad shoulders. "Well, yeah. Actually I had some business I had to courier off to my boss."

"Boss?"

"The company I work for is actually headquartered in Seattle."

Kissa was confused. Everyone had always thought Quinn worked for himself. "Okay, buster, start from the beginning."

"You sound just like Mikerra. Technically, I work for myself, but I'm contracted by an architectural firm in Seattle. As long as I get my work in on time, I can live here."

"But what about the buildings in Waco?"

"I still do freelancing. This way I can pick and choose what I want to do."

Okay, that sounded like the Quinn she grew up with. Always doing things on his timetable. "So your being on time is just a fluke?"

He reached for the plastic-coated menu. "Pretty much."

Kissa laughed as she reached for a disposable napkin. "Some things never change. Now, tell me about Mikerra and Drake."

"Not much to tell. I know she loves him, but it's all this other mess that's clouding her vision. I know the real reason why she came back, and I don't mean the half story she gave us in the hospital. I also know that guy has a price on her head."

"How on earth do you know that?"

"I have friends all around the world, Kissa. I guess you could say I'm connected. And my very reliable sources informed me Seth has an underground hit out on her."

"What exactly is that?"

"That is a hit that goes out only to certain hitters. Say, maybe the top five in the United States."

"So you're telling me that hit men are going to invade our town?"

"This is a new day. It could be a hit woman. The thing is you can't tell Mikerra. She's got enough on her mind already without her knowing this. We're going to need to stash her and Drake somewhere secure for a few days."

"What difference is a few days going to make?"

"A lot. Like I said, I have a lot of friends. I have a few in the agency, and I think I have a line on the hitter, but to get him, he's going to have to come here. There's a government agency that actually goes after hitters."

Kissa could actually see the wheels turning in

Quinn's brain. If they could get the hitter to come to Wright City, the agency guys could catch him or her. Would Mikerra be safe? "But will that really help anything?"

The waitress came to the table. The young woman announced the specials and took their orders of chicken-fried steak, mashed potatoes, and broccoli smothered in fattening cheese.

"I like a woman with a good appetite," Quinn announced after the waitress had departed.

Kissa grinned. "Mikerra and I thought you'd given up women after your divorce."

"Nah, only the wrong ones. Now if the right one comes along, I'd welcome her with open arms."

Kissa didn't get a chance to interrogate Quinn farther, because Mikerra and Drake walked inside the diner, attracting the attention of all the patrons. Kissa waved to the couple, and they headed over to the table. Kissa noticed the very relaxed look on Mikerra's face. Yep, she was in love.

Drake helped Mikerra with her chair, then sat beside her. Mikerra had the silliest grin plastered on her face.

"Well," Kissa said, "I guess I don't have to ask what you two have been up to."

Mikerra nodded. "No, you don't."

To anyone else, that answer would have seemed short, but Kissa knew that it only meant they'd chat about it later. After all, they'd been friends forever. So Kissa tried another, more important topic. "I'm glad you guys came up for air. Quinn and I have an idea to keep you guys safe."

"From what?" Mikerra asked, attempting to sound calm and failing miserably.

Kissa took a dramatic pause. "Come on, Mikerra.

You know what I'm talking about. You and Drake need to disappear for a few days, before someone lets it slip that you're Karen Mills."

Mikerra sighed. Actually, it sounded like a sob. "I know. Things are escalating out of control. I don't want my parents harmed in all this mess. I don't want Seth coming after them to get to me. We have the cabin at the lake. I used to go there when I was a teenager. It's pretty secluded. Most people don't know it's there."

Kissa nodded. "Good. We'll go check it out later today."

The waitress came with Kissa's and Quinn's food orders. She also took Drake's and Mikerra's meal requests and then left the table.

Kissa watched her best friend from childhood break down in a mass of tears. Drake wrapped Mikerra in his arms and comforted her. "Now, baby, it's going to all work out. You'll see." He kissed Mikerra's hair and reached for the napkin dispenser. He gently wiped her tears away. "I know you're frightened, and you have every right to be, but I won't let that bastard get anywhere near you. Promise."

Mikerra shook her head. "It's not me I'm worried about. I don't want anyone else getting hurt on my behalf."

Kissa cleared her throat. "Now, Mikerra, we're not going to have this discussion again. We're all in this together."

Mikerra looked at Kissa with tear-streaked eyes. "I just don't want you guys getting killed. One person's life has already been taken."

Okay, that was new, thought Kissa. "Who was killed?"

"Remember when I was getting ready to leave Manhattan and I was selling my car?" asked Mikerra.

"Yes," Kissa answered. "Some young guy bought your car."

"That young guy was carjacked the next day and was killed," Mikerra said.

Kissa could see how Mikerra had connected the dots. "But that had nothing to do with you. It was just a freak turn of events. You can't control someone else's behavior."

Mikerra nodded. "At first that was what I thought. But lately I've begun to wonder if they were after me instead. I didn't tell Seth I was selling the car. What if he had had a hit planned and that poor young guy was just an innocent victim?"

The table was quiet. Mikerra had posed a valid question. Kissa was now faced with the problem of having to burden her friend even more. "Mikerra, you could be right. I didn't want to tell you this, but Quinn has information that Seth has put out an underground hit on you."

The news should have forced more tears, but Mikerra only nodded. "I figured he had. The only thing in my favor is that I seldom used my given name on anything while I lived in New York. It might take him a minute to track me that way. I didn't mean for this to happen. I figured once I was gone, Seth would just move on to the next woman and forget about me."

Drake stared at her. "You can't bury your head in the sand about this, baby. I know at first I was in denial about what the military was doing to me, but you've got to keep going with the story. A lot of my friends are still in Iraq and could be part of the drug testing. I've already lost one friend to it. I don't want any more soldiers to die, either."

"Really, Drake? I didn't know what to think. I didn't know if it was worth continuing. I didn't want to lose what we're building together." Mikerra reached for another napkin and wiped her face. "I wasn't sure if you were on board with the idea or merely appeasing me."

Drake kissed her on the lips. "I'd say a lot from column A and a little from column B. But know that I'm one hundred percent behind you."

Mikerra smiled up at him. "Thank you, Drake. You don't know how much that means to me."

Kissa didn't think she could take one more second of this purely romantic scene without going into a diabetic fit. "Okay. Now that the romantic part of the meal is over, can we get down to the real business of saving our butts?"

Washington, D.C.

Sloan walked into his apartment, heading straight for his phone. He quickly dialed the airlines to change his flight. Too many people at the Pentagon wanted his itinerary at the last minute. Something didn't smell right.

Earlier that afternoon the body of a man had been found just three blocks from the Grotto. Sloan knew that body. Carl Bennett was a pro at what he did—extracting information and getting top dollar from the highest bidder. Someone had just stopped his clock, and Sloan knew exactly why. Carl had had information on Mikerra and had leaked her location most likely, and so he'd become a liability. Now Carl was dead, according to the local cable news network.

His cell phone rang. Sloan abandoned his call to

the airlines and looked at the display screen on the small phone. "Carter. Great." Sloan put the phone to his ear. "Hey, Carter. Just the brother I need to talk to. I need a favor."

"What else is new?"

"This is important," Sloan pleaded. "I need to borrow Bessie Coleman."

"Why would I let you borrow my plane? Remember the last time you did? No way, man. I'll fly you where you need to go."

Sloan didn't have time to get into a debate about the last time he took Carter's beloved Bessie, named after the first black female licensed pilot, and almost crashed the Cessna. "Hey, man, I told you I was really sorry about that."

"Yeah, yeah. Where we going?"

"Wright City."

"Your hometown? I thought you were flying to Podunk, Texas, tomorrow."

"I was, but something came up. It's for Mikerra." Sloan hated to use his ace in the hole, but he was a desperate man. He used his knowledge of Carter's weakness. Carter would do anything for Mikerra and had. "Can you or can't you?"

"Be there in one hour." Carter ended the call.

"Finally some cooperation," Sloan murmured as he put the cordless phone back on its base. He finished packing, adding to his clothes his Sig Sauer and extra clips of ammo. For once he hit Wright City, things were going to start happening too fast to think straight and worry about consequences. All he knew and cared about was that his dearest friends were in trouble, and he had the means to help. Even if that meant losing his own life in the process.

Chapter 19

Mikerra and Kissa toured the isolated two-room cabin. It would be perfect. All it needed was a good cleaning, food, and maybe a TV, and it would be just perfect.

Originally, Mikerra's father had bought the cabin to go fishing with her uncle, Herbert, all those years ago. But Uncle Herbert died in a car accident just as the cabin was completed. Her father didn't have the heart to sell it after that.

"I think this will work, Mikerra." Kissa wiped her finger on the coffee table, then wrote her name in the dust. "Of course, it needs a little cleaning. This could be a little love nest for you and Drake while the plot plays out."

Mikerra didn't like the idea. "I don't want you guys getting in harm's way. I think you and Quinn were overexaggerating earlier this afternoon. What if Quinn's contacts are wrong? How long will we be in hiding?"

Kissa continued to inspect the cabin. "One, two, three days at the most. Just think, you and Drake could have mind-blowing sex for three days."

Mikerra followed Kissa into the bedroom. "Yeah, right before he checks into the hospital for surgery." She sat on the couch and began coughing as the dust settled. "I can't believe he's willing to hide out here in the first place. Usually, he's like, 'I am a soldier, and therefore no one can defeat me.'"

Kissa sat by her on the couch. "That's just fear talking. You're scared and you have every right to be. There are several people that want you dead. Drake wants to be with you, and whatever it takes to make that happen, he's willing to do that. He loves you, Mikerra. You know it's the kind of love you always wanted. Unconditional."

Mikerra looked at her friend, trying to stay strong and not cry, but too many things were happening too fast. Her lips started quivering, and the first tear fell. "I know. I love him more than I thought possible."

"But?"

"Why can't I say that to him? I said it once, but I can't seem to say it again. It's like the words are stuck in my throat." Mikerra's heart felt lighter as she confessed this to her best friend. "I mean, I want to."

Kissa put her arms across Mikerra's shoulders and hugged her. "It's because you're scared."

"What am I scared of?" Mikerra wiped tears away.

"You're scared of what that love can mean. It could mean a deeper love than you're ready to invest in. It could mean forever, and that frightens you."

"You think Drake is the one?"

"I didn't say that," Kissa said in her practical voice.

Mikerra turned and faced her friend. "Tell me exactly what you mean."

Kissa shook her head. "Mikerra, this is something you're going to have to work out on your own. I could tell you, but that's not what you need. Love is a journey.

Everyone has to find their own path. You're going to have to decide what is important to you. Is Drake, the man, more important to you than Drake, the prizewinning story?"

No one knew Mikerra like Kissa. She knew how to ask the important questions that would only confuse Mikerra more. Mikerra knew she loved Drake with all her heart. But could she forgo the story that could rebuild her credibility as a journalist?

What good was her career if she didn't have the one man she loved? "Damn you, Kissa."

Kissa laughed. "That's my girl."

Wright City Memorial Airport

Sloan stepped out of the small plane and kissed the ground. He didn't think he would be so happy to see Wright City in all his thirty-nine years of his life.

Carter stepped off the plane, threw his bags at Sloan. "Man, get up. You're embarrassing me." He helped Sloan stand up.

"You tried to kill me!" Sloan grabbed his bags and headed for the small airport terminal. "You deliberately tried to run into that mountain, you played chicken with a commercial airliner, and then you didn't put the landing gear down until it was almost too late. If you didn't want to fly me here, all you had to do was say so."

Carter was right on his heels. "You know, Sloan, you used to be fun. You know I had to blow off a little steam. I'm right in the middle of my divorce. Monica is trying to take me to the cleaners."

Sloan had forgotten. Carter and his wife of two years were smack-dab in the middle of the messiest divorce this side of the capital. Luckily, no children were involved. "Sorry, man. But I'm still pissed at you."

"I got you here, didn't I?"

"In what condition? I think I peed in my pants. I don't think I can even get back on a plane again. I should sue you for mental anguish. I don't know how I'm getting back to D.C."

"You're such a drama queen," Carter said. "I'll take you back. I think I'm going to hang around Wright City and see what it's like to be in a town this small."

Sloan walked inside the small building. "Carter, you can't be serious. I told you what's at stake, and you want to stay?"

Carter shrugged. "Can't be any worse than living in D.C. for the last forty-five years. Besides, I'm doing this for Mikerra."

He watched the two men as they entered the excuse of an airport, bickering like an old married couple. They hadn't noticed his presence, which was good. He took out his cell phone and dialed a familiar number. He waited as the call connected. "It's me. I'm in Wright City. She's here."

Mikerra let herself into her house, ready to take a shower and go straight to bed. For the last few hours she and Kissa had cleaned the two-room cabin from top to bottom. They had also stocked the fridge with enough food to last her and Drake at least a week.

She threw her keys on the kitchen table as she headed upstairs. She was struggling out of her T-shirt when her doorbell rang. "That better not be Drake, Kissa, or Quinn," she muttered, slipping her shirt back on and stomping downstairs. She reached the door and pulled it open. "Oh my God! Sloan?"

He stepped inside her house and closed the door. "Why don't you say it a little louder? I'm sure the hitter didn't hear you." He hugged Mikerra. "It's good seeing you, Care Bear."

It took Mikerra a few minutes to collect her thoughts. Sloan was actually standing inside her house. "What are you doing here? You said you couldn't get away from D.C. until tomorrow."

Sloan, dressed in jeans, a T-shirt, and tennis shoes, reminding her of the nerdy friend she knew in high school, smiled at her. "Well, let's just say too many people wanted to know when I was leaving town and how long I'd be gone. Carter flew me down early. He claims he didn't have anything to do."

"Carter? My Carter?" Mikerra asked excitedly. "I haven't seen or heard from him since he helped me leave the city."

Sloan laughed at his friend. At least his flying with the insane Carter took Mikerra's mind off her troubles. "Yes. You know he's still got a thing for you. He'll do anything in his power to help you."

Mikerra nodded. Carter was a godsend. She'd met the attorney over fifteen years ago, when they both interned at the magazine. His job at the Justice Department was her saving grace. With all his connections, he was able to help her get away from New York with barely a trace.

Sloan took a seat on the couch. "This looks good on you." He patted the cushion next to him. "See, I told you coming back here was a good idea. You look relaxed, ready to conquer the world."

Mikerra wished that were true. "Right now I just

wish this mess was already over. Do you know Seth actually hired someone to kill me?"

Sloan nodded. "Yeah, I finally got a line on the hitter."

"Figures. I knew something else brought you home sooner than expected. So who is it? Not Ingus Machelli, I hope. I wouldn't want to be chopped into bite-size pieces."

"I can't believe you said that," Sloan said. "You know he's in jail for the botched attempted killing of that witness."

Mikerra vaguely remembered the sensational news story of a few years back. Ingus was supposed to kill Harper Killian, a mob informant, but Harper outsmarted the hired killer by slipping him a sleeping pill. Ingus fell asleep and was soon captured by the cops. "So who has the honors?"

"Walter Ging."

"Okay, now I'm really scared. Walter Ging never misses. At least with Ingus, I had a fighting chance, but Ging is the kind of hitter I really hate. He'd kill me slowly. Letting me hope there was a chance before he bashed my head in with a hammer." Mikerra took a deep breath, then another, attempting to calm down.

Sloan rubbed her back. "Look, I have it on good authority that he's still in New York. But someone has leaked your whereabouts, so I do know that Seth and his party are on their way here."

Well, that was something she'd never expected to happen. "How?"

"Bennett."

"That little sneak. I'm going to kill him."

"Too late. Someone blew his brains out right behind the Grotto."

Mikerra saw her life flashing before her eyes. If they

got Bennett, they were going to get her. She had to think of a way out, or at least a way to save Drake, Kissa, and Quinn from harm. "I have to do something."

Sloan nodded. "You need to write that story about Drake. That's going to be the sweetest revenge. How is Drake, anyway? Kissa told me about the tumor. I'm glad to hear David is working on it."

That brought everything into focus. In the last few hours, Mikerra had forgotten how serious this was for Drake. His life was on the line, too, but he wasn't sitting around playing the victim. She wouldn't either. "Yeah, David wants him to check into the hospital Sunday night. He's scheduled for surgery Monday morning. When the military finds out he can't report to his next post, they're going to be here, too."

Sloan shook his head. "Yeah, the military doesn't take kindly to civilians getting involved in a soldier's health. How did you get the rest of the info? Drake's records have a seal on them. Not even the president of our United States can get to them without proper authorization."

Mikerra smiled. "Quinn. You know I hate to admit it, Sloan, but he's still the best computer hacker this side of a federal prison."

Sloan laughed. "I should have known. Did you print the records? I would really like to verify a few things before I talk to Drake."

"Speaking of, I asked Drake about his friend that died mysteriously in Iraq, and I think it sounds like another cover-up."

"I think it sounds like a reporter is on to a big story," Sloan said. "I like the excited gleam in your eye. But I think Drake put it there."

Mikerra snorted. "Oh, please. This story is huge. It goes all the way to the Pentagon. General Mac-

Arthur has been calling about Drake's condition," Mikerra announced.

"What did David say?"

"Well, he was a little suspicious and told the general that Drake came in on his own."

"Good. Horace did seem edgy in the last meeting. A few pieces of the puzzle are falling into place, Mikerra. And the picture I'm getting is going to blow the lid on the administration. I could very well be out of a job when all this is over."

Mikerra grabbed his hand. "You know there's always a place right here in your hometown."

"Doing what?"

Mikerra shrugged. "I don't know. I'm sure there's something that the junior administrative assistant to the Joint Chiefs of Staff could do in this town. You know all the military secrets of all the branches. You could start your own military school."

"No thanks. How about I just wait and see how this thing plays out?"

Mikerra hoped that was still an option in the morning.

Chapter 20

Drake woke up early Wednesday morning with the feeling that something important was going to happen today. He'd had the same feeling the week before he left Iraq. A tingle in the pit of his stomach was a sure sign that something or someone was going to change his life.

His headaches had returned. A not-so-gentle thud at the base of his brain was making its way to the front of his head. His brain felt like it was on fast-forward. He took two of the pills David had prescribed for the pain and headed for the shower to prepare for the day.

After he was dressed in cargo shorts and a T-shirt, he headed downstairs for breakfast. As usual, his mother had fixed a breakfast large enough to feed his entire family, but it was only Drake and his dad at the morning meal. There were pancakes, scrambled eggs, bacon, hash browns, and toast. Drake didn't know where to start first.

Drake joined his father at the table. "Hey, Dad. Taking the day off?" Drake knew better. His father took off only when absolutely necessary, like for surgery. When Drake had returned home after serving eighteen months in Iraq, it was his mother who had picked him up at the airport in Dallas.

"No, I have to fly out this afternoon. I have a conference in Chicago for the rest of the week. So I'm leaving you in charge of your mother," he teased. "You have to make sure she doesn't go on a wild shopping spree while I'm gone." His father speared three pancakes and some bacon.

Drake nodded, reaching for the platter of eggs and spooning some on his plate. After he added some bacon to his plate, he glanced at his mother. She stood at the stove, shaking her head at his father's remark.

"Dad, I'll make sure she doesn't go on a shopping spree. But what about her boyfriend?" He looked at his mother and winked at her.

"Drake Alexander Harrington," Shirley said in that voice. "You know my boyfriend doesn't come around until I give the signal." She laughed as she took her seat at the table.

Drake's father shook his head at his wife. "It's a good thing I love you and know you have a warped sense of humor. Now you got the boy doing it, too." He leaned toward his wife and kissed her on the lips. "I'm sure going to miss that for two days."

Shirley smiled. "Well, when you get back, there'll be plenty waiting for you."

Drake watched his parents with pride. They acted more like newlyweds than the mature married couple they were. That was the kind of love he wanted. No matter what, he had to know that Mikerra would always be there, waiting for him with kisses.

"Drake, I didn't cook all this for you to let it get cold," Shirley scolded. She reached for his plate and headed for the microwave.

Before Drake could utter a word, his mother was pushing buttons on the microwave to reheat his food.

His father grinned at him. "I found it's better just to let her do her thing. How's the headaches?"

"I had one this morning. I took the medicine David gave me. But it's the first one I've had in a few days. I just wish this mess was already over."

"I know you do. I can't believe the military had a hand in this, but I guess it doesn't surprise me, especially listening to the Vietnam vets. Military soldiers have enough to worry about with the enemy without having to worry about the boys in the Pentagon, too."

Drake nodded. Finally, someone understood what he was going through. "Thanks, Dad. It took a while for me to realize what was what. Luckily, Mikerra is as stubborn as a mule and wouldn't give up."

His father gave one of his noncommittal nods and continued eating. "I know that look."

Drake was confused. "What look?"

"You're in love," his father said.

"Oh that. Yeah."

Terror was barking at Mikerra, waking her out of a sound sleep. "Not now, baby. Mommy needs another hour of sleep," she mumbled into her pillow. *Of all the days for Terror to want to go out early,* she thought sleepily.

The little dog wouldn't be deterred. He continued barking and then started jumping on Mikerra's bed.

Getting any more sleep was impossible. Mikerra opened her eyes and sat up. "All right, you mutt. We'll go for a walk." She pushed the covers back and walked to the bathroom.

"This wouldn't be so bad if Sloan hadn't shown up last night, unannounced," she told the mirror. Staying up until nearly dawn hadn't helped matters, either. With just a few hours of sleep, she wasn't ready to face the day, let alone her terrier. She pulled on some baggy shorts and a T-shirt, attire suitable for dog walking in Wright City at seven in the morning. She opened her bathroom door to find Terror waiting for her. "I know you're ready to go out. I still don't see why you can't use the backyard like a normal dog. No, we have to walk halfway across town so you can pee in the park."

She and Terror quietly walked out of the house so that they wouldn't wake Sloan as he slept on the sofa. After they were outside and in the humid morning air, Mikerra had to admit this felt good. "Okay, I have to admit this is what I needed, boy. Thank you for dragging me out of bed."

Terror barked and took off for the sidewalk.

Mikerra laughed. Before she knew it, her four-legged friend was almost out of her field of vision. She had to increase her pace from an amble to a power walk. As she rounded the corner of Hilman Street, she realized someone was watching her.

He turned a corner before she could get a good look at him. But she knew the tall man with short blond hair would be easy to pick out in Wright City. He looked like a hit man.

She had to get back home as quickly as possible. Apparently, Ging had arrived and was ready to get the job done. She whistled for Terror but couldn't find her little friend. "Terror?"

Since it was so early in the morning, not a bloody creature was stirring. No one to help her find her dog. No one to help her at all. No one but a hired killer. *Steady, girl,* she reminded herself. She took a deep breath and reassessed the situation. Terror was probably under the nearest oak tree, doing his business.

"Terror!" She continued walking in the direction of the park. Hopefully, she'd find her dog and she could return home. Her heart jumped with joy when she heard Terror answer her with a bark. He soon scampered to her, panting and most likely relieved. "There you are," Mikerra said. "I'm going to have to get you a leash if you keep this up."

Terror barked and jumped until Mikerra finally picked him up. "That's a good boy. Now we have to get home." She put Terror on the ground, and they started back to her house.

Mikerra knew she wasn't seeing things when she kept spying the tall, blond-haired man following her. She could pretend she didn't live on this street, but she knew the downside to living in a town this small was everyone knew where to find you. He probably already knew where she lived and even what time she got up this morning. Her best bet would be to act natural.

But how natural could she act, knowing her life was about to end?

He followed his quarry down the street. It wasn't a bad town, he thought. It had that Mayberry feel to it, and she felt safe enough to walk that excuse of a dog without a leash.

He could have killed her several times already, but the senator had made it very plain that he wanted to do the killing. All he had to do was find her. He'd done his part, but curiosity had gotten the better of him, and he wanted to know why the senator wanted one out-of-work reporter dead so much.

He stared straight ahead as she rounded another

corner. He knew she was trying to throw him off, but it was useless. He already had her home address and her parents' address. She had nowhere to run.

His cell phone vibrated in his pants pocket. Engaging his newfangled headset, he answered the call. "Ging."

"Have you found her?"

"Yes, as I said earlier. I have completed my part of this. When can I expect payment?"

"When I feel her cold, dead body in my hands. Not a moment before. Any word on the sergeant?"

"I was contracted for one thing. That information will cost you double."

"Damn, you are a thief. All right. Agreed."

"He's here. Haven't seen him, but according to the rumors at the diner, they are an item. So you've got twice your trouble."

"You let me worry about him. Just keep tabs on them. But don't hurt her."

"What about the sergeant?"

"Kill him."

Mikerra thanked the heavens as she unlocked the door to the house. The stranger had become distracted and she'd made her getaway, for all the good it was going to do. To his employer, which was most likely Seth, Walter Ging was worth his slight weight in bullets. He left nothing to chance and, most likely, already knew where she lived.

Sloan was missing from the couch. His brand-new sneakers were still parked right in front of it, so he had to still be in the house.

"Mikerra, is that you?" Sloan called from the kitchen.

"Yes, it's us," she said. "Terror had to go to the

bathroom." She walked into the kitchen. "You don't have to cook breakfast. I was going to make some omelets."

"No worries," Sloan said. "Mine will be better than those froufrou things you make, anyway. I'm making some real omelets."

Mikerra nodded, reaching into the cabinet for Terror's breakfast. "Speaking of real, I just saw Walter Ging. He has blond hair now."

"No way."

"Very way," Mikerra said dryly. "He was following me. Then he stopped abruptly. I think he got a phone call."

Sloan scooped an omelet onto a plate. "What do you mean?"

"You know how those Bluetooth headset things work. People think they still have to yell into the mouthpiece to be heard. He was talking quite loud. I just know he was talking to Seth. I bet Seth wants to kill me. He had Ging find me, but he wants to do the honors. How sick is that?"

Sloan motioned for her to sit at the breakfast table. When she did, he presented her with a plate with an omelet, bacon, and toast on it. "I'm not surprised, Mikerra. I told you he was bad business. And with you knowing all the secrets of Project Perfect, he can't afford for you to blow the lid on the story."

Sloan sat down at the table, with a plate, and they began eating. Mikerra ate the food with gusto. Was it the morning air that had made her so hungry, or was it the adrenaline from seeing the hired killer? "I probably should tell Drake what's going on."

Sloan looked up from his plate. "Why? I know this has to do with the military, but as long as he's at the cabin with you, he's perfectly safe."

Mikerra put her fork down and voiced her theory to

her friend. "Don't you see? Drake is only the second soldier to fall ill from the Project Perfect experiment. The first case was his friend Josh. He drowned in the shower, in less than a few inches of water. The army claimed that he probably slipped in the shower, but I think differently. I think he was killed, and it was made to look like an accident. The minute Drake went to the doctor, all this other mess started. Did you know the army has called his parents' house several times, wanting to know how his headaches are?"

Sloan shook his head. "I knew it was bad. But I didn't know it was this bad. This is bigger than I thought."

Mikerra nodded. She hadn't wanted to give it a name, but with all the facts before her, she didn't have a choice. "It's a scandal, Sloan. I know this will cost you your job and your lifestyle in D.C. We'll be lucky to escape with our lives."

"Care Bear, I'm not sorry you called me. I think it's time the world knew what the military is doing to innocent servicemen. What really sucks is soldiers will die because of this."

Mikerra's only thoughts were of Drake and how much he'd suffered. "Drake said he's in favor of me doing the story on it."

"That's because he loves you. I think he'd do just about anything for you," Sloan said.

"Yes, I know. I feel the same way."

Sloan nudged her. "So have you guys said the L word yet?"

"Well, it slipped out, and he didn't believe me. He thought I said it to get the story. Now I can't seem to get that word past my lips again." Mikerra pushed her plate away, trying to formulate her feelings for her old friend. "I mean, you know, I didn't mean to fall in love with him again, but you know what they say?"

Sloan stood. "Yes, you can't control who you fall in love with. So just because he has a tumor at the moment doesn't mean he can't return those feelings. Besides, he's having surgery on Monday."

Mikerra wiped her eyes with a napkin. The thought of Drake having to undergo something as serious as brain surgery just because Seth and his buddies wanted to make money infuriated her. "David is very positive about the procedure."

Sloan laughed at her. "Hey, I know about the no-sex rule until after surgery and the fact that you guys blew it the first day."

"Does Quinn tell everything he knows?" Mikerra muttered. Leave it to her bigmouthed brother to inform everyone that David had told her and Drake they couldn't have sex.

"Actually, it was Drake. He called this morning, while you and Terror were out. He sounded a little put out about it."

"Ha-ha," Mikerra said, smiling at Sloan's play on words. "So not funny."

"Oh, come on, Mikerra. Admit it. It's funny. You and Drake haven't seen each other in over twenty years, and you guys hit the sheets, and it's like we're back in high school."

Mikerra balled up her napkin and threw it at her friend since elementary school. "Only now I've gotten all you guys involved in my mess." She hated the thought of endangering them on her behalf. "If I had known all this was going to happen, I don't know if I would have returned here."

"Better on your home turf than the streets of New York," Sloan said. "Why don't you go take a shower while I finish cleaning the kitchen? Drake said he'd be over around lunchtime. I thought we could have lunch at Jay's."

Mikerra rose and headed out of the kitchen. "If I didn't know Jay was at least ten years older than we are, I'd swear you have the hots for that woman. You haven't even seen your mama, and you're trying to eat at the diner. That woman is going to blow a gasket."

"I already called Mom, and she's actually busy today. I'm meeting her at my grandmother's for dinner. That will give us time to work out what we're going to do about all this."

Mikerra felt grateful for her friends and their willingness to help her. "I can't say this enough, Sloan, but thanks."

He continued his task of cleaning up the kitchen and did not look in her direction. "That's what friends are for."

Chapter 21

Drake's brain still felt as if it were a movie stuck on fast-forward. He felt good enough to walk the few blocks to Mikerra's house.

What was it about Texas and the summer? Drake wondered as he walked along the sidewalk. It was hot, no doubt. It was June, and Central Texas sweltered, the temperature rising to nearly a hundred degrees every day, but the humidity didn't bother him. He was definitely dressed for the day in shorts, a T-shirt, and sandals, but that wasn't what put a spring in his step. This day was the day he was going to confess his love to Mikerra.

He arrived at her house and rang the doorbell. He heard Terror barking at the intrusion of noise. Drake smiled. If he had his way, Terror would take permanent residence at Mikerra's parents' house. The door opened, and Drake got his first shock of the morning.

"Drake! Good to see you!" Sloan ushered him inside the house like he owned the place. "Mikerra is upstairs getting dressed, so it'll be a few minutes," he said, closing the front door. He guided Drake to the couch to have a seat.

Drake wasn't sure what to make of his old friend being at his girlfriend's house. He was grateful Sloan could get away to help them, but still he didn't like another man at his woman's house, with or without his knowledge. Although he'd spoken with Sloan earlier, now it was time for real talk. "When did you get here?"

"Last night," Sloan said. "Oh, I get it. Why am I at your woman's house instead of my mama's house?"

Drake felt silly about his jealous thoughts. "Okay, maybe I am a little over the line, but you gotta admit, it looks strange."

"I got here kinda late last night and wanted to get with Mikerra as soon as possible." Sloan immediately backtracked. "I mean, to visit Mikerra and compare notes. It's weird, you know. It reminds me of when you guys were a couple in high school. You were super possessive then, too."

"I just want her to be safe, that's all."

Sloan laughed. "Drake, this is me. The man who had to listen to you whine about how Mikerra dumped you all those years ago. So don't try to use those tired playa-playa lines on me."

Drake laughed. Everyone could see right through him, and it was time he quit kidding himself. He knew he wanted to get those words of love out of his body, but was he confident enough to not hear her return those words? "Okay, you got me. I was thinking of confessing my love today. It feels like a block of cement weighing me down."

Sloan nodded. "I know how you feel, Drake. And I know Mikerra feels the same. But getting her to say it will be a battle all its own."

Drake already knew that. She'd said it once, and he'd accused her of trying to use him. Probably not the smartest thing to say to a troubled woman. Mikerra was keeping her feelings well hidden, and he had to know why. He had an idea that it had something to do with her past. And he wanted her to deal with that before they went any farther.

Sloan shook Drake's shoulder. He had been talking the entire time Drake was in la-la land. "Man, you were definitely in another place. I was asking you about your buddy Josh."

"Josh Hughes?"

"Yeah. Can you remember the details of his death? I mean the most intricate details."

"Yeah, I can remember that morning like it was yesterday. I didn't find him, but I was one of the first people on the scene." He didn't have to recall the events. They were lodged in his memory, right next to the ones he had of Mikerra telling him all those years ago that she couldn't love him. "I can still see Josh's face, all bloody from the fall, his blue eyes staring up at the ceiling. It was like he was surprised."

"Did Josh complain of any of the symptoms you're having now?"

"Yeah, he had a bad sinus infection for like two weeks. I mean it was bad. He said his eyesight had blurred, and he was always coughing some kind of stuff up. He'd have migraines, and he was always complaining about a pain behind his ears."

"Wow, Drake, you remember a lot," Sloan said. "Were you guys close?"

"I'd known Josh since boot camp. We ran into each other every so often over the years. In ranger training, we became really close and were tight after that. I really regret that I wasn't able to go to his funeral and pay my respects."

"I know, man. But if Mikerra can break this story, no more soldiers will die."

"If we don't die in the process. You know her ex wants her dead, too. Probably for what she knows about the Project Perfect testing. I still can't believe the military would do this to soldiers." The mere thought still infuriated Drake.

"It's not really the whole military. Just a select group of men, some of whom probably never really served in the military. They just see you guys as numbers in an experiment. And since you've been experiencing headaches and the tumor has formed, you've now become a liability they can't afford."

Drake knew that, too. Especially after the call he got from Mason. "They want to reassign me to Fort Hood, and they want me to report immediately. Luckily, my CO is almost a friend and called to warn me."

Sloan shook his head. "I just hope that didn't cost him his life."

Drake didn't like the bleak picture Sloan had painted, but there was little recourse at the moment. "Mason is a good soldier and knows how to handle himself. What are we going to do to keep Mikerra safe?"

"What are *you* doing to keep yourself safe?"

Drake was dumbfounded. He'd been so focused on Mikerra, he really hadn't given much thought to his own safety. Was he so taken by Mikerra that he would forsake his own life?

"He has me, Sloan," Mikerra said as she walked down the stairs. Terror was on her heels as she entered the living room.

The men rose like good Southern gentlemen and waited for her to take a seat next to Drake on the couch before they reclaimed theirs. "Now what's this about being in danger?" Mikerra glanced at Sloan, but her mind was on Drake. He looked too good in shorts. She was going to have to contain herself better or something when it came to looking at his chiseled body.

"I don't get a good-morning kiss or anything?" Drake whispered in her ear. "I missed you last night."

The feel of his hot breath against her skin was doing all the wrong things to her body, especially since David had suggested they refrain from such energy-zapping activities. Her body would listen to her brain as it demanded attention. Mikerra scooted away from him, or at least she tried to.

Drake's strong arms pulled her against him. "Now, about that kiss," he said just before letting his lips descend upon hers.

Mikerra didn't have time to remind him of his health. His tongue felt too good inside her mouth. Even more so when she joined in. Who knew how far they would have gone if Sloan hadn't cleared his throat?

"If you guys don't mind," Sloan said, holding back a laugh. "Can I get you to focus on something else besides each other? We do have a crisis here."

Drake released her mouth. "You were always the worrier, Sloan."

"Okay, Sloan. What's the next step?" Mikerra grabbed Drake's ever-moving hand. That man had her thinking, *To hell with everything*, and giving in to the passion.

"Well, I need to make a few calls. But since Ging is already here, McCaffrey must be on his way. When is the bigger question," said Sloan.

Mikerra leaned closer to Drake. "Why?"

Sloan looked at her. "We know that Seth wants to do the honors. Ging is just going to shadow you. Drake is a different situation entirely. They want Drake out of the picture, because he's the bigger threat. If word of his condition gets out, the Pentagon is going to have to answer a lot a questions they don't have answers for."

Mikerra took a deep breath. She knew exactly where this was leading. "You think we should hide out now, don't you?"

Sloan nodded. "Yes, I do, but it would be fruitless to leave now. Especially with Ging already knowing your location. We're going to have to go under the cover of darkness. We're also going to need Quinn and Kissa to help with this. So for now, act as normal as possible. Ging isn't going to harm you."

"What about Drake?"

"I got this, Care Bear," Sloan said. "As long as there's enough of us, he's okay."

"So we have to stay barricaded in the house?" asked Mikerra.

"We all know staying in the house isn't going to deter Ging. That's why I said, 'Do everything as normal.' We need him to think he hasn't been spotted." Sloan stood and walked to the table near the stairs. "I'll call Kissa and Quinn and tell them to meet us at the diner for lunch. I'm dying for some good old home cooking."

Massachusetts

Seth paced the area in front of the private air landing strip on the outskirts of Boston. Already his plan had failed. They were already several hours behind schedule, due to a stupid miscommunication. If he didn't know better, he'd think it was a curse.

A curse in the worst kind of way.

All he wanted to do was silence her. Let her know what she was going to miss by being dead.

"McCaffrey," a deep voice ground out.

He spun around and looked into the eyes of the man he deemed responsible for the mess. "What is it, Horace? Got the planes situated?"

General Horace MacArthur nodded. "Yeah, it was a maintenance mix-up. They serviced the wrong plane. We'll be set to go in about twenty minutes."

Seth stared at him. "You do realize we're already a half a day behind schedule. She could be ready to blab to somebody about the drug, and then we'll all be in trouble."

MacArthur stepped closer to him, invading his personal space. "If you don't calm down, you're going to blow it for all of us. You should've let Ging take her down, along with Harrington. If you had, this could be over without us having to go to Texas. Our hands would be clean, and we wouldn't have to let more people in on our plan. As it is now, there are ten people who know who shouldn't. You should have killed her months ago in New York. But instead, you had an innocent person killed because you didn't have your facts straight."

"And I told you this is personal. She has to pay for leaving me. No bitch leaves me unless I tell her she can."

"See? That's why we're in this mess. Your cocky attitude. You think no woman is immune to your charms. How many people do you plan on killing because you got overconfident? You got sloppy. You left important documents at her place, for her reporter's eyes to see, and now we're all paying for it."

"I will take care of it, Horace. Why don't you just monitor the reports from Iraq to see if any more soldiers have gotten sick and are exhibiting the usual symptoms?"

MacArthur looked at him incredulously. "Are you planning to have more soldiers killed? This has to stop here. We can't keep killing them when the symptoms start appearing. If more soldiers get sick, then the project dies in the water. I will not have more unnecessary deaths on my hands."

Seth refused to let that happen. He'd worked too hard for Project Perfect to die now. MacArthur, like Karen, had become a liability, and they both had to die.

Wright City

Quinn watched as Mikerra, Drake, Sloan, and Kissa walked into the diner. He hadn't seen Mikerra look so refreshed in years. It was all due to Drake, he knew. Her high school sweetie had put a spring in his sister's step, and he was thankful for that.

He waved them over to the large table he had reserved for them. He hoped that the events of the next few days would play out quickly and with as little bloodshed as possible. He'd already taken as many precautions as he could without raising a red flag with the local police. He'd made sure his permit to carry a concealed weapon was up to date. He'd been practicing his aim at the lake, and he'd switched from his trendy cell phone to a more practical walkie-talkie model.

He'd also purchased a similar phone for the cabin, since that was where Mikerra and Drake would end up, and they would definitely need one. He felt like a spy, or at least a really good government agent.

"Quinn, what a surprise. You never get anywhere on time," Mikerra accused as she sat down next to him. Drake sat next to her.

Quinn smiled at his sister. "I can when I need to." He glanced in Kissa's direction. "Hey, you." Kissa was dressed in baggy denim shorts and a T-shirt advertising her chiropractic clinic.

Kissa sat on the opposite side of Quinn. "Hey, yourself. What's this? Like the second time you've been early?"

"Something like that," Quinn said. "Hey, Sloan. Good to finally see you, man."

Sloan gave Quinn a nod in greeting. Sloan might have aged twenty years, but he still had that nerd look about him, Quinn mused. His casual outfit might scream Ralph Lauren, but his very slender physique still screamed nerd.

After everyone was seated and their orders were taken, Quinn decided to get right down to business. "So, is everybody on board with the plan?"

Mikerra looked at her brother. "Quinn, I don't want you getting into trouble on my behalf. Mom would kill me."

Quinn appreciated his big sister's concern, but it wasn't necessary. "Thanks, sis. I can say the same about you. I do think you need to come clean with the folks about why you're really back. I think everyone deserves a clean slate, and you know I'll never judge you, but they should know the truth."

Mikerra nodded. "I'm going to tell them tonight. I don't want some reporter knocking on the door, telling them I was fired from my job because I was sleeping with a married white senator from Boston."

Quinn reached for his sister's hand. "Baby, that's not what I mean. Actually, yes, it is what I mean, but you don't give yourself enough credit. You can't control whom you fall in love with."

"If I had been thinking, it wouldn't have been as terrible as it has been. Innocent people wouldn't be dead, and Seth wouldn't be tracking me down like a deer in hunting season." Mikerra grabbed a napkin and wiped her eyes.

Drake put his arm around Mikerra and drew her closer to him. "Baby, that's why it's called love. You had blinders on. You saw only the good side of him. When you saw the true side of him, you left. Don't beat yourself up about something you couldn't control. You mean everything to me."

Mikerra looked truly stunned. As if an eighteen-wheeler was barreling down the road toward her, ready to pounce. "I care for you, Drake."

Drake kissed her forehead. "I know. I love you, Care Bear."

Quinn gasped. He hadn't expected Drake to say those words, never mind in front of three other people. It was amazing. Now, if only his sister could say the same in return. But instead Mikerra burst into tears.

Jay was at the table in an instant. "What's wrong? The food is on its way. Promise."

Quinn laughed. "It's one of those girlie things, I guess."

Jay took a deep breath. "Did Drake finally tell her he loves her? It's about time. I wondered how many times he was going to eat here with her, knowing his mama fixes all his meals at home."

Quinn looked at Drake for confirmation or denial. Drake only shrugged his shoulders and continued comforting Mikerra. Yeah, they were in love, whether his sister wanted to admit it or not. "Well, it looks like another is down for the count."

Chapter 22

That evening Mikerra parked her SUV in front of her parents' two-story house and looked over at Drake as he unbuckled his seat belt. "Drake, I really appreciate you coming with me for moral support." She leaned over the console and kissed him on the cheek.

"Baby, you know I'll be by your side no matter what. Everyone has something in their life they'd like to forget. That's just part of life, baby. We couldn't have got to our age without some kind of baggage. I just want you to know nothing that you'll say tonight will shock me and make me run in the other direction."

"Thank you, Drake." The words were right there on the tip of her tongue. Three simple damn words and she couldn't say them again. *I love you. How hard is that, Mikerra? He said them, and you can, too,* she told herself.

As if he knew her very thoughts, he told her, "Mikerra, I'm not asking you to say you love me. I know your emotions are all over the place with all this hanging above our heads. The time will come."

She hated when he sounded practical and not like the jerk she'd had glimpses of the last ten days. Had it been only ten days since she'd laid eyes on him?

Where was her brain? It had taken Seth at least six months of flowers, candy, and dates to get this far. Drake had already been there the minute she saw him in the furniture store.

"Honey," Drake prodded gently. "Your mom is going to think we're making out in your SUV if we don't get in the house." He nodded over his shoulder. Her mother was standing on the porch and waving them inside.

Mikerra slowly came out of the funk she was in and focused on him. Then her mother came into view. "Oh, yeah. We better get inside." She opened her door and got out.

Drake met her and grabbed her hand. "It's going to be all right. You'll see. It might hurt like hell, revealing the truth, but it will be worth it." He kissed her forehead.

Mikerra wanted to believe him. She really did. But how did she tell the people who expected the most out of her that she'd failed them by having an extramarital affair and by enduring something else too horrible to mention?

Hand in hand, she and Drake entered the house, and Mikerra gathered her courage to tell her parents the details of her life. It was going to be the fall of Mikerra Stone.

"Mikerra, Drake, so glad you decided to get out of the car," Carolina teased. "I was beginning to think we were going to have to bring dinner outside."

Mikerra kissed her mother on the cheek. "Hey, Mom. Sorry about that. I do have something I need to discuss with you and Dad before we sit down to dinner."

"Can't it wait until after dinner?" asked Carolina.

Mikerra wanted to get this over with as soon as possible. "I'd rather do this now, Mom."

Her mother shrugged her shoulders. "Well, you know best. I'll get your father, and we'll meet you in the living room."

Mikerra nodded and led Drake to the love seat. After they were settled, he turned to her and asked, "Are you sure you want to do this now? Don't you want to lead up to it slowly?"

She shook her head. "No. It feels like a giant weight, and it's sitting on my chest, weighing me down with pain. I have to confess this now, or it's going to blow up in my face."

"Okay, honey." Drake kissed her on the lips. "This is your show."

She watched her parents saunter into the room and take a seat on the couch. "All right, Mikerra. The floor is yours. What's going on? I don't see a ring," said Carolina.

Mikerra gasped. "No, Mom. It's nothing like that. It's about why I came back home."

"I thought you were tired of living in New York," replied Carolina.

"Mom, please," Mikerra pleaded.

Her mother was silent.

"I told you guys that I was tired of living in New York, which in a sense was true," Mikerra explained. "But the real reason was that I was asked to leave my job as an editor and reporter because I was trying to end my relationship with a very powerful man."

"Isn't that against the law?" Carolina asked.

"Well, there are a few other details that will clear everything up for you. He is Senator Seth McCaffrey from Massachusetts."

"That idiot that's heading up the defense committee? The one that wants to send more troops to Iraq?" her father asked. "He got you fired?"

Mikerra nodded, tears sliding down her face. "Yes, I met him years ago, and before I knew it, I was involved with him. But I tried to end it last year, and he hit me and swore he'd kill me if I tried to leave him again. I didn't know this then, but women didn't leave him. He killed them or had them killed, but no woman kept breathing after the relationship ended. After that my boss started complaining about the quality of my work. He said I needed to start coming up with some fresh ideas for the reporters, or he'd put me back on the streets to find my own stories so I'd know a good story when it hit me."

Mikerra took a deep breath and continued the saga. "I knew Seth had gotten to him, and I knew as long as I was on the East Coast, Seth would see to it that he had a hand in my career and my life. He also knew that I knew about the serum."

"What serum?" Her father leaned forward and met her eyes. "If you know it's him, why can't you turn him in?"

Mikerra knew if she told her parents too much, they would be in as much danger as she, Drake, Quinn, Sloan, David, and Kissa were. She couldn't have that on her conscience. "The less you guys know about this, the better. Let's just say it's very dangerous."

Her father rose and began to pace the room. "What I don't understand is, if you knew about the serum and the harm it has caused, why didn't you do something about it? Why didn't you get the information to someone who could help you?"

Mikerra lowered her head in shame. "I was selfish. I wanted that story but was too afraid that something awful would happen if it got out."

"So you *sat* on the story?" her father asked incredulously. "Mikerra, I thought that was why you wanted to become a journalist, to change the world. Not let some no-good man make you afraid to do what's right."

Mikerra bit her lower lip. "I know, Daddy. I'm sorry. I was scared. I could have possibly caused two people their lives. I'm not proud of what I did, but I'm doing everything I can to make this right."

Her father stopped in front of her and kneeled so that they were eye level. "Honey, you know I'm behind what you do, and I'll help you in any way I can to make this right."

Mikerra wiped her eyes, hating that the worst of the story was yet to come. "Thank you, Daddy. You might want to hold that thought until I finish."

Carolina nodded in sympathy, as if she knew the hardest blow was coming.

"Well, after my boss kept complaining about my job performance, I was put back on the streets," Mikerra told them.

"A beat?" her father asked, taking his seat next to her mother.

"Yes, Daddy. I had a certain part to cover. They gave me fashion and the society pages. Two things I really hate. I had to attend modeling shows, interview models, and attend those ritzy society dos, hoping something exciting happened. Seth was at most of the society dos in his official capacity as chairman of the defense committee, and his wife was some kind of social climber. That's when I knew I had to make a clean getaway. It took six months of planning and secrecy, but I did it. I started experiencing stomachaches, headaches a few months before I finally left. I went to the doctor, and he told me I didn't have an ulcer, but I was pregnant."

Carolina gasped. "Pregnant? With a married man's

baby? But wait." She paused. "You're not pregnant now. What happened?"

Mikerra had forgotten Drake was sitting next to her until she felt his large hand caressing her back, encouraging her to get it all out.

"I had a miscarriage," Mikerra admitted. "I didn't want Seth's baby, but I couldn't bring myself to get an abortion. It just seemed like adding more fuel to the fire. One night I started cramping real bad. Luckily, a friend drove me to the hospital before I started bleeding really bad. I had nightmares about it for months. That's when I knew I had to change everything about me." She wiped the endless flow of tears.

Her mother was crying now. "Mikerra, don't torture yourself. That was beyond your control. I knew something was wrong with you when we had our weekly chats, but I would have never dreamed it was of this magnitude. You've carried this around for too long."

"And I pay for that every month. I have horrible periods, and my OB said that given what happened along with my age, getting pregnant again will be difficult."

"Oh, baby," Carolina said. She walked over to Mikerra and held her hand. "Nothing you've told us would make us ashamed of you. I just want you to find some happiness after all the pain you've suffered."

Mikerra knew she'd found happiness with Drake, but could she give that a voice? "Thank you, Mom. I just want this whole ordeal to be over, and I don't want you guys harmed. I wanted you to know the truth in case reporters descend on you."

Her father laughed. "Big-city reporters in Wright City? I doubt this would cause that much commotion. If I ever see that Seth, he'll have to answer to me."

Mikerra sniffed, trying to hold back more tears. "Well, Dad, you might get your wish. He's on his way here. He had me tracked down, and he wants to kill me."

"Kill?" her parents said in unison.

Drake spoke up when Mikerra tried to explain and words failed her. "Yes, Mr. Stone, Mrs. Stone. You see, Seth is on the committee that is pushing the Project Perfect serum. Suffice it to say, both Mikerra and I are flies in his ointment. So we're both in danger."

Carolina looked at Mikerra. "How did you finally make your getaway?"

"I had help. A friend in the Justice Department had my mail rerouted and sold my condo and my car. It was like Karen Mills ceased to exist, and Mikerra Stone was born." She felt bad about the guy who purchased her car. "Unfortunately, the person who bought my car, a young man, was carjacked the next day and killed."

"Oh, dear. This has all the markings of one of those mysteries you read, honey," her mother said to her father. "You need to get away," she said to Mikerra.

Mikerra patted her mom's hand. "That's the tricky part. Seth wants me so bad, he has hired a hitter."

"What on earth is a hitter?" Carolina rose and went back to her seat.

Mikerra would have laughed if the situation hadn't been so critical. "A hitter is a hit man. You know, like a wiseguy."

"He hired someone to kill you because you left his married behind?" asked her father.

"That's it in a nutshell," Mikerra answered dryly. "He wanted the hitter to find me, but not kill me. He wants that little honor for himself."

"Men suck," Carolina proclaimed. "Except for present company," she amended quickly.

"Thank you, baby," her father told her mother.

"You guys need a place to lie low until all the players are here. Then the sheriff can do his thing."

"We are going to the cabin." Mikerra didn't tell her parents when. If they didn't know, then they couldn't tell.

"Well, it sounds romantic to me," Carolina said. "Now that that's all over, I say, let's eat."

Mikerra laughed, realizing exactly where she'd got her large appetite.

Chapter 23

"Are you sure you don't mind me staying with you tonight?" Drake asked Mikerra as she unlocked the door to her house. He wanted to stay with her because after her confession to her parents, something still wasn't right. She might have just poured out her soul to her parents, but she wasn't free from herself.

"I don't mind, Drake," she said softly. "As long as you remember the rules."

He remembered the rules. No one would let him forget David's rule, or suggestion, that he and Mikerra abstain from sex until further notice. But he couldn't let her sleep alone, not in the mood she was in. She needed comforting, and he was the only man for the job.

"Yes, Care Bear, I remember. No sex until David says it's okay," he told her, knowing there was no way in hell he'd be able to keep his hands to himself.

She smiled at him as she opened the door to her house. "Okay, you can stay." She entered the house, and he followed her inside. She locked the door and motioned for him to sit on the couch.

He sat down beside her and took her hand. "You

know this isn't just about sex, don't you? I meant what I said. I know you think my brain isn't up to par, but it is. You're probably right. I do feel like my brain is on a roller coaster sometimes and I'll never be able to catch up. It might take me longer to get there, but I do know what I'm saying."

She leaned against him. "I know you meant what you said, but I just can't return those words to you. I care a lot about you, but you know what I just went through with Seth. I just don't trust my heart right now."

He knew she was trying to keep him at a distance. Drake was well aware of the maneuver because he'd used it for so many years on so many women. But now it was different. He wanted to show Mikerra what their love could be. But how could he do that when he didn't know the answer to that himself? "I'm not asking for you to say it. I know you care. That's enough for now."

"Really?" She looked up at him with teary brown eyes. She'd never looked more beautiful or more scared.

"Yes, Mikerra," he lied. "I can wait until you feel what I feel. I know you need closure with Seth."

She shook her head. "No, I'm okay. I mean, it was my mistake, and I paid dearly for it."

He caressed her, knowing she had to get it out or it would haunt her forever. "Mikerra, when you said you pay for it every month, what exactly did you mean?"

For a moment he didn't think she'd heard him, because she didn't answer. Then he heard it. A sniffle. A chest-heaving sigh. Then the dam burst. She was crying full force and uncontrollably. "It's because . . . ," she wailed. "It's because, uh, uh . . ."

She was bordering on hysteria. Drake pulled her onto his lap and whispered in her ear. "Now, baby, calm down. Just let it out."

He waited patiently while she attempted to explain why she was crying so hard, but the tears only came faster. He felt as helpless as a child as he listened to the gut-wrenching sobs. He wanted to comfort her but had no idea what he was comforting her for. So he hugged her, whispered comforting words to her, and let her cry.

She cried until she started hiccuping. Drake slid her off his lap and went to the kitchen to get her some water. When he returned to the living room, she was just as he had left her on the couch, crying softly. He decided she was going to need something stronger than water. He walked to her makeshift bar in one corner of the room and poured her two fingers of brandy.

He handed her the glass. "Drink this. It'll help." He sat beside her.

She took a baby sip at first. Then she knocked the rest back like a seasoned drinker. "Thank you," she whispered.

He noticed she didn't apologize for crying, which she didn't need to. "I'm here whenever you're ready to talk."

She nodded and leaned against him. "I don't know if you want to hear this."

"I told you that nothing you can say will change how I feel about you. Not now. Not ever." He meant that with all his heart. He just hoped he was man enough to handle it.

She took a deep breath. "Well, when I had the miscarriage, it was Seth's fault. Once I found out I was pregnant, I wanted to make a clean break from him and start over, but he wasn't having it. He pushed me down, and I hit my head on the coffee table. When I opened my eyes again, I was in the hospital and had lost the baby."

Drake tempered his anger. Mikerra needed a comforting shoulder, not someone in a rage, he reminded himself. "Did he take you to the hospital?"

She shook her head. "No, my neighbor heard the noise and found me. She called the paramedics and probably saved my life. That was the turning point. I knew I would have to leave New York if I ever hoped to get my life back."

"Mikerra, that doesn't matter to me. All that matters is that we're together." Drake was thankful for all the intense training he had received in the military. It would take everything he had not to let his emotions show on his face.

"You don't have to pretend for me, Drake. I know every man wants a son."

"I want you."

She studied him carefully, as if deciding whether or not she could believe his words. "Drake, I know you think you want me."

There was only one way to remove any doubt from Mikerra's stubborn mind. He kissed her with all the pent-up frustration of a man with a mission on his mind. He had to remove any doubt in her brain.

At first she was hesitant and tried to pull away. But when he slipped his tongue inside her mouth, he knew he had her. As the kiss deepened, she held him closer, wrapping her arms around him.

She abruptly ended the kiss and stood. "You tricked me," she accused. "Now it's my turn." She held out her hand.

His eyes met hers, and she was smiling. "I just wanted to show you that it doesn't matter." He took her hand and rose. "Would it matter if I told you that

David told me that after surgery I might not be able to father a child? Would you leave me?"

He had shocked her. "No, I wouldn't. I'd stay with you no matter what you could or couldn't do." She looked him over and asked, "Is it true?"

"Does it matter?"

"No."

Drake hugged her tightly. He couldn't hide his erection, and he didn't try. He heard her giggle as she disentangled herself from him. "We're not having sex tonight. So I hope that is going away soon."

He knew that night was going to test him like no military strategy ever had. "I got this, baby."

She led him upstairs. "You just make sure you keep it."

Later, as Mikerra lay next to Drake in her darkened bedroom, his earlier words rang in her head. Had he said that bit about not being able to father a child to comfort her in her sorrow? She listened to him breathe slow and steady, well on his way to slumber land. She nudged him awake.

"Drake?" She turned on the bedside lamp and faced him.

"Yes?" He didn't open his eyes. "You know we can't," he mumbled.

"I thought you said tonight wasn't about sex?" she teased him. She kissed his closed eyelids.

"You know you shouldn't tease a man like that. That's just wrong," he said, finally opening his eyes. "You know David only said we should try to refrain from having sex. He said nothing about foreplay." His large hands went to the waistband of her shorts.

She stopped his hands. "Oh, no, you don't. I want

to know if you were telling the truth earlier. Did David really mention infertility?"

He sighed. "What does that have to do with the price of condoms?"

She laughed. Most people would have finished the clichéd saying with the words *the price of eggs*. Not her Drake. He went right to the heart of the matter. "You know, for someone who can't have sex, you seem to be preoccupied with it."

He pulled her closer to him. "Hey, every time I'm close to you, I start thinking about sex. I can't help it. You make me crazy."

"You didn't answer my question," she reminded him. She felt him move his leg between hers. The feeling of his very rigid erection was unmistakable. She tried to move away, but it was useless. He had all but trapped her body under his.

"That's because the question didn't deserve an answer." He kissed her long and hard. "Now, why don't you turn off the light, so we can pretend to get some sleep?"

"But, Drake," she pleaded.

"Woman, there's nothing to discuss. The matter has been settled. Most likely, we won't be conceiving. Do I have to kiss you into submission, or what?"

Mikerra wanted to see how far he'd go. "I'll take the 'or what' option."

Drake moved on top of her and kissed her. "Remember, you asked for this." His large hands moved under her nightshirt and caressed her breasts.

Mikerra gasped as he gently squeezed her breasts. The sensation was addictive, and she wanted so much more. Her nightshirt was soon sailing across the room, but she didn't care. She wanted to feel more of him. She grabbed at his shirt. Drake groaned and tore the shirt from his muscular body. Her hands glided over his well-developed chest.

Drake resumed his kissing, and then he abruptly stopped. "Did you hear something downstairs?" he whispered in her ear. "I thought it might be Terror, but it sounds like it's a two-legged creature."

Mikerra thought she'd heard a noise earlier but wasn't sure. "But who could it be? You think it's the hitter?" She looked around for her nightshirt. It was lying in a heap in the corner of the room. She slipped out of the bed and pulled the nightshirt over her head.

Drake was doing the same. "Could be." He motioned for her to be quiet. He formed his thumb and forefinger into a gun, asking her if she had one.

She nodded, opened her nightstand drawer, and took out the nine-millimeter gun and handed it to him. He waved her back as he made his way to the door. He opened the door when he heard Terror growl at what he presumed was an intruder.

Mikerra decided enough was enough. She stood behind Drake.

"Go to the bathroom," he demanded.

"No," she countered. "We're in this together. Besides, it's my gun."

"I don't have time to argue with you," he said in a hushed voice. "Follow me."

Mikerra heard the clipped tone in his voice and knew Drake was pissed, but there wasn't time to go into it. He grabbed her with his free hand, making sure she was behind him, and they descended the stairs.

Before they made it halfway down the stairs, they heard the front door open, and two men ran out. Drake ran to the door in hopes of catching them, and Mikerra hurried after him. She didn't want him to get hurt for her. Luckily, the men were halfway down the block when Drake lost them.

He was doubled over and wheezing by the time Mikerra caught up with him. "Damn. If I was in shape, I would have caught those bastards and snapped their necks."

Mikerra didn't doubt it for one second. She'd forgotten that quickly that Drake was Special Forces and had had special training. He could very well have killed those men without a second thought. If she could have found her voice, she probably would have screamed.

"Are you okay?" Drake asked when he finally caught his breath.

Mikerra nodded, reaching for him.

They hugged in the middle of the street. Drake led her back to the house. Mikerra looked around the living room, but nothing was out of place. "I wonder what they wanted," she said, walking into her home office.

"I think you just found your answer, Care Bear." Drake picked up the piece of paper lying on the floor. It was a printout of her life, or what Seth knew about it, and featured a recent photograph. "Your cover has definitely been blown, baby. I think we need to get out of here now."

She knew it, too. They sprang into action. Mikerra went to pack a small bag, and soon they were on their way to Drake's to do the same. After they dropped Terror at her parents' house, they headed to the cabin at the lake.

Mikerra unlocked the door to the cabin and threw down her bag. She looked around the two-room place with pride. She and Kissa had cleaned that place within an inch of their lives.

"It seems homey," Drake commented, dropping the other bags on the floor.

"My parents don't use it much. Dad says it has too many memories for him. But Mom comes out here every now and then. I used to love to come out here when I was a teenager." She felt she had to keep some kind of chatter going or she'd go nuts.

"Mikerra," he crooned. "Stop."

"What?"

He walked over to her and placed those large hands on her shoulders. "Stop this. You don't have to fill every silent moment with conversation. You're scared out of your mind. Me too. But you've got to get a hold of yourself. We can't afford to be distracted, and you flipping out would be a distraction."

She laughed nervously. "Okay. I promise not to flip out until this mess is over."

Drake walked around the large room. "That's all I can ask for."

Mikerra watched him, shaking her head. Being in an isolated cabin with the man of her dreams was the stuff romance novels were made of. But being in a cabin with the man she loved and with not so much as a condom between them was an accident waiting to happen. Good thing neither of them had anything to worry about in that department.

Chapter 24

Thursday

Seth paced the excuse of a hotel room. Two double beds barely fit into the dimly lit room, reminding him of a bad spy movie. Being in this state of mind was about to push him over the edge. Too many things were happening at one time.

It was bad enough they'd had to land near Austin the night before. But they'd also had to explain to the dim-witted, too-young representative of the FAA why the wrong flight plans had been filed. The flight was supposed to terminate in Wright City, but the pilot had penciled in Washington City, which was located fifty miles outside of Austin and had a small airport.

When the entire mess was finally sorted out and Seth discovered they were at least an hour from their destination, the pilot decided he needed some rest and wasn't flying any farther. So they were stuck in Washington City's version of a Holiday Inn.

General MacArthur sat on one of the double beds in the small room, looking at him curiously. "Seth, since we're stuck here, anyway, might as well make the best of it and finish reading the report. You might learn something." He handed the folder to him.

"What is it, Horace? You got some news on Karen?" He opened the folder.

MacArthur's annoying cell phone alerted them that a call was coming through. "Mac," he said. He listened to the caller with all the attention of planning a military strategy. "Did you get her or the soldier?"

Did MacArthur's goons screw up and kill Karen by mistake? "They can't kill her," Seth said.

MacArthur held up a large hand to Seth, silencing him. "What do you mean they got away? You had the upper hand, you idiot. Go back there and finish the job."

Seth shook his head. Another sign that doom was just around the corner, and there wasn't a thing they could do about it.

"All right. Calm down. We'll rent a car and be there as quick as we can. Keep me updated." He snapped the phone shut.

Seth stopped pacing long enough to see the worry on MacArthur's pale face. "Something wrong?"

"Yeah, something is wrong. No one in town knows Karen Mills. They do know a Carolina Stone, who has a daughter who was a journalist and just returned to Wright City. Her name is Mikerra. Karen is her pen name. That's why you had such a hard time finding her."

Seth closed his eyes against all the fury he felt. He felt betrayed. Karen, Mikerra, or whatever her name was, had betrayed him and played him like an all-day sucker. He'd given her the world, and she'd repaid him by lying to him all those years.

* * *

Sloan woke to the ringing phone on his bedside table. His eyes focused on the caller ID display. It was the phone Quinn had left out at the cabin, which meant only one thing. Trouble with a capital T.

He reached for the phone. "What's wrong?"

"Oh, Sloan," Mikerra said in a strangled sob. "They broke into my house late last night, so Drake and I came out here early this morning."

Well, he was up now. "How did you get out there? Did you erase the car tracks? Do you have your gun?"

"Slow down," she whispered. "Drake is still asleep. I took my SUV, and before you get all crazy, I didn't have an option. I'm on my way to erase my car tracks now. And with all the craziness, I didn't bring the gun."

Sloan was up and pacing the room. "Okay, Mikerra, listen to me. Don't you leave that cabin for anything! You don't have any protection. Jesus Christ, what were you thinking! I'm going to come out there later with Kissa and Quinn, but I need to check in with the sheriff first."

"How am I supposed to make Drake stay inside the cabin all day?"

"You're a woman. Better yet, you're his woman. Do what you have to. Even if that means making love, do it. Move around the cabin as little as possible."

"Yes, sir!"

He knew he sounded like an ass, but he had no other option. "I'm sorry, honey, but this has just escalated to super serious. Be in touch." He ended the call.

He was reaching for a pair of shorts when he noticed he had a missed call on his cell phone. Closer inspection told him it was a text message. He read the short note and muttered a curse. "Now what?"

He reached for the cordless phone and dialed Quinn's number. "Hey, man, it's go time."

"Damn, I had hoped we'd have more time."

"No, man. Meet me at the entrance to the lake in about an hour."

"Got it. I'll get Kissa."

Sloan felt the adrenaline waking his slender body. He didn't like violence and tried to avoid it at any cost, but these were two of his best friends, and he had to help. Even if it meant his life would hang in the balance.

He slipped on the pair of shorts, a T-shirt, and tennis shoes. He grabbed his backpack for just this occasion. He opened his bedroom door and walked to the kitchen. His mother greeted him as he left.

"You be careful, Sloan."

How did she know? "Mom?"

"Yes, I know about the trouble that's coming. I'm your mother, and I know you just don't come home in the middle of the week all the way from Washington unless it's really important. I'm fine. Your father is fine. I know about the stranger that's been watching Mikerra's house. It's all over town."

He looked at his mother, not wanting to tell her how serious it was, but he didn't want her to have false expectations, either. "Mom, you're right. This is big, and I feel like it's my fault it got this far. If anyone calls looking for me, you don't know where I am or that I'm in town." He hugged his mother and kissed her on the cheek. "I love you."

His mother hugged him once more and nodded. "Go do what you have to, son."

Sloan smiled. "I'll be careful. Promise." He walked out of the house without another word.

* * *

Carter woke up early in the quaint hotel room. *Quaint* was a nice word for the cramped but clean room. He hadn't expected to sleep so soundly in the very frilly room, decorated with flowers and lace all over the place. When was the last time he'd had a good night's rest? He was glad Sloan had convinced him to fly to this little Podunk town. Initially he'd had another reason for calling Sloan. He wanted Mikerra, and now that he was once again single, he was going to stake his claim. Although he didn't have a car and had to walk everywhere, he was still glad he'd come. He wanted to help Mikerra.

After he showered and dressed, he headed for the town's only diner, a few blocks from the hotel. The hotel's receptionist swore by the place, so he just had to check it out. Born and raised in D.C., Carter hadn't known the feel of a small town, and now he envied Sloan for being from this place. As he walked the four blocks to the restaurant, he met people on the street, and they greeted him as if they had known him for years.

He made it to the storefront diner and entered. The atmosphere of the diner was like a beacon in a storm. It was large as diners went, but it still felt cozy. He watched the tall, slender African American woman take orders and move around the room with fluid grace and precision. The place just felt right. Then he recognized the feeling. He was home.

"Are you going to stand there staring into space, with that silly look on your face, or do you want a table?" the slender woman asked him. "You're blocking paying customers from coming in, so you're going to need to make a decision."

Carter laughed as his dream of a docile Southern woman flew out the window. This woman wasn't docile. She had attitude and plenty of it. "No, ma'am. I'd like a table. For one," he added, for no reason.

"I'm not a ma'am. I'm Jay." She looked him up and down. "Visitin' these parts? You sound like a Yankee." She motioned for him to follow her.

They arrived at a table tucked in a corner of the room, where he could people watch if he wanted. But he didn't. He wanted to watch Jay. Her skin was a few shades darker than his pecan brown skin. Some would have called her skin tone chocolate with a shot of fudge mixed in. She was as thin as a rail and had the build of a runner. Her long black hair was pulled back in a ponytail. If he were a guessing man, he'd put her age near his. Or at least a man could hope.

"You decide what you're eating? Or you just imagining what you're going to eat?"

While Jay wasn't what Carter considered docile, he decided at that moment, she was definite what he wanted. "Does this place have specials?" He figured two could play this game of verbal sparring.

She smiled at his attempt at verbal foreplay. "We sho' does, sir. Even in Texas we have specials, sir." She curtsied and took out her notepad. "Today, in honor of a Yankee in our midst, we are serving bagels, cream cheese, and lox. For the rest of the crowd, the special is grits, eggs, and bacon for three bucks, and that includes a bottomless cup of gourmet coffee."

Carter laughed. "I do beg your pardon, Jay. I will take the Southern special, if that's not breaking the rules."

Jay smiled at him. "I like a man who has a backbone. Your order will be a few minutes. Why don't you read a copy of the *Wright City Record*—that's the local paper—while your order is being prepared?"

"Thank you, Jay."

"The paper is free. If you decide to take it with you, it's okay." She turned and walked to another table.

Carter glanced around the crowded diner. From the looks of the place, the diner obviously did well. Jay and two other waitresses worked the room well and efficiently.

"Coffee, sir?"

"Sure, kid." Carter watched the young man pour the coffee and hurry to another table.

Carter enjoyed his coffee as he waited for his first Southern meal.

Drake forced his eyes open. The previous night had seen one crazy event after another, culminating with his and Mikerra's arrival at the cabin in the middle of the night, like wanted outlaws. He had trouble focusing his eyes. He concentrated on the ceiling fan whirling around soundlessly, hoping it would soon bring everything into focus.

He grabbed the sheet for balance as the room started spinning counterclockwise. He had to do something. Wimping out and calling for Mikerra was not an option. Over twenty years in the United States armed forces would not allow it. He slammed his eyes shut and took a deep breath. His heart thudded against his chest in anticipation. He took another deep breath and forced himself to calm down. Mikerra needed him now. He couldn't fail her. He opened his eyes slowly, and the room was still out of focus, but not as bad as before. The ceiling fan tilted, and everything became clear.

"Hey, would you like breakfast?" Mikerra stood in the doorway, watching him carefully.

He shook his head, wondering how long she'd been there. "Not hungry."

Mikerra was at his side in an instant, sitting next to him on the bed. "What's wrong, baby?" She caressed his face gently.

Drake didn't want to sound as pathetic as he felt, but the concern in her voice unnerved him, making him feel like less of a man. "Nothing is wrong." He pushed her hand away.

She took a deep breath, reining in her temper. "Drake, now is not the time to play super soldier. If you're hurting, you have to let me know." She put the back of her hand against his face, checking his temperature, and the stern look on her face dared him to challenge her. "You feel a little warm."

He didn't like her treating him like he was a child. Moving her hand, he said, "I feel fine. I just moved too fast this morning. Everything is okay."

"Drake, don't get all pissy with me. I know how much this is costing you. I wasn't implying you didn't know how to take care of yourself. Why can't you let me help you?"

"Why can't you say you love me? You said it once when you needed my okay on the story. Why can't you say it again? Or is once your limit?"

Mikerra didn't know the answer to that question. She knew she did love him, but for some strange reason, she couldn't give those words a voice. Too much had happened when she had said those words in the past. Seth had used those very words against her when she first discovered Project Perfect.

"You wouldn't release that story if you loved me. You wouldn't write that column about the unnecessary deaths in the war on terror if you loved me," he had said on more than one occasion.

Mikerra had vowed that if she ever got out of that predicament, she'd never get in it again. No matter if it cost her the one man she loved with all her heart.

"Mikerra, I asked you a question." Drake stared back at her with dark eyes that didn't look quite there.

Angering him wouldn't help either of them and would only make their time in the cabin unbearable. "I know you asked me a question, Drake, and I don't have an answer for you. I'm being brutally honest here. I do care for you and only want the best for you."

"But?"

"I don't know if I'm what's best for you. I have a massive cloud hanging over my head. Seth wants to kill me. I knew about the serum before and didn't do anything about it. This time I have to finish what I started. I have to write that story."

"Why don't you let me decide what's best for me? I think you're it. I can wait for you to be more sure of your feelings. I don't care if you have to go before a Senate committee. I'd still want you in my life. I'll stand behind you whatever you do. You made me realize the military was killing me, and although it was tough to swallow, I'm glad you stayed on my case."

"Thank you, Drake. You're right. As long as you want me, I'm right here. Have you taken your meds?"

He shook his head. "Not yet. I will soon."

Mikerra rose and walked to the door. "Breakfast will be ready in about twenty minutes. I talked to Sloan, and he wants us to stay inside. He's coming out with Quinn and Kissa later." She thought Drake would flip his military lid over Sloan giving orders, but as usual he surprised her.

"Yeah, we don't want the enemy to know we're

here. Although I think they know. But no use giving them more ammo against us," Drake said in an unusually calm voice.

Mikerra relaxed against the door, proud she'd avoided the biggest skirmish of them all.

Kissa reached for her ringing bedside phone. A licensed chiropractor, she was seldom called out on an emergency. It was barely daybreak, and someone had dared dial her phone number. "Hello," she said, clearing her throat.

"Baby," Marc Phillips cooed. "How are you doing?"

Of all the days for her no-account ex-husband to call, she mused. "Hello, Marc."

"I don't even get a good morning?"

He wanted something, she knew. She hadn't been married to him for ten years not to know his tactics of manipulation. He tried to butter her up by buying her expensive pieces of jewelry, furs, trips, and just about anything else he could think of. In the spirit of girl power, she'd take the gifts, but each time Marc brought up the subject of reconciling, she always told him no. "What is it, Marc?"

"Markissa, we were husband and wife," he reminded her. "I think you owe me something."

"Like you owed me when I caught you in bed with the twins?"

"I knew you'd bring them up."

"They were in *my* bed with you, I might add."

Marc sighed. "Let it go, baby. Let it go. Okay, I messed up. Can't you forgive me and let us move on from that?"

She thought about the many nights she'd cried herself to sleep, thinking she'd failed her husband by forcing him into the arms of other women, but in reality it was her too good-looking husband who had failed her. "No, I can't. We're divorced, remember?"

"Yeah, about that."

She swore under her breath. "What is it?"

"Some goober from the Joint Chiefs of Staff called me, looking for you."

"What did you tell them?"

"You're not even going to deny you've done something wrong?"

"Marc, what are you talking about?"

"I'm talking about trying to illegally obtain government documents. Just because you're a chiropractor doesn't give you the right to harass government officials, baby."

"I'm not your baby, and I haven't broken the law. They have. What did you tell them?"

"That I'm no longer responsible for you. And I gave them your address in that excuse of a town you live in. I can't have my name linked to a scandal."

"You are a scandal." Kissa ended the call, then called Quinn and described her previous conversation.

"I'm on my way to get you," Quinn said in a rush. "Somebody broke into Mikerra's house last night. She and Drake went to the cabin. I'm sorry your ex called."

"Thanks, Quinn."

"I wouldn't let anything happen to you, Kissa. Mikerra would have my hide if I did."

"I feel the same way about her. I'm glad she and Drake are picking up the pieces and are in love. It's kind of funny seeing her so happy. It gives me hope that there's somebody out there for me."

Quinn chuckled. "Maybe he's closer than you think. Bye."

Kissa gasped as Quinn's last statement filtered through her slow-moving brain. Was he actually stating what she had felt in her heart already? *Talk about bad timing*, she thought, struggling into blue jeans and a T-shirt. The last thing she needed was to fall head over heels for Quinn Stone.

Chapter 25

"Repeat that again," Seth demanded as they drove to Wright City. "I just know you didn't just tell me that woman was living in Manhattan all this time under a damn alias." If he wasn't driving the blasted rental car, he'd slam his fist into the dashboard.

General MacArthur cleared his throat and quoted from his previous cell phone conversation. "I just confirmed Mikerra Candace Stone is Karen Mills. Didn't you ever look at her ID? Check her out? Anything? I mean, you were sleeping with her for over five years."

"Yeah, I checked her out, and her name is Karen Mills. The condo she had was under Karen Mills. The bank account I slipped money into every month for the last three years was under Karen Mills. Everything in her apartment said Karen Mills. Even when I had a check run on her, Karen Mills came up. Shouldn't there have been some kind of red flag saying she was using an alias?"

MacArthur nodded. "It means she had help from within the government structure. Only someone with a very high security clearance, one rivaling that of the president, could make all this happen without any flags going up."

Seth realized that. Now. "That's probably why she was so evasive about her past. She never wanted to talk about her parents, siblings, or even this godforsaken town we're headed to. I could wring her neck for that alone." And for getting pregnant, which was her fault, too, he thought.

Horace looked sideways at him. "Listen to you. You sound like a man who's pissed because the woman he loves has left him. This isn't about you getting revenge. This is about the information about the serum getting out. We've already killed five people trying to keep this secret from the press. If there are many more deaths, there'll be questions, and fingers are going to start pointing. I don't want any of those fingers pointed at me."

"You think I'm going to crack under the pressure. I want her dead, and you need the sergeant out of the picture. Ging is there, making sure they don't leave that excuse of a town. So what's the problem? Don't forget I have a thirty-year marriage at stake if any of this gets out. Celeste could take me to the cleaners if she even thought I was having an affair. Not to mention the end of my career."

MacArthur held up a large hand to stop his rampage. "We both have a lot at stake and don't want any more publicity about this, due to your carelessness."

Seth took a deep breath and forced himself to calm down. "All right." He took another deep breath. Arguing with the general was getting him nowhere fast. "Who do you think helped her?"

"I don't know."

Seth pondered how she could have kept her true identity a secret from him. He'd listened to her babble on and on about how she wanted to write novels, not edit magazine articles, but not one word on Mikerra Stone. "Maybe it was someone in the Justice Department or someone who has a CIA clearance. They could have altered her identity, and it wouldn't have caused a red flag."

MacArthur nodded. "Possibly. But it's really a moot point now. The fact is that she did have help, and whoever it was that helped her alter her identity also helped her get out of New York without so much as a valid forwarding address. The forwarding address we have for her ends in Chicago."

Seth thought it was pretty important to him. Mikerra had betrayed him to the highest degree, and she would have to pay the ultimate price. But he would have to finish this business on his own. And then he'd take care of MacArthur.

Mikerra was beginning to get nervous. Drake had been in the bedroom for over an hour and hadn't come out for breakfast. Did he fall back to sleep? Did he pass out?

Calm down, she thought. He was probably just tired from all the events leading up to this forced seclusion, she reminded herself. With a more relaxed demeanor, she sat at the breakfast table and drank a cup of coffee while she waited.

She took in the scenery out the window of the cabin. It was beautiful. If she and Drake weren't hiding from hired killers, the government, and who knew who else, this cabin could be a romantic love nest. But when did gunplay have anything to do with romance?

"Hey, you look deep in thought," Drake said, sitting down in the chair opposite her at the table.

Mikerra blinked. She hadn't heard him walk into the main room. "I was just thinking," she replied.

"About what?"

Mikerra sighed. She didn't want to admit he'd been on her mind. "Nothing really. Thinking about how much trouble I am in and how I can possibly fix it." She glanced at him. "Breakfast is ready. I can fix a plate for you."

He shook his head. "No, I can fix my own, thank you."

She could tell by the clipped tone in his voice, she'd offended him again. With him being so defensive about his thought processes and just about anything she said, Mikerra wondered how would they survive the next couple of days without having a serious argument.

He rose, walked to the stove, grabbed a plate, and began piling food on it. He sat down without another word. She watched him shovel food in his mouth. He had effectively put up a barrier between them that she wouldn't be breaching anytime soon.

Thankfully, the walkie-talkie cell phone chirped to life. Mikerra made her escape into the next room and closed the door. She knew it was Sloan. "Hey, I'm so glad you called."

"What are you guys fighting about?"

"How did you know?"

"Mikerra, you know you guys are made for each other. I know he's defensive right now, and you're probably trying to overcompensate for what you view as brain damage," Sloan said in his practical voice.

"Okay, maybe I'm being too protective of him. I just don't want him to get hurt."

"He's a grown man," Sloan reminded her. "He can

think for himself. I'm surprised you're not cutting his meat for him."

Mikerra was silent. She'd come very near, cutting the eggs into bite-size pieces. Did she view Drake as an invalid?

"Damn, girl. He has brain cancer, but it's in the beginning stages, so he's functioning normally. Yeah, some things may confuse or baffle him, but he can still think and has his motor skills. Why are you trying to take away his man card?"

"I'm not, Sloan. Really I'm not. I'm just trying to help."

"Well, you're not helping. You're hurting. Treat him like normal. I called to tell you that I'm waiting on your brother, but as usual he's late."

Mikerra let out a choked laugh that soon turned into a sob. She held back the rest of her cry, vowing not to fall apart during this crisis. "Call Quinn and remind him."

"No need. He just drove up. See you in a bit."

Mikerra put the walkie-talkie phone back on its base and sat on the bed, wishing the whole mess would just go away and knowing that it wouldn't. "Now, Mikerra," she told herself, "you're just going to have to deal with Drake. This is for your story."

With that, she rose, with her head held high, and went back to the main room and faced Drake.

He had finished eating and was now on the couch, watching the portable DVD player that her parents had left on one of their visits. She took a seat next to him.

"Drake," she began in her most gentle voice. "If we're going to be here together, we're both going to have to relax."

"I'm relaxed," he said in a tight voice. "I have no

problem adapting to my environment. I'm an airborne ranger. That's what I do."

"Don't use that military tone with me, Drake. I mean that with us being in such close quarters, we're bound to get on each other's nerves. I just don't want you taking the high road all the time. I'm just trying to help."

He turned to her. "If you want to help me, tell me you love me."

"You know I can't."

"Can't or won't?" He grabbed her hand and caressed it gently. "I need for you to tell me something. I thought I could live without you saying that you love me, but I can't. I'm a man, Mikerra. I need to hear those words, just like any other person on this earth."

Mikerra opened her mouth to say something, anything, to get that hurt look off his face. But any words she might have said would only make matters worse. If she said she loved him, she'd be giving in to the moment. She didn't want a repeat of Seth. She wanted Drake to love her unconditionally. She knew she loved him, but she just couldn't give it a voice.

Her mother had always told her that love cost something. And she had to be prepared to give that something up. Was she ready to give up anything for love? Could she actually drag Drake farther into the maze that had become her life?

Drake hadn't expected an answer from Mikerra. He'd hoped he could bully her into an answer, but each time he pushed her, he got only that vacant stare in her eyes. A definite nonanswer.

"Okay, Mikerra, don't answer me." He rose and headed for the door. "I need some air."

"Sloan said not to go outside."

At that moment he didn't give a damn about Sloan, or the people who were out to get them, but he did care about her. So he retreated. "Fine." He heard the distinct sound of tires on the gravel road leading to the cabin. "Get away from the window. I hear a vehicle."

"You know I can take care of myself."

"Really?" He didn't want to fight with her, but a little misdirection of anger never hurt. If she was angry at him, maybe she'd finally let her guard down. It was a big gamble, but what else could he do? He was a man, so he pushed. "I said stay away from the window. Either close the curtains and hide behind the couch, or I'm going to make the choice for you."

She was shocked, yes. Too shocked to do anything but close the curtains and hide behind the couch. Drake smiled in satisfaction. Then he noticed it was Sloan and Quinn. Closer inspection revealed that Kissa was also riding with Quinn. "It's just Sloan, Quinn, and Kissa."

Mikerra rose from her hiding place. "Good," she said, walking to the door.

"Don't you dare open that door!" Drake commanded, with a little too much force in his voice. "You don't know if the shooter is in place and is just waiting for you to open the door and kill you. You're going to put everyone's life at stake by not thinking."

She gasped, realizing he was right. "Oh God, you're right. Ging will just have a field day with me acting like an idiot." She moved away from the door.

Drake had her just where he wanted her. Why didn't he feel a sense of victory? Mikerra was looking to him for answers. But he wanted the old Mikerra back. The Mikerra that fought all her own battles and dared anyone to help.

"Drake, how will they get into the house?"

"You'll see." He walked to the back of the cabin. "The front door is too obvious, and the back door is the next obvious place. They're coming through the side window."

"What?"

"It's called a soft entry," Drake told her. "It's an entry with no weapons drawn and through an alternate entrance."

Mikerra looked up at him. "Oh." Soon Quinn, Sloan, and Kissa entered the cabin.

Drake was happy to see them. Maybe Sloan had good news. He could use some. He shook Sloan's hand. "Man, I hope you have something good to tell me."

Sloan shook his head, sliding the backpack from his thin shoulders. "I wish I did, but I do have something you can use." He took out a folder and handed the contents to Drake. "This is what they've been giving you for the last twelve months. Mikerra was right. You are part of a test on one hundred to two hundred men. I'm not sure of the true number because there are two sets of papers going around Washington, in select circles, mind you."

"Yeah, after the initial shock wore off, I realized she knew what she was talking about." Drake glanced in Mikerra's direction. She was staring directly at him. She mouthed her silent apologies to him.

Sloan continued his bad news. "That's just the tip of the iceberg. Now that we all know what's going on, we're all in danger. But you two are in it up to your eyeballs. Since you've been sick, you are now a liability they can't have. It was okay when you were seeing the military doctors, but now that both Senator McCaffrey and General MacArthur know you've been to a regular doctor, you pose a threat."

Drake didn't like the sound of anything he was hearing. Again Mikerra was right. *Damn.* Why hadn't he just listened to her in the first place? "Seems like someone should have said something."

"They were under strict orders. You're in Special Forces and in the battle unit. You've been red flagged."

Drake knew what his friend wasn't telling him. The military was slowly becoming like the Mafia. Once you were in, you were in for life. An order took precedence over any moral choices one might have. How many times had he taken a life in the name of the job? He'd done things for the military he'd not been necessarily proud of, but he'd still done them. So the doctor lying to him about his headaches didn't seem so far-fetched.

Sloan stood directly in front of Drake. "Drake, do you understand what's going on?"

Drake nodded, feeling absolutely like the biggest fool this side of the White House. "Yeah, man, I understand. My job of over twenty years is trying to kill me. Got it."

"That's pretty much it in a nutshell. I've been checking into Josh Hughes's death, and I think Mikerra hit the nail on the head. His records were sealed tighter than the Kennedy conspiracy papers. But, luckily, I got the best hacker in the world at my fingertips." Sloan patted Quinn's back. "Quinn got the information for me. The official death cert says he slipped in a shower and hit his head on the knob on the way down, resulting in a brain hemorrhage. But the real death cert reveals a gunshot wound."

"What?" Drake sat down on the couch, not liking the way the conversation was going. "You mean, they killed Josh 'cause he was having headaches, like the ones I'm having right now?"

Sloan nodded. "Yeah, it's that nutshell thing again. I'm real sorry, Drake." He sat by Drake. "See, that serum they've been giving you is supposed to make your body stronger. The idea behind Project Perfect is to make the soldier almost indestructible. Like if you got shot, the serum should heal your body, and you could keep fighting with little or no recuperation time."

"But?" said Drake.

"Yes, there's a but," Sloan admitted. "While it's making your body stronger, it's also breaking down much-needed red blood cells and aging your body at twice the normal speed. If your headaches had gone untreated, you'd be dead within six months from the brain tumor."

"So why'd they have to kill Josh?" asked Drake.

Sloan patted Drake's knee. "The same reason they're after you. They can't have any links to the project. Josh died in the shower in a freak accident, or that's the story the military is sticking with. His mother didn't believe it, and she made some noise for about six months after his death. But no one else ever looked into it."

"We're in the middle of a war," Drake said. "Who's going to look twice at a freak accident? Those bastards are getting away with murder."

Sloan shook his head. "Not if we can beat them at their own game. That's why I need you guys to stay here. Kissa will drive Mikerra's SUV back to town, and maybe that will throw Seth and Ging off track for a little bit."

Sloan's cell phone rang. "It's probably my mom." He looked down at his display and frowned. "This is crazy." He shook his head and answered the phone. "Yes. Who? Jonelle." The rest of his conversation was lost to Drake and the others as Sloan went into the bedroom and closed the door.

Drake let the information slowly filter through his brain. Mikerra had been right the whole damn time. He shuddered thinking about what might have happened if she hadn't been so stubborn and dug her heels in about his headaches. He looked up at her. "I'm sorry, Care Bear. I should have listened to you in the first place. Part of me doesn't want to believe it, but the proof is right here." He tapped his head with his forefinger. "I'm sorry for doubting you."

Mikerra sat by him. She had tears in her eyes and wrapped her arms around him. "You called me Care Bear! You haven't called me that all morning. I thought you were still mad at me."

She felt so good in his arms. Drake knew she didn't pity him anymore. "I could never stay mad at you for long, baby. I'm mad about our situation, and I feel like less of a man 'cause I can't take care of you like I want to, but I know this is for the best."

Mikerra kissed him. "Oh, Drake, I promise to get us out of this. And when we do, I'm going to write that story."

Drake wrapped her in an embrace. He felt her fear and frustration, because it matched his. He also noticed she didn't utter one word about love.

Chapter 26

Sloan closed the door, separating him from the others. "Now, tell me this again. Why are you calling me, Jonelle? I'm not your boss," Sloan said. None of this was making sense.

"Because I know where you are and why you're there," Jonelle said.

"Okay, Jonelle. You're going to have to explain this to me again."

She sighed dramatically. "Okay, Sloan. I overheard Mr. McCaffrey discussing your flight plans a few days ago with the general. I didn't like what I was hearing, so I deterred them the best I could."

She just wasn't making any sense. Sloan knew Seth's secretary was on her own planet on occasion, and apparently today was one of those times. "Now, Jonelle, perhaps you misunderstood him. After all, Seth asked me for my itinerary earlier in the week."

"No, I did not misunderstand, Sloan. I heard the general ordering a plane. Yesterday Mr. McCaffrey told me to call with the GPS location of Wright City, and I knew that's where you were going. I gave them the coordinates for Washington City, Texas."

Sloan rubbed his head in frustration. "Jonelle, I'm a little pressed for time. Cut to the chase."

"All right. Joshua Hughes was my son."

Oh, that little statement had all his attention. "His mother's name is Margaret Hughes. I know you're not her."

"You came to my home and took my statement right after Josh's so-called accident last year. I was a hundred pounds heavier, and depression was my life."

Sloan tried to remember the events. The Joint Chiefs had been getting a little nervous about Josh's mother's threats and had sent him to Boston to interview her. But that woman was a plump, mousy brunette who couldn't seem to stop crying. Jonelle was a slender redhead and very much in control of her world, most days. Something wasn't adding up. "Okay, Jonelle, start from the beginning."

"That's better," she said in her nasally Boston accent. "Josh had complained of headaches, nausea, and severe stomach cramps each time he called home from Iraq. I thought it was like being in Mexico. You know, don't drink the water. I told him to go to the doctor. Now I wish I'd never told him to go. His death is my fault."

"No, it's not, Jonelle. You thought you were doing the right thing. You had no idea the military was killing your son. How did you come to work for Seth?"

"It was part of a plan. I knew he had something to do with it. A few months before Josh died, he became very paranoid. He said he knew they were going to kill him. I just thought it was the war getting to him, and at first I disregarded it."

Sloan was hooked. "What changed your mind?"

"When I learned of Josh's death. I know my son would have been careful. He wouldn't have slipped in a shower. Some general called me and told me that Josh's body would be on the next plane home."

"Did you order an autopsy?"

"That was the plan, but the same general called me about two days later and said there had been some kind of mix-up at Bethesda and Josh's body had been cremated. I couldn't even see my baby one last time."

Damn. That also meant there wouldn't be a body to exhume. Sloan suddenly felt sympathy for Jonelle. "What happened next?"

"Well, after my repeated attempts to get Josh's death investigated, including talking to you, I took matters into my own hands. My husband retired and we moved to D.C."

"How did you get a job with Seth?" Sloan knew those positions had waiting lists a mile long due to all the political hopefuls.

"I have a cousin," was all she said.

Sloan nodded, putting the pieces together. Jonelle had somehow got the job with Seth and had probably monitored his movements. *Revenge.* He wondered what the woman had in store for the morally corrupt senator.

"Anyway, Sloan. I called to tell you that they are on the way to Wright City. The senator was really edgy yesterday. He had me call your house several times when the general told him you took off early."

"Where's the general?"

"Out of the office until next week," Jonelle said.

Damn. It was go time, Sloan realized. "Thanks, Jonelle. I'll be in touch."

"You just get the people who killed my boy."

Those idiots had a lot to answer for. And Sloan would make sure they paid for taking Josh Hughes's life. "Already working on it." He folded his phone closed. He had some real thinking he needed to do and not enough time to do it.

A soft knock alerted him that the door was opening. Mikerra peeked her head around the door. "Hey, are you coming out, or what?"

"Sure."

She stepped farther inside the room and closed the door. "What's wrong?"

"I think I'm in over my head, Mikerra. I think we all are."

"Sloan, what are you talking about?"

"Josh Hughes."

"Drake's friend that died in Iraq?"

"Yeah, I just got some news that brought everything into focus. And you're one hundred percent correct. This is big. This is no witnesses big. So if we want to come out of this alive, we've got to stay on our toes."

She didn't make a sound. She didn't blink. She fainted. Mikerra hit the floor with a thud.

Before Sloan could reach her, Drake burst into the room, followed by Quinn and Kissa. Drake picked up Mikerra and placed her on the bed.

"What the hell happened, Sloan?" Drake gently patted Mikerra's face, bringing her back to consciousness.

"I told her more about the trouble we're in. I guess I should have sugarcoated it a little bit," Sloan admitted.

Mikerra came awake slowly. "I'm okay." She sat up against the pillows. She held Drake's hand. "Thank you, baby."

Sloan was happy to see his friend almost back to normal. "Sorry, guys, but I have more bad news." He had the attention of the room. "It's about the phone call I just got." Sloan proceeded to tell his friends exactly how much danger they were all in.

"So what's the next step?" Drake looked from Sloan to Mikerra to Kissa to Quinn and back to Mikerra. She was still lying on the bed. He wanted nothing more than to climb on the bed beside her, but that wasn't an option at the moment.

"Our next step," Sloan said, really getting into the role of leader, "is to hide our tracks to this place. Quinn gave Mikerra a walkie-talkie cell phone so you and Mikerra have a way to communicate with us. The best plan is for Quinn, Kissa, and me to have as little contact with you guys as possible. Just in case phone lines have been tapped or someone is watching us. Ging is in town, and Seth is just a few hours away, so things are really going to heat up soon. Mikerra, you have your gun?"

Mikerra shook her head but said nothing.

Drake really wished she would snap out of whatever had her brain on overload. Was she nervous that Seth was this close and might exact his revenge, or was it something even worse? "So you're suggesting we just lie in wait for Ging and Seth to make their move?" He sat down on the edge of the bed.

"I've got some government help coming, but not till this afternoon," Sloan explained. "That's why I want you guys to lie low. Maybe Ging doesn't know about this place yet. The longer he doesn't know, the better. I would like for them to be the ones killed in a hail of gunfire, not us."

Mikerra waved good-bye to her friends as they left the cabin a few hours later. The plans had been laid

out, and everything had been settled. She and Drake
would have to stay at the cabin until all this was over.
There was nothing worse than being isolated with the
only man she'd ever really wanted and not being able
to touch him. How was she going to survive the next
few days?

"Mikerra?" Drake nudged her. "We'd better get
inside." He placed his large hands on her waist and
guided her to the front door.

"Yes, we had better." She tried to move her leaden
feet.

"Need me to carry you inside?"

Mikerra forced herself to move. "No, I'm quite capable of walking on my own."

"Yeah, right." He scooped her up in his strong arms
and carried her inside the house. He placed her on
the couch and marched back and closed the door.
"Mikerra, it's okay to admit you're scared of Seth."

"I'm scared, but not about Seth," she admitted.
Might as well be honest with the man who held her
heart.

He sat beside her and wrapped her in his arms.
"Well, what's on your mind?"

She didn't want to tell him. But he deserved the
truth. "I'm not worried about Seth. I know things
look pretty bleak for both of us right now, but I know
we'll come out of this."

"I just wonder how we'll come out of this."

"Drake, you're the reason I'm preoccupied."

He dropped his arms and moved away from her.
"Why would I do that to you?"

Now she'd done it. Drake was acting defensive
again. "Drake, it's not you. It's me. I can't control my
emotions, and I need to put a lid on them, or we're
going to be in trouble."

"Oh, I get it. You want me."

Damn him for being so cocky, she thought. But he hit the nail on the head, so to speak. "I know now is not the time or the place. But you're the reason I can't concentrate on my situation. And the last thing we need is to have sex. Remember David's orders, which we've already disobeyed once."

He slid closer to her and pulled her on his lap. "Why don't you let me worry about David and his orders?" He kissed her softly.

Mikerra could feel her resolve slipping away as his tongue teased hers. She tried to pull away so she could at least remind him that they couldn't start making out. Each time she tried, Drake increased the pressure of his kiss. Finally, she had an opportunity when Dràke moved from torturing her mouth to tantalizing her neck with hot kisses.

"Drake, you have to stop," she barely got out. His hands crept under her T-shirt. He unsnapped her bra and squeezed her breasts gently. Mikerra gasped with pleasure. This man was going to be her downfall.

"Why?" He pulled her T-shirt over her head. "If this is it, Care Bear, I think we should go out in a blaze of glory. What's the use of abstaining from sex if we'll be dead before I can have surgery?"

She didn't like his question, but he did have a point. "That would be admitting defeat, wouldn't it? I think we can beat Seth at his own game. His need for revenge is too great for him to let anyone else hurt me, so I think we can get him."

He tossed her bra on the floor. "How about a little incentive, then?" He took a breast in his mouth.

As he suckled her breast, Mikerra saw the last of her resolve walk out of the room. She'd pay for this moment of weakness, she knew, but for the life of her, she didn't care. She shuddered as Drake took more of her breast in his mouth. His tongue played with an erect nipple as his free hand tormented the other breast.

She felt him shift her in his lap, then realized she was airborne. He carried her into the bedroom and placed her on the bed. He hurriedly stripped off his clothes and joined her on the bed.

She thought he would continue on the frenzied path to lovemaking, but he slowed the pace from pleasure to torture. He kissed her lips, cheeks, neck, and lingered on her breasts. Mikerra couldn't ignore the intense pleasure she felt. "Drake!"

He didn't answer her. Kissing her stomach and moving lower, inch by delicious inch, seemed more important. He moved between her thighs, kissing his way to her center. He kissed her softly before his tongue entered her body. Mikerra jumped at the invasion as his experienced mouth worked magic on her body. She let go of all the tension, frustration, and anxiety that gripped her. She let go with a scream so loud that if Ging was anywhere in a five-mile radius of the remote cabin, he would have heard her.

"Just relax. I'm not done yet," Drake said against her moist folds.

"I am relaxed." She moved her legs farther apart and reached for a pillow to cover her mouth, smothering her screams of pleasure. She had a feeling the next orgasm was not going to be pretty.

He placed his hands on either side of her hips. "We'll just have to see about that." He continued worshipping the most womanly part of her body.

Time blurred for Mikerra. She remembered only bits and pieces of the event. She remembered covering her face so her screams of delight couldn't be heard, but Drake wasn't having that.

"Oh, no, baby. I want to hear every ear-piercing yell." He removed the pillow from her face and continued feasting on her.

Mikerra granted Drake's wish.

Chapter 27

Mikerra's eyes sprang open later that afternoon. What had she done? She felt Drake's large, naked body shift closer to hers in bed and knew exactly what she had done. She'd had sex with him. Knowing that it was against doctor's orders hadn't stopped either of them. Nothing could have stopped the passion in that room.

Drake had been fantastic. She couldn't deny it for a second. Even if her body wasn't exhausted, she'd still know Drake had rocked her world. Her heart told her so.

Now they were in a pickle. She and Drake had made love against David's wishes, and now Drake might pay the ultimate cost. How was she supposed to live with that? What if he died before he had the opportunity to have surgery because they had given in to passion and had had sex? She had to think this through. She threw back the sheet and sat up.

Drake's hand shot out and wrapped around her waist. "Where do you think you're going?" He pulled her back in bed, against him. "You're not going anywhere. Not that you have any options, anyway."

"Drake, I probably just killed you." She couldn't hold back the tears.

He kissed her forehead. "Care Bear, I'm a grown man with over twenty years' service in the United States Army. I make my own decisions. I wanted to make love with you, so I did. I jump out of planes, Mikerra. One thing I do know is that life is temporary. I don't want to live one more day without you. Not being able to touch you these last few days has been pure insanity for me. I can't and won't live like that. So don't think *you* seduced me into making love. It was a mutual decision. We both wanted it."

She couldn't deny it. He was right. "Okay, Drake, but what happens when this is all over and you have your surgery and you're too weak from us having sex to heal properly?"

He pulled her closer. He bit her playfully on the ear, sending all kinds of shivers down her body. Was there any part of her body immune to Drake?

"Baby, you're good, but you're not that good." He pulled her on top of him. "I feel just fine, and even if I didn't, that's not your worry."

"Yes, it is. I'm supposed to keep you alive, not kill you with sex."

He entered her while she was ranting and raving. She gasped, moving against him instinctively. Forgetting her little tirade, Mikerra leaned down and kissed him like she was starving and Drake's lips were her last chance at food.

When she finally pulled away, they were both panting for air. Drake smiled up at her. "Now, what were you saying about me being too tired or too feeble to rock your world?"

She knew she had a goofy look on her face. She was deliriously happy. Now would have been the perfect

time for her to voice her true feelings for him. Fortu-
nately, Drake took that moment to pay homage to her
breasts, and any thought process Mikerra would have
been capable of was totally shot to hell.

The next time Mikerra woke, Drake was sound
asleep beside her. Sound asleep as in snoring very
loudly. His arms were around her, and his head was
nuzzled against her ear. It should have been painful,
but Mikerra felt safe and secure for the first time in a
long time. Nothing could touch her as long as she was
in Drake's strong arms.

Friday morning Drake was having the most wonderful dream. Probably more of a fantasy, he realized. He
was flying. Or he was floating. Whatever he was doing,
he liked it and hoped it never ended. It actually felt
like he was engulfed in the hottest wet dream ever.

He forced his eyes open and found he was exactly
right. Except for the small fact that Mikerra was making
his dream a reality. She tasted him eagerly, taking as
much of him in her mouth as she could. Drake stared
at the ceiling as Mikerra took him to the moon.

"Oh, baby," Drake moaned. He reached for her,
but she waved him away. Drake knew if she didn't stop
soon, he'd explode before he could get started.

"No, this is for you," Mikerra said. She continued
her task, working her magic and driving him wild.

Drake rolled his head from side to side, enjoying
the morning's activities. He reached for her again,
not to make her stop but to increase the pressure, but
she waved him away again. "I wanted to surprise you."

"You did," he breathed, giving up control to the
woman he loved. "You did." He took a deep breath,
raised his hips off the bed, and exploded.

Mikerra sat up next to him. "Good morning, baby."

Drake's chest heaved up and down until his breathing became regular. "Yes, it is." He wrapped his arms around her waist. "Yes, it is. A very good morning, baby. I love you."

He didn't expect her to return his sentiments, but it would have been nice. Mikerra stared back at him with tears in her eyes. The words were there, but she was going to need help getting them out.

Seth stomped inside Wright City Memorial Airport, wanting to kill someone, anyone. He wasn't particular at that moment about whom. If MacArthur whined about one more thing, he would be first. All Seth wanted to do was find Karen/Mikerra and kill her.

He approached the makeshift information center, which consisted of a cheap card table that was being used as a desk, behind which sat an old woman. He guessed her age to be around sixty or seventy. How could this woman give him information? She probably couldn't remember what day it was.

Her blue eyes met his, with a smile. "New in town?" She closed her romance novel and folded her wrinkled, spotted hands one over the other. "What can I help you with?"

Seth knew charm would get him farther than waving his nine-mil at the old woman. "Yes, ma'am. I'm here to visit an old friend." He patted his jacket, pretending to look for a slip of paper with an address.

"I know just about everybody in town. What's your friend's name? Maybe I know him or his parents," she said in a kindly voice.

"Actually, it's a woman. Her name is Karen . . . I mean, Mikerra Stone."

"Oh, you mean Mike's daughter. She's a journalist in New York. We're all very proud of her. You know, when she graduated from high school, she shot out of Wright City like lightning, saying she was going to be a prizewinning journalist, and she became one. But they always come back."

"Yes, you were telling me her address," Seth lied. He didn't want the woman to wander off on some mundane subject.

"Was I? I didn't catch your name?"

She was slick, Seth mused. He could use her on his team. Nothing probably got by her. He was confident no one knew his name this far south, so he told her.

"The senator from Massachusetts? I hear you're quite the Romeo with the ladies. I don't know how your wife stands it. My husband, James, was like that. Had a wandering eye, but I soon fixed that."

Seth was quickly losing his patience. "Ma'am, do you know where I can find Mikerra Stone or not?"

"You know what I did?"

Seth was beginning to wonder if he would ever get the answer he was looking for. He sighed. She was worse than any lobbyist. "What?"

"I killed him."

Seth wondered if she was having an Alzheimer's moment or if it was just wishful thinking. "How did you do it?"

She smiled, apparently very proud of her naughty actions. "I poisoned his food. He ate dinner and left for one of his meetings and died on top of that slut, Percie Simmons."

"Remind me never to piss you off," Seth said. "Now, where does Mikerra live?"

"I don't rightly know. Heard she just bought a place on Hilman Street."

Seth, through gritted teeth, thanked the woman and decided she was most likely nuts. He looked around for a city map and became furious when he couldn't find one. He decided to chance it and hoped the old lady was only half crazy.

Chapter 28

Kissa woke the next morning in a strange room. Strange because she didn't recognize any of the furnishings and didn't know why her queen-size sleigh bed had suddenly changed into a king-size four-poster bed.

Think, girl, she thought. What happened last night? Then it all came crashing back like a bad dream. Maybe not exactly a bad dream, but it had been a dream of some sort. Quinn had invited her over for dinner. She had figured he'd just order takeout from either the pizza parlor or the Chinese restaurant, but he'd shocked her. Quinn had fixed a real meal. They'd dined on grilled steaks, baked potatoes, salad, and lots of wine.

She felt someone shift in bed next to her. A large hand drew her closer to a nude male body. A very awake body, it turned out.

"Good morning," Quinn murmured.

She'd slept with Quinn? Where had her brain escaped to? How was she going to explain this to Mikerra? Her body tensed as she realized that she was also very naked in bed with Quinn, her best friend's younger brother. Oh, she was in so much trouble.

"Kissa?" Quinn shifted his body even closer to hers. "What's wrong?"

She turned over so that she faced him. He even looked good in the morning. His light brown eyes danced in the morning light sneaking through the wooden blinds. Who would have thought Quinn's house would be so beautiful and homey on the inside? "What exactly happened last night?"

He grinned slyly. "I could say maybe a little too much liquor and not enough food. But I'd rather say it was a mutual thing. You don't remember any of it, I take it?"

She gathered the sheet closer to her body. She glanced at Quinn's very chiseled body. He was gorgeous. "I remember having dinner and you showing me around your trees out back. You're into making your own wine." She snapped her fingers and grabbed her head. "Ow! You got me drunk on homemade wine?"

"I didn't get you drunk," Quinn said shortly. "You drank of your own accord. I told you it was a little strong, but you drank, anyway. That's when you finally let go and loosened up."

"What do you mean?"

He pulled her into his arms and kissed her softly. His lips tasted like nectar, probably from the wine. "I mean, after about your third glass of wine, you finally started talking about yourself. I love my sister, and I like Drake well enough, but that was all you talked about for about an hour. When I couldn't take it anymore, I had to kiss you to shut you up."

"I did not," Kissa said. "I do not babble, Quentin Stone!"

He laughed and pulled away the sheet, revealing her naked body. "Yes, you do. Just like now. I know you're worried about Mikerra and Drake, but they're perfectly safe." He moved closer to her.

"You're having them watched?"

"Of course," he said against her throat. "You think I'm leaving my sister's safety to Sloan? You smell good." He nuzzled her neck and gently bit her ear.

How could he multitask at a time like this? Kissa couldn't think of anything but the sensations Quinn was creating in her body. She needed to focus, but it was almost impossible when Quinn's hot mouth engulfed the tips of her breasts. The only thing she saw was stars.

The next time Kissa opened her eyes, the bed was missing Quinn. She struggled to sit up, but her body complained with every move she made. What had Quinn done to her?

At that moment Quinn walked in, with a wooden breakfast tray decorated with a small vase of wildflowers. He was dressed in a T-shirt and baggy cargo shorts, and had no shoes on. "I brought you breakfast, Kissa." He sat the tray on the nightstand next to the bed. "I know we have a lot to discuss, and one day soon we'll sit down and talk about what we want. But know this, Markissa Jackson Phillips, I want you and have wanted you for a long time."

She opened her mouth to speak, but Quinn solved that dilemma for her. He kissed her. She was getting lost in his tender kiss when good sense reared its ugly head. She knew Quinn was a lot of fun, but what about after the fun? "Quinn, I don't know. I mean, you're my best friend's little brother. I don't regret last night, or what I can remember of it, but this is treading on dangerous ground."

He looked at her, dismissing her prior speech. He handed her the tray. "Okay, Kissa. You think I'm some kind of novelty boy toy, but you'll find that I'm going to be around a long time."

Kissa ate a forkful of eggs. They were delicious. "Quinn, you're only thirty-five." She ate some more eggs and bacon. "This is really good."

"You're only four years older than me. You're going to have to come up with something better than that to get rid of me."

The age card had been her last hope. She didn't know what the future would hold. Who did? "Quinn, you just got out of a bad marriage."

"So did you."

Kissa sighed. This was not working out like she had hoped. "I know, Quinn."

"Why don't we table this discussion until you finish eating? I think this is important enough that we can work through any issue you could possibly have."

"I don't know about this, Quinn."

"What don't you know?"

"About this?"

"Eat." He sat on the bed and pointed to her food.

Kissa opened her mouth to protest, but Quinn gave her his serious face. "I mean it, baby. Eat."

So she did.

Seth looked into the intense blue eyes of a killer. They were standing in the deserted parking lot of a strip mall on the outskirts of Wright City. He stood before the famous Walter Ging, hoping to make sense of this fiasco.

Never in his fifty-five years would he have imagined that killing one woman would entail so many detours.

But here he was, standing in front of the biggest detour of them all. "So you think you know where Mikerra and the soldier are? Do you think you can actually do your job and kill the bastard?"

Ging looked back at him, equally pissed. "I did my part. I found her once. When I could have killed her, you told me not to. You wanted that honor. Well, I am giving you that honor. It's not my problem that you took so damn long getting here that she and her lover have gone to ground and I can't lay my hands on them."

"He's not her lover!" Seth spat at the hired killer. "I will not let you talk about her in that fashion."

Ging smiled crookedly. "Sounds like she still has you by the cajones. Man, you act like you still want her. Is that why you told me not to kill her, but to kill her lover?"

Seth's anger soared. This freaking idiot was trying to bait him on purpose. He grabbed Ging by the collar of his designer knockoff shirt. "How many times do I have to tell you, he's not her lover?"

Ging wriggled free from Seth's hold and grinned. "Well, from what I saw through my night-vision goggles, I'd say they are lovers. Anytime I see action like that, I have to say their relationship has been consummated several times over."

The words whirled around in Seth's brain a few minutes before he reacted. Before his brain could tell his heart not to react, it was too late. He gave Walter Ging a left uppercut he wouldn't soon forget.

Seth shook the pain from his hand. "When I want commentary, I'll turn on CNN. Now, I have an address on Hilman Street. I'll check it out and get back to you. Try to be ready to move when I call."

From his position on the hard pavement, Ging nodded. Blood spurted out of his mouth. "Be in touch."

The next morning, Carter finished his breakfast with a sigh. The receptionist at the hotel was correct. Jay's Diner had the best food he'd tasted in years. He couldn't remember when he'd had such a delicious meal.

"You have to leave," Jay told him as she cleared the dishes from his table. "People are beginning to think you're some kind of government cop or something."

Carter smiled at her. "Well, I'm not. I'm actually an attorney."

"Just as bad."

He liked Jay, even if she hadn't jumped up and down when he mentioned his occupation. She'd said what was on her mind and damned the consequences. "Hey, I'm also a pilot. Maybe I can take you for a ride?"

She stacked the dishes on a tray and raised her hand. The young man who had poured his coffee earlier rushed to the table and picked up the tray and hurried away. Jay called after him. "Brandon, after you finish the breakfast dishes, you can leave."

"Cool. Thanks, Mom."

"He's your son?" Carter should have known his fantasy wouldn't last long. She was probably blissfully married, with a house full of kids.

"Yes, he is. He's working to make a little extra spending money for some computer game. His father refused to buy it."

"And you're going against your husband like this?" He liked her spunk.

"No, I'm doing it because it's an educational game.

My ex-husband thinks Brandon spends too much time studying. I don't agree."

"Good for you. Stick up for your principles." He placed a five-dollar bill on the table. "Give this to your son."

Jay shook her head. "No, he's getting paid for cleaning tables."

He pushed the money toward Jay. "Please, let me do this. I'd hate to let a good mind go to waste."

"I guess I owe you one for this." She took the money and stuffed it in her jeans pocket. "No charge for breakfast."

"No, I insist on paying. Let me do this. It marks the start of my metamorphic change."

"What?"

"Well, Jay, let's just say I'm at a crossroads in my life. And visiting your charming town has cleared up a lot of things for me. I just decided that I'm going to move here."

"What about your job?"

"Well, like I said, I'm an attorney. A town this size can never have too many lawyers."

Jay shook her head. "Is your wife going to just up and move here?"

He smiled in satisfaction. "I'm going through a divorce, and I don't think she'd really care where I am one way or another."

Jay laughed. "I know that feeling."

Carter laughed as well. "Well, Jay, you better put the Yankee special on your menu permanently."

Jay's brown eyes glittered. "I think I need some incentive for that. You have to earn a spot on my menu."

"My plane is ready when you are."

"I don't really like flying."

"I wasn't talking about my airplane."

* * *

Kissa sat in the solitude of her bedroom, trying to figure out what had happened in the last twenty-four hours. Quinn was in her living room, watching television, while she showered and changed.

She had slept with Quinn and didn't regret it for one second. From what she could recall, he'd been a wonderful and caring lover. In short, Quinn was the direct opposite of the man she thought she knew. He was very tactile. She giggled at the thought of how hands-on a lover Quinn Stone actually was.

A timid knock interrupted her dressing. She was still in her silk bathrobe, and her hair was a mess. "I'm not quite ready, Quinn."

"Duh! I want to come in."

But Kissa wasn't quite ready for that much intimacy with Quinn. He probably wanted to pick out what she was wearing or inspect her bedroom. "Just give me five minutes."

"Baby, I want to talk, and I figure I can do that while you dress or undress."

Kissa laughed. What was it about men? They always compared everything to sex or something sex-related. Why was she being so uptight, anyway? "All right. Come in." It wasn't like he hadn't seen her intimately already.

He opened the door and walked directly to the perfectly made-up bed. He sat down on the queen-size bed, testing the mattress for firmness. "Hey, this feels pretty good. We'll have to test this out later."

"Quinn, you're impossible," Kissa said, laughing. "We're supposed to be helping your sister and my best friend, Mikerra."

"I know. Everything is fine. My sources have

informed me that Seth is here and has been inquiring about her."

"Does he know about the lake?" Kissa hurried over to her large walk-in closet, reached for the first pair of jeans she found, and slipped them on. "We have to get going to the cabin. We have to warn her."

Quinn stood and stopped her retreat to the bathroom. "And tell her what? The best thing for Mikerra and Drake is for them not to know. Mikerra will just sit there and drive herself crazy over all that's wrong in her life. I don't want her to worry."

She was touched by his concern for his sister. "I don't want anything to happen to them, either. Are you sure they'll be safe?"

He pulled her in his arms, and they fell back on the bed. "Yes, they are safe for the moment. I told you I'm having them watched. They are perfectly fine. The only thing those two need is a box of condoms."

"They're not supposed to have sex. Drake is supposed to be saving his strength," Kissa said, wiggling free from Quinn's embrace. She let her robe slide off her shoulders. She laughed at Quinn's disappointed face. She already had on a T-shirt.

"Man, that's just wrong. I was ready to watch you dress, and you shoot a brother down like that."

"Forget about it. Where's your walkie-talkie phone? I want to call Mikerra."

He shook his head. "You'll see her soon enough."

"That means they're still at it. Where does he get the strength?"

"Unfortunately, from the same drug that's killing him," Quinn said dryly.

Kissa sat on the bed and embraced Quinn in a comforting hug. In that instant she knew. She had fallen head over heels for Quinn Stone in just twenty-four hours.

"Did you hear something?" Drake asked Mikerra as they watched a movie on the portable DVD player. Since Quinn and Kissa's brief visit earlier, he'd been on high alert.

"No, I didn't hear anything. Maybe it was from the movie." She snuggled closer to him. "You think Quinn told us everything?"

"All that he could, baby." Drake knew that was a lie. When he and Quinn had been alone, Quinn had told him the real deal. But neither man wanted Mikerra to worry needlessly. Besides, she only put herself in a state by worrying. And he needed her to stay focused.

"Drake, I know you. You're hiding something. What did Quinn tell you?"

"That he had us watched, and that he knows how many times we had sex today to prove it."

"Please tell me you're kidding!"

"I wish I could." Drake wanted Mikerra's mind on something, anything, other than their problems. He couldn't tell her that Seth had positioned himself outside the cabin and was waiting for the right moment to pounce.

"I'm going to kill Quinn," Mikerra murmured. "You know, he looked different today. If I didn't know better, I'd swear he had a woman, but I know that is highly unlikely."

Drake smiled to himself. Quinn was different today, all right. While he'd told Drake of Seth's whereabouts, he'd confessed his night with Kissa. Quinn had sworn Drake to secrecy. So actually, Drake was keeping two things from Mikerra. But after tonight he could confess everything to her.

"Mikerra, I think we need to talk about our future. I want to be with you, but I don't know if the army is going to give me a dishonorable discharge since they know that I've been getting outside medical attention."

"I want to be with you, too, Drake. No matter what. There's nothing between us that can't be worked out, right?"

"Nice try, Mikerra. What's wrong?"

"I don't understand what you mean."

"I mean, I know you're going to give me the speech about you having too much hanging over your head to give me your heart. Oh, come on, baby. I know what's in your trash can, and I'm cool with it. Hell, I'm having brain surgery in a few days, and I don't know what's going to happen to me, but I do know whatever time I have left on this earth, I want to be with you."

"I want that."

Drake had hoped she'd finally say the words she'd been holding on to like a gold bar at Fort Knox. If he ever got the chance, he was going to shoot Seth himself. Just to make sure the bastard was dead and could never hurt Mikerra again.

"Drake?" She called his name softly while her hands roamed his chest. "Are you okay? We were pretty active today. Maybe you need to rest?"

"Do *you* need to rest? You're probably tired as well. Remember, you asked me to stop."

Mikerra laughed. "Yes, I did, didn't I? I can't believe you have all this stamina. I don't think I'll ever be able to keep up with you."

"Oh, you know that doesn't matter. Actually, this

may sound a little perverted, but I really like it when you beg me to stop."

She elbowed him in the stomach. "That is perverted."

A loud noise came from the porch. Drake immediately turned off the DVD player and motioned for Mikerra to be quiet. He heard the noise again. Loud footsteps on the front steps of the cabin announced the intruder's every move. Quinn's idea of putting brush and rocks on the steps didn't sound too silly now.

Drake knew all the windows were locked, but that wouldn't do much good against a gun and an experienced hit man. And he knew Mikerra wouldn't go hide in another room. She was ready to face her past. Sloan had left his gun, along with a round of ammo, but those were in the bedroom. Ging probably already had them in his sights, but Drake had to try. "I'm going to get the gun," he whispered.

He went into the bedroom, grabbed the gym bag containing the gun and ammo, and headed back to Mikerra. She looked at the bag and shook her head. "Why don't they just get it over with, already?"

"He's waiting for the cover of darkness," Drake said, sitting beside her on the couch. "It's a basic maneuver. He's figuring that we'll turn on the lights, and it will be like shooting ducks in a barrel."

"Oh, that's awful. But I wonder if it's just Ging out there." She glanced at the window. "Or if Seth and his goons are out there, too?"

"How many goons does he usually have with him?"

She shrugged. "Sometimes two, but no more than three men."

That didn't set well with Drake. He had counted on Ging, Seth, and the general. But if Seth had brought some of his goons with him, and the general had done the same, there could be at least seven to ten men out there ready to kill. He was definitely going to need some backup. Still seated, he looked around for the walkie-talkie phone.

"I've gotta call Sloan or Quinn." He rose and began looking frantically for the phone.

He was too focused on finding the phone, or he would never have walked past the window, letting his guard down. By the time he realized his tactical error, it was too late. Something very hot pierced his chest, and he fell to the floor. Mikerra ran to him, but her vision was blurry. Her mouth opened and closed. He knew she was saying something, but he couldn't hear a word.

Chapter 29

"Drake, get up!" Mikerra pounded Drake on his chest, hoping against hope that he could somehow cling to life. "Baby, please don't die on me! I love you." She couldn't believe she had actually said the words aloud. Now. They'd been hovering at the back of her throat for the last few days.

Now the one man who needed to hear them couldn't, because he'd just taken a bullet marked for her. Mikerra brushed away her tears and looked for something in the small cabin to stop the bleeding. Why on earth had he been standing by the window at that precise moment? The sniper's bullet had been on the mark, hitting Drake square in the chest.

They had thought they'd be safe at the isolated cabin by the lake, thought no one would think to look in the middle of nowhere, but this was the government. And they wanted both Drake and Mikerra dead.

Drake moaned as Mikerra wiped at the steady stream of blood pumping out of his chest like a Texas oil well. She needed to put pressure on the wound to stop the flow of blood. She spied a white T-shirt on the chair. Her mother would be so proud of her instincts now. She rolled the T-shirt into a tight ball and pressed it against the wound.

Mikerra leaned down and kissed him on the forehead. "I love you, Drake. Always have and always will." She just hoped she could keep him alive until help arrived.

"I love you, too."

Mikerra's hands shook. She looked down at Drake, and his eyes were open. "Baby, hang on! I hope Sloan will be back soon."

Drake shook his head. "We need to shoot our way out."

"Nice idea, but I don't see how. That's an underground hitter out there. He'll kill us." Mikerra rubbed his head gently.

Drake coughed and spat up blood. She was going to have to do something and fast. She crawled to the nearest window and noticed there were only two men out there. Apparently, they didn't think they needed much man power to take down an army ranger and a journalist.

"Care Bear," Drake whispered.

"I'm going to get you some help, Drake."

He struggled to a half-sitting position. "How?"

Well, that was a good question. "Maybe we can draw them closer and knock them out."

He shook his head. "Think like a soldier. Kill them."

"I can't take a life," Mikerra countered. "I just can't."

"Us or them. You decide." He coughed and passed out.

Mikerra scurried back to Drake and saw dribbles of blood ooze out of his sweet mouth. Her decision had been made. If it took the last ounce of her strength to save Drake, then the price wasn't too high. She crawled her way to the couch and rifled through the gym bag Sloan had left the day before. She took out the nine-millimeter gun and the clip of ammo and stared at her enemy. The last time she was face-to-face with a gun, Seth was holding it to her temple, daring her to end their affair.

"No woman leaves Seth McCaffrey," he'd told her in that quiet voice. "And you're sure not going to be the first."

Mikerra wondered whether he would have killed her then if she hadn't passed out.

Seth paced the area behind the parked SUV at the end of the road, blocking public entrance to Wright City's only lake. This was supposed to be simple. This was supposed to be clean. This was supposed to have been over months ago. Karen, Mikerra now—how hard was it to call her by her given name—and that soldier should have been dead days ago. *This is what happens when you send idiots to do a man's job,* he told himself. He should have killed her months ago, when he had the chance. He wouldn't be making a second mistake.

He picked up the walkie-talkie, barking orders as he continued to pace. "Status report."

"Not sure. I still see some movement in the cabin. Don't know if I hit him or the girl. Don't know if it's a clean kill or not."

Idiots. He was about to get reamed by the Senate committee because of idiots. "Look, I know it's dark, but can you use those two-thousand-dollar night-vision goggles you demanded and give me some solid answers? If the girl is still alive, don't kill her. I want that privilege for myself."

"But, sir," Ging said in a patronizing voice.

"But me no buts, or I'll have your ass serving the rest of your military career on the front lines in Iraq."

"I'm a civilian, sir."

"I don't give a damn. I can have anyone sent to the front. Got me?"

"Yes, sir."

"Call me back with approximate answers and nothing else." He signed off.

Mikerra watched Drake's perfectly still body and prayed that he was still with her. If things had gone accordingly, he would be getting ready for brain surgery and would not have a bullet lodged in his chest. Instead, they were stuck in a cabin miles away from nowhere, not exactly the best situation.

She took a deep breath and took stock of the situation: if there were two shooters, maybe she could take them out. If she focused on what needed to be done, she could protect Drake and save them both.

"What's wrong?" Drake asked quietly.

Mikerra moved closer to him and caressed his jaw lovingly. "Nothing. Just how this great plan didn't work. How I messed up three more lives and I shouldn't have come back here."

Drake studied her intently. "Mikerra, you came back here because this is home. But that's not what you're thinking about. You're worried about last night."

She hated that he knew her so well. "That's not important right now. Save your strength."

His gaze went to the gun and the clip of ammo beside it. "Can you load?"

He reached for her hand and picked it up. "Baby,

you need to be ready to shoot. Load." He turned his head to the window. "I hear something."

Mikerra did, too. It was the distinct noise of someone on the porch. "I have to move you. If he sees you, he might shoot you again."

Drake nodded. The little conversation they'd had had cost him the last bit of energy he had. Mikerra searched the cabin for some bedclothes. Luckily, she found several crisp white sheets. She made a pallet from the sheets and attempted to move the 230-pound man alone. Although Drake outweighed her only by seventy pounds, Mikerra found his deadweight too much to handle, but she refused to give up. She gave it one more try and managed to move him out of the line of fire, so to speak. At least now she had him secure behind the couch and out of sight.

"I like a strong woman. Makes me feel safe." He smiled and passed out again.

"You make me feel safe."

She went back to the gun and quickly loaded the clip. Familiar with nine-millimeter guns, Mikerra pulled back the slide, extracting the bullet from the magazine and allowing the ammo to slide safely into position and await penetration from the firing pin. "Now let's see where this moron is hiding." The hair on the back of her neck rose as she heard the creaking of the wood porch as it gave under their assailant's weight. As her vision adjusted to the night, she made out the masculine form. *About six feet,* she guessed. *Definitely a man, or a woman with the world's flattest chest,* she mused. It had to be Ging, ready to make his move. She also made out the shape of the rifle he was carrying.

Drake was right. Again. It was going to boil down to

them or him. Her only option was to take this man out. Why was this so hard? The Joint Chiefs of Staff had no problem offering up the lives of a hundred innocent soldiers. Why was it so hard to shoot one man, who was probably up to his neck in all this, anyway?

On her hands and knees, Mikerra crawled to the window. Using the window's edge for leverage, she aimed her gun, closed her eyes, and squeezed the trigger. On instinct she hid back in the shadows, just in case.

"I'm hit!" Ging cried out.

Mikerra cursed silently. She was going to have to shoot him again, and his cry also meant there really was someone else out there.

"Don't shoot her!"

Mikerra's blood chilled when she recognized that voice coming through Ging's walkie-talkie loud and clear. Seth. She really was going to die and probably very brutally.

"I want that honor," Seth added.

Mikerra realized this was zero hour, minute, second, or whatever. She found strength somewhere in her body and took a second shot. This time she heard the distinct thud of a body falling on the porch and down the concrete steps. If Ging wasn't dead from the shot, he was dead from the fall. But now she had to contend with Seth, and his wrath was going to kill one of them. But who?

The question was answered with the sound of the front door lock being blasted off and the door flying open. It was go time.

Seth strode into the small cabin as if he had all the time in the world. His slender frame was encased in all black. He looked like an assassin. A black T-shirt molded his taut upper body, and black jeans wrapped around his runner's legs. His brown hair peeked out from under his black unmarked baseball cap.

Mikerra fought every nerve in her body and stood her ground. She wanted to run for cover, but she had to keep Drake safe. Hopefully, it won't cost her her life.

Seth looked at Mikerra and grinned. She scrambled to her feet, making sure to keep the gun hidden behind her back. For every step he took toward her, she took one in the opposite direction and away from Drake.

"Now, Karen, don't make this harder than it has to be. You know there's no way out of this. I have planned this for too long for you and that soldier to mess things up."

"I won't say anything about Project Perfect, Seth."

"You know I can't trust you. You know too much about the project, about the variables, and about me. I can't have a journalist armed with that much information against me. I plan to run for president, you know. I'm going to be bigger than Kennedy."

Mikerra didn't bother to refute his statements. Seth was very proud of his Irish heritage, but to think he would be larger than the thirty-fifth president of the United States was going over the edge. But she couldn't upset him. Not until she could get a clean shot.

"Where is he?" Seth snarled.

"Who?"

Seth reached behind his back and extracted a pistol and pointed it at her. "I guess we're going to do this the hard way." He motioned her toward the couch. "Sit down."

But she couldn't sit there. Drake was behind the couch. And she couldn't let anything happen to him. She had done enough to him already. "I'm fine. Why don't you just do what you came here to do?"

He looked her up and down before walking to the couch and sitting down. "In due time. You've lost weight."

Mikerra sighed, hoping against hope that Drake wouldn't make a sound and give away the game. "Whatever."

Seth jumped up from the couch and stalked toward her. "You know how I hate that."

Before she could utter a saucy retort for this man who had caused her so much pain, he'd wrapped his slender fingers around her throat and was choking the very life out of her.

In a few short months, she'd shed forty pounds and fallen in love with Drake. Mikerra had forgotten how much control Seth had had over her life, including her speech. If she could survive just another minute, she'd be able to shoot him. She couldn't squeeze the trigger. It was jammed.

"What the . . ." Seth mumbled and crumpled to the floor.

"Drake!" yelled Mikerra.

Drake stood there leaning against the back of the couch for support. He was still holding the small-caliber pistol in his hand. Mikerra cried, running to his side. Drake threw the pistol on the couch. He smiled at her. "Bastard."

She wrapped her arms around him and hugged him. "Oh, baby. You were great."

"I just nicked him, honey." Drake nodded to the pistol. "It's Mom's little pistol." He sagged against the couch but quickly regained his stance.

Mikerra felt rather than heard Seth's presence behind her.

"Good. I didn't think he was dead. Now I can finish this and get out of this godforsaken place," Seth muttered.

Mikerra's eyes met Drake's. This was it. She eyed the pistol on the couch cushion. As she slowly turned around to face Seth, she dipped slightly to pick up the pistol in what she hoped was a smooth motion. With the small pearl-handled pistol securely in her palm, she faced Seth.

Seth faced her, smiling. "He only nicked my shoulder. He's a damn army ranger, and that's the best he could do? Is this what American taxpayer dollars are being spent on? A soldier that can't shoot?"

Mikerra didn't like Seth's smug tone. She didn't like the man. She didn't like what she had become in his company, and she didn't like what he and those idiots had done to innocent soldiers. "No, but this is the best I can do." She raised the pistol to waist level and squeezed the trigger. The bullet ripped into Seth's abdomen.

Seth fell backward, striking his head on the fireplace.

"If the bullet didn't get him, the fall did," Drake said. "You think there's anyone else outside?"

Mikerra heard the familiar sound of tires spinning on the gravel. Someone was attempting to get out of the area as quickly as possible. "I think they just left." She went to Drake's side and helped him sit on the couch. "Why don't you lie down while I call the paramedics?"

Mikerra called the sheriff's office, which in turn called for medical help. Then she called Sloan. Drake lay on the couch, floating in and out of consciousness. His body was tired, and all he wanted to do was rest, but Mikerra wasn't having it. She sat down next to him on the floor and talked nonstop. She hadn't shut her mouth since she shot Seth. Why had she turned into chatty Cathy all of a sudden? he wondered.

"I can't believe I took a life. But you know, I thought I would feel more remorse, you know, like those people on TV when they're slinging snot everywhere, talking about how sorry they are. Seth would have killed us and just walked away and covered his tracks. I almost wish I could have inflicted more pain. Yeah, that would have been better. There should have been a way to make him gain a hundred pounds, like I did."

Drake laughed through his pain. His chest was really hurting, but Mikerra kept on babbling. He knew she was bordering on hysteria. "Baby," he said softly.

"I just wish we could have done something more to him," she said, clearly not hearing a word he'd said.

"Baby."

That time she heard him. "Are you hurting more? Maybe you need to sit up instead? You need water? There's plenty in the fridge."

He was going to have to be firm with her, or she'd start babbling again. "Baby, you have got to calm down."

Mikerra laughed nervously. "I'm fine." She glanced at Seth's body and sighed. "Do you know I tried to break up with him at least a dozen times, but each time he convinced me that I'd be nothing without his backing, and I was stupid enough to believe him?" She picked up the small pistol and held it in her hand.

"Not stupid," Drake whispered, wanting to do more than hold her free hand for comfort.

She took a deep breath. A lone tear streaked down her face. "Not stupid. Weak maybe, and delusional, of course, but thanks to you, I'm better now. Better than I've been in a long time. Drake, I love you."

He smiled at her, noticing the solid tone in her voice. "I love you, too, baby."

Mikerra leaned over him and kissed him gently on the lips. "You know, every time I think about what Seth and those idiots have done to you, I just get mad all over again. I wish he wasn't dead, so I could kill him again."

"But, baby, he's dead, and he won't hurt anyone again."

"That's not good enough." She aimed the small pistol at Seth's already dead body and pulled the trigger. "There. I feel better."

Drake chuckled. "I'm glad. Are you sure you're okay?"

She caressed his stomach and upper body, carefully avoiding the wound. "Yes, I'm just fine."

"You know I want to be with you."

Mikerra looked at him with a blank expression on her face. "I know you are going to qualify that statement, but let me say this, Drake."

He nodded, swallowing the lump of anxiety in his throat.

"We don't know what the future may hold for either of us. I know that more than likely you're not going to be in the military anymore, and they're probably going to fight your discharge as much as possible. The last thing the army is going to want to admit is that it was injecting soldiers with deadly experimental drugs without their knowledge. I'm going to be with you every step of the way."

"But, Mikerra."

"No. I'm not listening. If you think you're going to send me away after all we've been through together, just forget it."

Drake had known this woman for most of his childhood; they'd been high school sweethearts; and now, after a twenty-one-year separation, they were together again. He knew she was just as stubborn as he. He'd had every intention of telling her she'd be better off without him, but now he knew that was useless. He was licked and he liked it.

Chapter 30

When Mikerra and Drake arrived at the hospital, officials from the army were waiting for them. How did they know so soon? They wanted to speak with Drake, but David refused, immediately ordering Drake into surgery.

Many hours later Mikerra sat next to Drake's hospital bed, waiting for him to return from surgery. Everything had gotten tied up in a neat ball. Seth's cohorts were sitting in jail. Seth's and Ging's bodies had been taken to the city morgue. The FBI, Homeland Security, and the local sheriff had questioned Mikerra about the whole dirty mess.

Now Mikerra and the two men dressed in green sat in the small room, staring at each other, sizing each other up. Would they kick Drake out of the army? Would they still want him dead?

She quickly refuted that notion. Too many people knew the real story now, including the FBI. Heads would definitely roll, and this time it wasn't going to be hers.

The door swung open, and David walked into the

room, smiling. "Mikerra, can I have a word with you in my office?"

The army men immediately stood. "We can leave, Doctor. As long as we're allowed to speak to the master sergeant."

David nodded. "He's not very alert at the moment, but as soon as he's coherent, and I think he's up to your questions, you may speak to him briefly. I don't want you trying to get him to sign anything at this time. He's just had brain surgery," David said in a very unfriendly voice. "It wouldn't be legal for you to question him at length at this time."

The men nodded and left the room.

Mikerra's heart rate accelerated as David took a seat on the bed. "David, did everything go okay?"

"It went better than okay. Thankfully, the drugs in his system decelerated the bleeding from the gunshot wound. He has a chest wound and shouldn't have been conscious after he was shot, let alone able to get a shot off at McCaffrey. It was like his body had already started healing itself from the serum."

Mikerra nodded. "Well, that's the least it should have done, since it was killing him."

"I was also able to stop the cancer growth, and he'll need therapy for about six months. And I'm sure our boys in green aren't going to like what I'm about to tell them."

"What's that?"

David smiled. "That Drake should have a medical discharge, and it should be one hundred percent disability."

Mikerra knew that would break Drake's heart. "I agree with you, but getting Drake to see the light might be difficult."

David rose and headed for the door. "I do have an

insurance policy. Shirley Harrington is all for anything that's going to cost the military money. She says her prayers have been answered."

"Oh, no. It's as good as done, then."

David laughed, opening the door. "Drake should be back in the room in about an hour. Shirley's been pacing the waiting room. She said she'd be in here as soon as she calmed down."

A month later Mikerra sat in her mother's kitchen, praying that her headache would stop. Since Drake's release from the hospital three weeks ago and his discharge from the army two weeks ago, her life had been one crisis after another.

Drake didn't mind being discharged from the army. He'd accepted it like a true soldier. He did mind therapy. It took Mikerra, Mikerra's mom, his mom, and his dad to convince him that he needed it.

Then there was the military. Initially, they'd refused to grant him any disability status. The first ruling was for 30 percent disability. The army claimed that Drake could eventually work, but that was before Mikerra's story hit the news a few days later. Every pro-anything group was demanding that the remaining soldiers who had been part of the experiment get tested for cancer and be pulled from the war zone immediately.

The last hearing was held yesterday, and they were awaiting the official decision. As if the army really had a choice. Mikerra knew they had to give Drake 100 percent disability and pay for all his future medical bills.

"Mikerra, why don't you drink some herbal tea?" Her mother placed a cup of tea in front of her that had an awful aroma. "Maybe some crackers."

"Mom, I have a headache. Plus, I promised Drake's mom I'd sit with him while she went shopping today."

"You go over there every day, anyway. How's he doing? I know Shirley was very worried when he was first released."

Mikerra remembered that as well. Those first days had been agonizing and scary for everyone. Drake had been restless and had had trouble expressing his thoughts and walking, but he had bounced back quickly and had regained his motor skills. "Pretty good. Just antsy. He wants to start exercising, but David said it's too soon. They're still testing his motor skills."

"You mean, like reading, writing, that kind of thing?" Carolina plopped down in the chair beside her. "Oh, my God, I know he had brain surgery, but I just didn't realize it was that bad." She reached for a napkin and wiped her eyes.

"Mom, it's okay. David said they're the standard tests after brain surgery, and with David catching any problems so early, Drake is doing great. Why don't you come with me today? You can see for yourself."

"No, honey. I think you and Drake have bigger things to discuss."

Mikerra stared at her mother. "Mom, what are you talking about?"

"Have you guys discussed the future? I mean, he's obviously staying here for now, but for how long?"

"We haven't talked about it since that night in the cabin, and I wouldn't feel right discussing it now, when he's not all the way back."

"You just said he's doing great. Are you going to wait until the baby gets here to tell him?"

Mikerra gasped and put her hand over her mouth. She'd suspected she was pregnant, but she knew the likelihood of that occurring this late in the game was next to nothings. "Mom, I'm probably just going through the change early."

"Not this early. Baby, I can see the signs. He knocked you up."

Mikerra had a fit of giggles. "Mom! I can't believe you said that. I'm not pregnant."

Carolina nodded. "I'm sure all those headaches are just stress-related. As long as you aren't throwing up and your breasts aren't swelling, you're safe."

But Mikerra had been having all the normal symptoms of pregnancy; plus, she was late. And she was never late. Even the herbal tea was giving her stomach a fight for superiority at the moment. "Mom, it just isn't possible." She felt the first tears slide down her face.

"Oh, baby, I think so. I didn't want to say this, but I noticed your face has been looking a little puffy this week. Initially, I thought that maybe Drake was mad about the story going national and that you'd been crying about that."

Mikerra wiped her eyes. "No, he was pleased. The other soldiers are being pulled from Iraq and will soon be on their way home, according to Sloan."

"Well, baby, if you wait until he's all better, the baby might already be here. What are you going to do? Introduce them?"

Mikerra shook her head. She'd made a horrible situation worse. What if she was actually pregnant with Drake's child? They'd had unprotected sex at the cabin, and she had actually gotten pregnant!

Her mother rubbed her shoulder, trying to comfort her. "Now look, Mikerra, there's nothing wrong with being pregnant. I know you're helping Drake with his recovery, but we can all pitch in and help. And since this is my first grandchild, I would like it to get here healthy. So I don't want you to stress out about anything."

"Thanks, Mom, but I think I should at least take a pregnancy test before I start rearranging my life."

"Don't need no test. I've been around pregnant women all my life. I know the look. I'd say around four or five weeks."

Well, if nothing else cinched it, that did. It had been four weeks to the date since their time at the cabin and the one time he hadn't used a condom.

Was this the straw that would break Drake?

Drake watched as his mother fixed his breakfast. It was useless trying to argue with this woman. She'd argue with God, most likely. Trying to explain to his mother that he wanted only cereal for breakfast was fruitless. So he would eat the pancakes, bacon, and eggs like a good son.

"Mom, you know you don't have to wait for Mikerra to get here. I've lived alone before, and I'm capable of staying alone for a few minutes."

Shirley placed an oversize plate in front of him. "I know that, baby, but I want to. Isn't your doctor's appointment tomorrow?"

"Yes."

"I probably should plan to go with you, too, in case Mikerra isn't able to go."

His mother was talking in riddles. Again. "Mom, spit it out."

"Have you guys talked about the future?"

He should have known this was coming. "We talked about it a little the night I got shot, but I can't be with her now. She's taking care of me. I don't have anything to offer her."

"Drake, you have plenty to offer her. You're financially stable, and you have a good education and a good heart. What else is there?"

"I can't give her children," he said quietly. He spared his mother Mikerra's revelations that night at her parents' house. "David said it might not be possible."

His mother snorted. "I think you don't have to worry about that. I believe this time the great doctor is wrong."

"I appreciate the confidence, but how on earth can you be so sure? David said that with neutralizing the drugs the army gave me, he couldn't guarantee anything."

"Well, I know this is going to sound crazy, but I have the feeling that she's pregnant. The last few days I've heard her throwing up in the bathroom when she comes over to see you."

"Maybe it's just stress."

"Maybe it's just a baby."

"Mom, be serious. We're both almost forty. What would we do with a baby?"

"Love it. Just wait until she gets here. She's going to head straight for the bathroom."

Despite the absurdity of it, Drake realized his mother could possibly be right. Was Mikerra hiding this from him? Why was she hiding this from him?

He didn't have to wait long to test his mother's theory. Mikerra entered the house a little while later, courtesy of her own key, and headed straight for the bathroom.

"See, baby? I told you," whispered Shirley.

"It would have been nice if *she* had."

His mother pulled him into the kitchen so Mikerra

wouldn't hear them. "Now, don't you go accusing her of anything. Let her tell you in her own time."

"When?"

"When what?" Mikerra walked into the kitchen and took a seat at the table.

The breakfast dishes had been cleared away, and there was no evidence of cooked food in the kitchen. But the look that crossed Mikerra's face said that the aroma was still there and in full force. Her honey brown complexion had taken on an unhealthy green pallor.

Drake stood rooted to the spot. He'd been in combat, but he had no idea what to do to help her. Luckily, his mom sprang into action.

Shirley grabbed some crackers and gave them to Mikerra. "Chew these. It'll settle your stomach. It's just morning sickness." Shirley smiled and left the kitchen.

Mikerra stuffed the crackers in her mouth, and a few minutes later, her complexion was back to normal. "I guess everyone knew before I did."

"Not me." Drake sat beside her at the table. "Why didn't you say something?"

She continued nibbling on the crackers. "I just found out about an hour ago. My mom told me I was pregnant. I haven't taken a test or anything official."

Drake nodded, instantly understanding. "I meant what I said in the cabin."

She shook her head. "I did, too, but I think it's unfair to you right now."

"How do you know what's in my heart?" Drake replied. "Yeah, when I laid eyes on you almost two months ago, I never dreamed it would end up like this, but it was fate."

She was shoveling those crackers in her mouth at

an alarming rate. Drake grabbed her hands so she had to look at him. "Mikerra, you know I'm waiting to hear what the board says about my disability. I've saved pretty well over the years, but I probably don't have the financial portfolio you do. However, I can offer you my heart. You know I love you and want to be with you at any cost."

"Why do I feel like you are going to qualify this statement?"

"Look at me, baby. You or Mom has to drive me to therapy and just about anyplace else. Who knows when I'll be able to drive? What happens when this isn't fun for you anymore? I shipped most of my things to my brother in Dallas before I was deployed, and I still have to collect everything. Helping me get settled and being pregnant might be too much."

She wiggled her hands free and stood up. "Are you quite finished?" She walked to the door.

"Yes."

"You don't think I'm strong enough. You think I can't do it. You think I'm going to run. Look at me, Drake."

He looked her up and down.

"I might have taken the easy way out before, but I'm here for the long haul. If you don't trust me enough to believe that, cool. I don't want anything but your love and trust. I might have one, but I don't have the other. And I'm having the baby." She walked out of the kitchen and out of the house.

Drake sat at the table, wondering what the hell had just happened. He had intended to question her about the baby, but somehow things had got twisted and she had walked out of his life.

His mother sauntered into the kitchen, with her

Coach bag on her shoulder and her keys in her hand. "Come on."

"Where?"

"To Mikerra's. You've got to make this right. And once and for all, can you please let what happened over twenty years ago go? You can't keep throwing that in her face, especially when you didn't go after her in the first place."

Drake threw his hands up in surrender. Yes, it was time to eat some crow. He had definitely earned the honor.

But Mikerra wasn't at her house. Or at her parents'. Where was she? "Let's try Quinn's," Drake said, settling into the passenger seat. "Mrs. Stone said she hasn't seen Mikerra or heard from her since she left to come to our house."

Shirley grunted and put the SUV in gear. They headed to Quinn's house. As they turned onto Oak Street, Drake muttered a curse. "She's not here, either." Only Quinn's Silverado was parked in front of his house.

Drake rested his head against the leather headrest, trying to imagine what could have happened to her in such a short span of time. "I can't live without her again."

"So why give her all that 'I don't have much' spiel? You're not looking at what's important. She convinced you something was wrong with you when you had those headaches, she's been beside you every step of the way, and you try to play head games with her. She's not some military strategy. She's a person with feelings, and now she's pregnant with your child and missing."

His mother knew how to cut him down to size, no

matter what, Drake realized. And she was exactly right. Mikerra had been there, and he had taken her for granted. Now he was paying the highest price. "Mom, go to the lake."

"Where you got shot?"

"Yes. I think she's at the lake. She used to go there when we were in school, when she wanted to be alone."

He hoped he was right.

His mother didn't say anything about how crazy the idea sounded. She just drove. When they arrived at the lake, his heart was thumping loudly against his chest. In the distance he saw Mikerra's SUV. *Thank God*. He wasn't letting her out of his sight ever again.

Shirley stopped the SUV and Drake jumped out. He ran to the driver's side of Mikerra's SUV, but he didn't like what he saw. Mikerra was inside the SUV and out cold. The windows were up and it was August. She was going to suffocate or die of heat stroke. He tried the door handle; the door opened, and he reached for Mikerra.

"Baby," he whispered.

She moaned and struggled to sit up. "What happened?"

He pulled her in his arms and hugged her. "I was just about to ask you the same thing." He helped her out of the SUV. "You need some air."

She took a deep breath. Then another. She leaned against the SUV. "I came out here to think. But I was so mad at you, I couldn't think straight. Then I was mad at myself for getting mad at you. Then Sloan called me and told me that they want me to appear at the Senate hearing next month, to discuss PP One-ninety-two."

Drake didn't care about any of that. He had his woman back in his arms, and that was where she was staying. "I was wrong, Mikerra. I was holding on to what happened our senior year. We were different people then. I was holding on to something that was clouding my view."

She inhaled deeply and blotted her forehead with the back of her hand. "And now?"

He didn't have to think about now. He thought about forever. "I want to hold on to you."

She smiled up at him. "Good. 'Cause I think I'm going to pass out."

When Mikerra opened her eyes, the bright lights blinded her. She was lying in a hospital bed. How on earth did she get here? Drake was sitting next to the bed, his large hands clasping hers.

"Hey, Care Bear. How are you feeling?"

"What happened?" She glanced around the room, noticing monitors and machines, which all made erratic noises. "What's all that noise for?" She also noticed that several bouquets of red roses lined the windowsill.

He looked at the machines as if he'd never seen them before. "For you. You passed out yesterday."

"Yesterday?" Mikerra's free hand rubbed her forehead. "Are you telling me I lost an entire day?"

"Yes, that's what I'm telling you. I've never been so scared as I was last night. Your mom came in and took one look at you and started crying. Your dad had to take her home. I stayed with you. Promise me you won't do that again."

"Do what?"

"Pass out on me. I thought I had lost you. David kept you overnight for observation. Everything is fine.

The baby is fine. He said I could take you home this morning."

Home? "Drake, what are you talking about?"

He grinned at her. "I guess you don't remember yesterday."

"Apparently not," she said, staring at him. She knew he was leaving out something big. "Why don't you tell me exactly what's going on?"

"I asked you to marry me last night."

She vaguely remembered it but thought it was just a dream. "What did I say?"

"You mean you don't remember? That was some of my best work. I'm hurt, baby."

She could tell by his playful banter he didn't mean it. "Why don't you give me an instant replay? That way I can give you an answer."

"I happen to like the answer you gave me last night," he said.

"Humor me."

"All right. It was right after David came and said that, yes, you're pregnant and you're about four weeks along."

"You don't have to marry me just because I'm pregnant, Drake."

"I knew you'd say something like that. First, it was because of the tumor and because you didn't think I was in control of my faculties, and now it's because you think I don't love you enough. I love you, with or without the baby. I want us to be together. Whether you have to drive me every place I need to go or not. I want you."

Mikerra wanted him in the same way. She just didn't want him to regret it later. "Are you sure, baby?"

"Just as sure as I am that I love you and want to get married as soon as possible."

Mikerra wiped the tears from her eyes. "Well, I'm that sure, too. I want to get married as quickly as we can manage it."

Drake rose from the chair. "How about now?"

"Now? You can't be serious. You have to have a marriage license application, a preacher or a judge, and witnesses."

"I think I can manage that." He opened the door and Mikerra's parents sauntered in, along with Quinn and Kissa. Drake's parents and his brother, Dylan, and his wife also filled the small room. Judge Wilbur Harding walked inside the room and handed Drake a piece of paper, and that was when it all hit home. They were actually going to get married in the hospital.

Drake walked to Mikerra's bedside and reached for her hand. He slipped the three-carat diamond ring on her engagement-ring finger. "Would you do me the honor of marrying me?"

It might not be the big church wedding she had in mind, but the result was the same. She was marrying the man she loved.

Epilogue

Six months later

Mikerra glanced out the kitchen window, laughing at the scene before her. Drake was playing catch with Terror in the backyard. Actually, it was quite comical watching big, tall Drake frolic around with the tiny dog.

She rubbed her ever-expanding stomach. She was twenty-eight weeks along in her pregnancy, and she was still amazed every time she felt the baby move. The last six months had been a blur to both her and Drake.

After their marriage at the hospital, they had both settled into the union as if it were second nature. Drake had been honorably discharged from the army due to medical reasons. Mikerra had been offered a seven-figure book deal for a tell-all chronicling her relationship with Senator McCaffrey, his death, and the project's ultimate demise.

Quinn and Kissa were officially a couple now and were even considering the M word. Mikerra couldn't be happier for her baby brother and her best friend. Quinn was introducing Kissa to a life she never knew existed. Although, his free-spirited soul was giving practical Kissa a run for her money.

Instead of Sloan getting fired for helping Drake and Mikerra, he had been commended and promoted to the post of assistant press secretary in the new presidential administration.

David had received a commendation from the president for his willingness to stand up for what was right. He had also been promoted to chief of staff at the hospital.

She watched Drake with tears in her eyes. He'd been through so much in the last eight months, but he was her brave soldier. After the army finally admitted to the drug testing, Drake was awarded three million dollars in damages. Mikerra saw it as blood money, as an attempt to buy their silence.

Drake was still going through physical therapy and hating every minute of it. Now that Mikerra's pregnancy had progressed and she was in her last trimester, she was on bed rest. Drake's mom or her mom had to drive Drake to therapy.

He hated that and had made no qualms about hiding it. "I don't see why I have to be driven to therapy," he'd told Mikerra. "What happens when you go into labor? I'll have to drive you to the hospital then."

It would have been a good argument anywhere but in Wright City. The hospital was ten minutes away at the most. Her parents lived less than five minutes away, and his only a few minutes more, but Mikerra hadn't wanted to point that out to him. He looked too cute when he was venting.

"Hey, what are you doing up?" Drake asked, walking inside the house with Terror on his heels. "You're supposed to be sleeping, remember? You promised me last night, right before you seduced me, that you'd take a nap this morning."

She nodded. She would have promised him the moon and all the stars to get him to have sex. "I know, but you know how I hate sleeping alone." She walked over to him and put her arms around him. "I'd probably get to sleep quicker if you were in bed with me."

He kissed her forehead. "Don't think I don't know what you're doing. Because I can spot a maneuver when I see one."

She looked up at his handsome face. She wondered what on earth she'd seen in him twenty-one years ago, when he was a skinny, immature jock. Not the handsome, caring, and virile man he was now. "Is it working?"

He picked her up and kissed her. "Why don't you tell me?" He carried her upstairs and planted her on the bed. "Now, woman, you're taking your morning nap. I don't want my daughter coming into this world tired 'cause her stubborn mama wouldn't take care of herself while she was pregnant."

Mikerra knew she had to at least pretend she was going to sleep, or they would discuss this all day. She patted the space beside her. "You know, this would go a lot faster if you just lay down with me."

Drake laughed and did as she asked. "All right, Care Bear. You win, this time." He put his arms around her and kissed her ear. "But you haven't won the war."

Mikerra snuggled against him, loving the feel of his hard body against hers. It had been an incredible journey toward love, but Mikerra was glad it had taken them over twenty years to get there. It made her appreciate their relationship that much more. "Oh, I'm counting on it."